LEGION I:
LORDS
OF FIRE

VAN ALLEN PLEXICO

WHITE ROCKET BOOKS

For Wayne Reinagel,
Present at the creation.

This book is also available as a limited edition hardcover from White Rocket Books.

This is a work of fiction. All the characters and events portrayed in this book are either products of the author's imagination or are used fictitiously.

LEGION I: LORDS OF FIRE (THE SHATTERING)
Copyright 2013 by Van Allen Plexico
Cover art by Mark Williams
Cover design by Van Allen Plexico

A White Rocket Book
www.whiterocketbooks.com

ISBN-13: 978-0692021422

ISBN-10: 0692021426

New paperback edition: April 2014
First hardcover printing: March 2014
First paperback printing: January 2013

0 9 8 7 6 5 4 3 2 1

AFTER THE GODS,
BEFORE THE SHATTERING...

It is the 17th Millennium, and the fabled Terran Alliance that first carried mankind into the depths of the galaxy has fallen, replaced by four lesser but still grand empires. Mightiest of all is the Anatolian Empire, ruled for centuries by the Rahkmanov Dynasty. The Empire is protected by three great army divisions under the overall command of First Legion General Hideo Nakamura.

The wars in Heaven that spilled over into our universe are now long over, though the damage they wrought cannot be fully calculated. Much that was known is now lost. The old gods have nearly all vanished into the depths of the galaxy—or into their own private cosmos. Now they mostly survive as memories and as icons worshipped by the masses, along lines strictly laid down by the Imperial Ecclesiarchy—the Holy Church of Those Who Remain—and enforced by the Holy Inquisition. The cults for a few of the most dangerous gods are legally banned, with severe punishments for those who are discovered to be worshipping them.

Starships use a thin but accessible layer of the gods' transcendent dimension known as "the Above" as a shortcut to traverse the vast distances of the galaxy, and the "Aether" network transmits messages through that higher plane for instantaneous communications; but humans have lost all other access to that divine realm— and also to "the Below," the underverse that serves as home to demonic beings and other hideous and nightmarish entities.

But not all of the old gods are dead, and a doorway into the underverse is about to be reopened...

"In our youths, our hearts were touched with fire."
—Oliver Wendell Holmes

"Not all that dwell in Hell are demons, nor do all demons dwell in Hell."
— Doran Karah, Reflections, 18th Millennium

"All things, oh priests, are on fire."
— The Buddha

DRAMATIS PERSONAE

Imperial First Legion: Key Personnel
General Hideo Nakamura, "The Supreme,"
  commander of First Legion and Commander-in-Chief
  of the Imperial military
Colonel Nikolai Barmakid, "The Cunning," adjutant to
  General Nakamura
Colonel Ezekial Tamerlane, "The Relentless," Chief of
  Imperial Security; longtime friend and confidante of
  General Nakamura
Major Konstans Belisarius, "The Belligerent"

Other Personnel of Note, First Legion:
Major Niobe Arani, Special Forces officer
Major Den Senjanik, Special Forces officer
Major Shae, assignment unknown
Captain Durin, Special Forces officer
Sergeant Garner, assigned to support Special Forces
  operations on Trezibond
Lieutenants Singh, Reilly, Dalton and **Westerfeld**:
  assigned to Tamerlane's expedition to NM-156
Lieutenants Torval, Landau, Keefe and **Ling**: assigned
  to Gen. Nakamura's support team

Imperial Second Legion: Key Personnel
General Esteban Attila, "The Bold"
Colonel Ioan Iapetus, "The Unyielding"
Major Berens Barbarossa, "The Daring"

Imperial Third Legion: Key Personnel
General Abdul-Rashid Beyzit, "The Thunderbolt"
Colonel Arnem Agrippa, "The Golden"
Major Yevgeni Vostok, "The Cold"
Major Selim Iksander, "The Lightning"

The Royal Family
Janus IV Rahkmanov, Emperor of Anatolia, one of the
  four Empires of Mankind
Lisbeth Salome Rahkmanov, Empress Consort
Augustin Rahkmanov, Archduke and Heir Apparent
Marens Rahkmanov, Princess

The Emperor's Guard (selected members)
Osman, Captain of the Guard (Emerald armor)
Zeyid, Guardsman (Ruby armor)
Abdul, Guardsman (Sapphire armor)
Rashid, Guardsman (Garnet armor)

Planetary Governors of Note
Amon Rameses, "The Undying," Governor of
Ahknaton
Suleyman Mehmet, Governor of Bursa
Iyesu Tokugawa, Governor of Edo

The Holy Inquisition
Gabriel Stanishur, Grand Inquisitor
Lorval Chopra, Inquisitor's Aide
Leisle Delain, Inquisitor's Aide

The Ecclesiarchy—
The Holy Church of Those Who Remain
Wallin Zoric, Ecclesiarch
Salid Donnan, High Priest
Edan Reichenbach, Warrior-Priest
Father Octavion, Warrior-Priest

Some of "Those Who Remain":
Selected gods of the Empire

Alaria, goddess of beauty
Amenophis, god of death and resurrection; favored by
    the citizens of Ahknaton
Baranak, god of battle; once the possessor of the
    Sword of Baranak, a weapon of incalculable power
    that can also slice through dimensional barriers
Goraddon, god of persuasion; disciple of Vorthan
Karilyne, goddess of battle and lover of Baranak
Korvak, god of the current
Lucian, god of evil and mischief, rebellion and non-
    conformity
Malachek, god of wisdom
Vodina, temperamental goddess of the waters and
    the Furies
Vorthan, god of toil; later worshipped as a god of fire
    and death

PROLOGUE

By the time the lasers began to fire their murderous crisscross pattern, slicing deeply into the metal on either side of the shaft, Tamerlane had already cut his cable and dropped to the hard concrete floor some fifteen meters below.

Despite his best efforts he landed hard. Rolling over, he popped up and took a quick inventory of himself. Nothing broken; just a few places that would bruise over soon enough. No more time to waste; the beam weapons that had narrowly missed him above, as he'd descended into the deep, round, three-meter-wide access passage of this central vault complex by a thin cable, would be working their way down to his level at any moment. They were moving much slower than normal, due to the computer virus he'd introduced into the local network a few moments earlier—and that was the only reason he was still alive now. Once the beams reached the bottom of the shaft where he stood, the jet-black deflector suit he wore over his uniform would protect him from that type of firepower for approximately two seconds—if he was lucky. Then he'd be sliced into a thousand very small pieces.

He spun about, eyes moving across the gleaming silver surface that curved all around him, looking for the access hatch. It was there, somewhere—all of his sources agreed on that point. Unfortunately, none of them agreed on exactly what it looked like, or how to open it. If there was a potential bottleneck in the whole operation, this might well be it.

Save for a single line that looked to run, like a ring, all the way around at a height of about one meter from the floor, the metal appeared seamless. He moved forward, choosing a spot at random, and ran his gloved hand across it. Nothing.

The crisscrossing beams were ten meters above his head now. Nine. Melting metal hissed above his head.

He moved around the circular floor quickly, fingertips sliding along, lenses in his goggles magnifying what he was seeing and analyzing it for any clues to the location of the hidden hatch.

Eight meters above him now. Seven. The hum of the lasers and the crackle as they ate into the metal grew much louder.

He'd traveled over halfway around the circle, and still nothing. Time was running out. He spun about, abandoning the careful search for a more general impression, and saw very clearly that the shaft wall was just as smooth and unbroken on the half he hadn't inspected yet.

His sources had all been wrong. There was no access hatch. And of course he couldn't go back up. He was trapped here at the bottom of the steel and concrete well, and he was going to die.

Six meters. Five.

And the worst part was that he had never *wanted* to do this. He had never envisioned himself as a thief of any kind—much less a thief attempting to steal the most valuable, the most priceless artifact in history.

Sometimes greatness is thrust upon you, they say. Hmm. Sometimes thievery is, too, apparently.

Four meters. Three. He crouched down, still searching, the bottom of the shaft now lit up like a neon bulb by the blazing beams of death just overhead.

But there was nothing to find. No hatch, no seams at all—other than that one ring all the way around. But it never intersected anything vertical that might indicate a doorway. And it wasn't as if the entire bottom of the shaft could—

Wait.

Two meters overhead. The sound was deafening.

Could it be?

Reaching out, he pressed at the wall just below the seam. There came a click, almost inaudible over the noise of the energy beams. And then the entire circular wall from the seam line down retracted smoothly into the floor. This revealed four narrow passageways leading off in different directions.

One meter. No time to think. Just *go.*

He sprang forward, into the nearest passage, just as the energy beams dropped below the one meter mark. A few stray shots passed just over his head before the circular wall that had dropped down moved back up into position, blocking off the way he had come but also deflecting the beams.

Tamerlane rolled over on his back and lay there for a few seconds, just breathing. He tugged his goggles off and wiped at the sweat running across his face and down from his close-cropped black hair.

Another obstacle down. How many more to go?

Tamerlane crawled through the access tunnel, cursing his fate in general and idly wondering if there was any chance he was in the right one of the four passageways. Luck had been with him so far; luck, plus a much more advanced brand of technology than had been anticipated by the people who had built this facility.

No ordinary burglar could have gotten anything like this far.

He'd overcome half a dozen deathtraps already, and still had no idea how close to his prize he'd gotten. But there was no turning back now. In truth, there had been no turning back from the moment this assignment—this utterly insane assignment—had been given to him. But there was simply no refusing the person who'd chosen him for it.

So here he was, deep in the bowels of the most secure storage complex in the galaxy: the vaults of Candis. A complex inviolate from the intrusions of man and god for thousands of years. And he was attempting to steal the single most valuable item in those vaults.

And—most murderous irony of all—if he succeeded, his reward would likely be to lose his job, his career.

But, again, there was no saying "no" to the person who'd given him this assignment.

So onward he crawled, and eventually he reached the end of the access tunnel and emerged into a small room about four meters to a side. Accessing his very secure and encrypted Aether link, he mentally studied the stolen plans he'd acquired and was pleased to see they matched up again. It took only seconds to locate the right spot. He stepped forward, attached two small, white discs to the gleaming wall, and ducked back into the tunnel.

The explosions were simultaneous and very contained. They would do no more to alert the actual human beings monitoring the vaults than would his earlier adventure with the lasers, given the computer virus currently churning its way through the complex's artificial intelligence array and overriding the sensors and visual scanners. That couldn't be counted on to work for much longer, though; even if the computers were fooled, a random guard patrol might easily spot the signs of his presence. He had to speed things up, move things along.

He hopped back out of the side tunnel and inspected his handiwork. The two explosives had done their job; the door between this chamber and the next was now hanging open. Forgetting what lay ahead, he ran through it—and stepped out into nothingness.

He teetered on the edge of the drop for half a second, his eyes widening and his pulse surging, before he fell forward and tumbled down toward his death.

In the split second before he'd fallen, however, he'd remembered what lay on the far side of the doorway, and he'd gotten his fingers on the dial at his waist, attached to a small box on his belt. He twisted it sharply and his rapid descent abruptly halted. The suddenness of it nearly broke his neck, but clearly it was preferable to the other way his drop could have ended: the floor of this shaft lay only a few dozen meters below.

Adjusting the dial, he rose gently into the air and drifted forward at the same time, reaching the doorway opposite the one he'd passed through in only a few seconds. The device at his belt, working just as it had been designed to do, repelled the specific type of material the floor of the shaft was made from. He couldn't exactly push the planet away from him, but the converse was just as good: It pushed him away—up and away, and through the doorway. His feet touched the floor and he switched it off.

Surely only seconds remained before his computer virus was eliminated by the complex's defenses. Any moment now, everyone on Candis would know he was there, and a few seconds after that, he would be captured or killed. His rank, his status, wouldn't matter a bit. Candis was not part of the Imperial government. It had always operated as a private, independent entity, and it had the clout and the wealth to maintain that status. It had always been able to assert that it offered the galaxy the one thing no one else could offer: absolute security from theft by god as well as by man, and it charged fees commensurate with such a claim.

Of course, Tamerlane was testing that assertion at the moment.

He raced the length of the corridor, hoping beyond hope that he was in reality where the stolen blueprints seemed to indicate he was. Time was running out—if he was wrong, if he had chosen incorrectly back in the first shaft, he was done, finished.

The corridor opened onto a long, broad, high-ceilinged space with lights lining every surface. The center of the room was nearly filled by a plinth in the shape of a long rectangle, rising to waist-height. Its top surface was covered in a material like black velvet.

Upon it lay the single most valuable, most priceless object known to man.

Despite the press of time, Tamerlane could not resist standing there for a moment, staring down at it.

It gleamed golden in the bright white light. Its edge appeared as sharp as ever it had been. The curving lines inscribed into its surface matched the records in precise detail.

Despite himself, despite everything he'd been through on this insane, unwanted operation, Tamerlane smiled.

He took a small, black cube from one pocket and squeezed it, and quickly it expanded into a long, narrow carrying bag complete with shoulder strap. He opened it and lay it on the plinth.

Then, full of reverence, he reached down and lifted the Sword of Baranak.

Tamerlane floated back up the shaft on waves of magnetic/gravitic repulsion. The sword was secure within the bag he'd brought for it, hanging from his back.

A quick check of the Aether connection told him the computer virus would be overcome in mere seconds.

He reached the top of the shaft, and for once found the maintenance tunnel there just as it had been described to him—this time, thankfully, at full height, so that he wouldn't have to crawl. His boots touched the floor again and he raced along, reaching the far end and the doorway that led out very quickly. Four access panels covered the wall on the left just before the door, and he pulled the one on the bottom open, drawer-like, as the plan had called for him to do. There was a hollow space there, between rows of electronic components. He pulled the black bag containing the sword off his back and wedged it into the space—right where the highly trusted and skilled agent currently posing as a maintenance man for the facility would find it in a few days, once things had died down a bit. That man would have no trouble picking it up from its new, much less secure hiding spot—especially now that its trademark radiant energy signature was blanked by the super-high-tech insulating bag that now contained it. He would carry it out and smuggle it aboard a ship that would take it away from Candis for good. And deliver it to he who had ordered the theft in the first place.

Tamerlane stood, removed his belt and unzipped his deflector suit. He bent down again and stuffed those items into the space next to the sword. He pushed the drawer closed, straightened up, and smoothed out the uniform he'd been wearing beneath the black suit. Then he opened the door and stepped out. A ping via his Aether connection indicated that the computer virus had been eliminated—alarms were blaring to life all over the complex.

The staff was good, there was no disputing that. Armed men were already racing about as he moved smoothly away from the doorway he'd just exited and strode for the central office. As he arrived, he was met by an official of the local administration; the man's face was pained, his eyebrows knitted.

"Colonel Tamerlane! Sir!"

"What's the trouble?" Tamerlane asked, feigning confusion.

"We're getting readings that there's been a break-in," the man replied, his expression betraying his bewilderment. "Someone has apparently penetrated all the way to the innermost levels of the facility."

"What?"

The man's face was reddening. "And—even worse, Colonel—the section they have accessed is part of the Imperial collection. The Emperor's crown jewels!"

"The jewels?" Tamerlane made himself appear shocked to hear this. He took a step backward, his eyes widening. "But—is that even possible? No thief could get anywhere close to this far in. Candis is impossible to rob. Everyone knows that."

"Of course, yes," the man said, his agitation ratcheting upward as reports came in across the local network; Tamerlane was intercepting them via his own connection, which he'd secretly hacked, and was reading them just as quickly, so that he knew virtually everything the complex's staff knew. "I'm certain it must be a mistake—an error in the system, somehow. And yet—" If anything, his expression grew even more distressed as more reports came in, now that the virus had cleared the network. "By all of Those Who Remain—something *has* happened…"

"Alright, see to it, then," he told the man, releasing him to frantically scramble away, seeking more information. He couldn't help but feel sorry for the guy; Candis had never been robbed on any real scale in all the centuries of the complex's existence, and certainly not of an object of the incalculable value of the Sword of Baranak. Heads would roll—of that, there was no doubt.

Unfortunately, one of those heads might well be Tamerlane's own. After all, he wasn't just the thief who had stolen the sword. He was also the senior Imperial officer assigned to keep it safe. He had, in effect, stolen it from himself.

The only thing stranger than that was the identity of the party he had stolen it for.

"This is what you get for accepting the 'promotion' General Nakamura arranged for you," he whispered to himself as he strode toward the central command office. "This is what you get for ever moving up the chain of command at all, when you were perfectly content as a mid-level legionary. You're now both the most wanted criminal in the galaxy—though nobody knows it was *you*, hopefully—and, as Imperial liaison here, the guy who let the most valuable object in history get stolen from right under his nose—and from the most secure vault in the galaxy."

He walked into the command center—and into utter chaos. Just before he immersed himself in it, ready to put on the performance of his life, he asked himself one last thing:

I wonder why the Emperor ordered me to steal the sword in the first place?

BOOK ONE

THE ROAD TO DAMASCUS

1

s it true what they say, Major?" asked the lieutenant as he snapped his flight pack onto his belt.

"What's that, soldier?"

"That you're descended from Those Who Remain," the lieutenant replied, as the other three figures in the room looked up from their own work, intrigued. "That you're a child of the gods."

Marcus Ezekial Tamerlane snorted a sort of half-laugh at that.

"Don't believe everything you hear, Lieutenant—" Tamerlane paused, leaned forward, and pretended to read the man's name off the patch on the chest of his dark blue uniform. "—Singh." He smiled then, not mockingly but with genuine warmth. "Stories get around. Take them all with a, whaddyacall it—"

"A grain of salt," Singh supplied. He looked somewhat abashed. "Yes, sir. Understood."

"You'll have to forgive Lt. Singh, Major," came the voice of a female soldier behind them. "He watches all those celebrity and gossip shows. He's convinced half of humanity has divine origins."

23

"Hey, Dalton," Singh protested. "It's true. Have you seen the new lady that co-hosts the sports show on Five? I've heard they've got proof she's descended from one of the main goddesses, but they're keeping it from the public."

"She's not really my type," Lieutenant Dalton said, snorting and shooting Singh a look. Her straight, medium-length black hair shimmered as she moved.

"Alright," Tamerlane interrupted them. "At ease, lieutenants." He winked. "I'm pretty sure it's more about the latest augmetic surgical techniques than it is about having Karilyne as your great-great-grandmother."

"Is that your secret, too, Major?" Dalton asked with a wink.

"I'll never tell," Tamerlane chuckled.

"Major," came a voice over the Aether connection at that moment, "we're down."

Tamerlane nodded. "Thank you, Captain Radikov." He smoothed out the wrinkles in his own bright red uniform, gold insignia gleaming in the ship's artificial lighting. He gazed momentarily at the major's emblem he wore—an insignia that only saddened him, since it represented his demotion several weeks earlier—and then turned to face his team. "Everyone ready?"

One last quick check of environment and flight packs, and then the four soldiers signaled in the affirmative.

Tamerlane checked the power level on his holstered Mark IV service blast pistol—a weapon capable of firing a blob of extremely dangerous superheated plasma over a remarkably long distance—and confirmed that it was fully charged. He didn't expect to find trouble here on this barren rock, but one never knew. Then he looked to Singh. "How about the sensor unit?"

Singh patted the big black cube that rested beside him. At his mental signal, its lifter units engaged and it rose to hover a foot or so above the deck. "I've got it," he said.

"Then activate your protective fields, everyone, and let's go."

As they switched on the little boxes at their belts that generated human-compatible spheres of air pressure and atmosphere around each of them, Tamerlane sent a command through the Aether and in response the door that constituted almost all of the rear wall of the cabin slid open. They stared out into a gray dawn, a howling windstorm, and very little visibility.

"NM-156 is such a lovely planet," Dalton observed dryly.

"So lovely, they haven't ever bothered to give it a proper name," Reilly muttered.

"Shields to full power," the major ordered. "Looks like this stuff could cut right through us if we're not careful." A pause as he stared out into the swirling chaos for another couple of seconds. "Communications via Aether," he added needlessly; they wouldn't be able to hear one another speak verbally in this environment over a distance of more than a couple of feet. "Go to visual scanning mode. Our target is somewhere out there, but the captain hasn't been able to pinpoint it precisely with the ship's sensors, so it's up to us."

Without waiting for any responses, Tamerlane simply leapt from the dull gray metal deck of the Imperial starship *Donbas* and out into the storm. His boots never touched the ground; his flight pack engaged instantly, generating shimmering blue electromagnetic waves of force around him that held him aloft and propelled him forward.

Dalton followed hot on his heels, just ahead of Specialists Westerfeld and Reilly. Singh watched them go, envious, then frowned down at the big box that floated beside him and was his responsibility. "Come on then, you," he muttered to it, pulling it along behind him.

At the front of the procession, Tamerlane lofted as high as the flight pack would allow, spinning in a slow circle to take in the surroundings. The storm actually served to hide the worst of it all, for this was an ugly place; all rugged grays and washed-out browns. Desert terrain under an unforgiving mud-smear sky. No vegetation to be seen—no life at all—not even when he switched to deep scans.

"Anybody reading anything?" he called back to the others over their Aether link. "It has to be around here somewhere."

The ship's sensors had registered a power surge—a single point of intense, exotic energy—while still in orbit, but had not been quite able to precisely locate it. From one moment to the next, the readings had fluctuated from powerful to almost nonexistent. And since what they were here looking for would quite likely show up on sensors as just that—one small object of immense power—they had hurried down to investigate.

"Nothing so far," Dalton responded. The others echoed her report.

Tamerlane cursed. How could the reading have been so intense way up in orbit, but not show up at all now—right here on the ground?

Dalton continued, "Major—if I may ask—what makes anyone think there's anything of value on this rock? I mean, odd energy readings are one thing, but—?"

"The word came from higher up the chain of command, is all I know," Tamerlane replied. "An ancient and very powerful artifact might be here."

"And the Ecclesiarchy wants it," Westerfeld growled. "So here we are."

"You didn't hear me say that," Tamerlane replied. But everyone could hear the acknowledgement in his tone.

"The Sword," Dalton interjected. "The Sword of Baranak."

"What?" Westerfeld sounded incredulous. "You don't seriously believe that rumor—that somebody actually stole the Sword? There's no way!"

"I've heard it from more than one source," Dalton shot back.

"That just means you have multiple bad sources," retorted Westerfeld.

"The government itself hasn't said it was stolen," noted Reilly.

"Of course they haven't," Dalton replied. "They don't want to admit how badly they've screwed up, allowing something that important and valuable to be taken. It was all over the news outlets just as a rumor. Can you imagine the media firestorm if the government came right out and *admitted* it was true?"

"It just couldn't happen," Reilly insisted. "Nobody could get into the Imperial Palace. The security has got to be just unimaginable there. It's a joke to even think about."

"*If* it was in the palace," Dalton said.

"If? Okay, well then—if it wasn't there, where was it?" asked Westerfeld, scorn now filling his voice. "According to your unimpeachable sources, that is."

"Candis."

A moment's silence, and then both Westerfeld and Reilly snorted laughter.

"Okay—that's even funnier," Westerfeld chuckled. "If it really was stored on Candis, that would only make it *harder* to steal. It's secure from both human *and* supernatural thieves!"

"How about we focus on the job at hand, people," Tamerlane said, breaking into their conversation. "Word is the Emperor himself is interested in what we accomplish here, so let's take this seriously."

Even as he spoke the words, Tamerlane regretted having to withhold so much of the truth from his team. *If only General Nakamura hadn't reassigned me a year ago to Imperial Security, and thus gotten me mixed up in this insanity,* he thought bitterly. *I wouldn't have had to be the one to steal the Sword. I wouldn't have caught a bunch of the blame afterward for letting it get stolen. And I wouldn't have been busted down to major, and stuck on a rock like this—still neck-deep in whatever the Emperor is up to with the Sword. But, as always, I follow orders—I do as I'm told. And so here I am...*

"No readings at all, Major," Reilly reported, breaking Tamerlane's train of thought.

"Okay, let's form a perimeter and circle around," Tamerlane ordered after a few more seconds. "We'll divide up the area and—"

"Major," Westerfeld signaled, interrupting him. "I think maybe I have something here."

Tamerlane switched to tactical view, the Aether now displaying for him in his vision a layout of the area as they had mapped it so far, with glowing points for each of the troopers. He found Westerfeld's mark and saw that the man had already circled around somewhat to the west.

"Alright—everyone converge on Westerfeld," he ordered. "Singh—you and the box still with us back there?"

"I'm coming along, Major. It's a little slower going for me—for *us*. Be there in a minute."

Tamerlane sent a string of commands via the Aether link to his flight pack and swooped down towards where Westerfeld was standing. As he approached, the swirling waves of dust parted enough that he could make out a vast cliff face just beyond. He blinked at that—if he'd kept flying along as he'd been doing, he quite possibly would have run smack into it.

Dalton and Reilly landed behind him and they hurried forward to see what Westerfeld was pointing at. Tamerlane paused to locate Singh, still a good distance behind them, then turned and stared at what had been discovered. Involuntarily he took a step back.

It was a doorway. That much was very apparent. And it was big—a perfectly smooth, rectangular opening in the cliff face, at least fifty feet tall and thirty feet wide.

"Wow," Dalton muttered.

"…Yeah," Reilly agreed. "Not a natural phenomenon, I'd guess."

Both of them stood stock-still, heads inclined backwards, gazing up at it.

Tamerlane snapped a small scanner from his belt and held it up, pointing it at the opening. He ordered his Aether link to bring up the results and share them across the network.

"The readings are fluctuating," Dalton observed. "There's…something…in there, but it's not constant. Almost like it's…"

"Shifting in and out of existence," Westerfeld suggested.

"Or in and out of this universe," Tamerlane said. "Singh—get a move on." He switched channels. "Captain Radikov. We've found a kind of doorway into the side of this mountain. We're going to check it out."

"I'm seeing the images now, Major," Radikov responded from aboard the *Donbas*. "I'm sure I don't have to suggest that you and your team take care."

"Safety is our top priority," Tamerlane replied with a smile. "We'll get back to you when we know more."

As Tamerlane switched off the link to the ship, Singh's voice noted, "I thought finding the source of the energy readings was our top priority, Major."

"That's second, Lieutenant. If we get ourselves killed somehow, finding whatever-it-is won't do us much good." He gazed up at the gaping entryway again, then added, "Hurry up!"

"I'm here, sir," Singh replied, and Tamerlane turned to see the man trundling up, the big black floating box still in tow. "Be fair—you guys had it easy, getting to fly."

Tamerlane ignored him and motioned forward. Together, the five of them passed through the doorway and entered a darkened cave.

Within a couple of seconds everyone had switched to infrared and sensor, but there simply wasn't much to see.

Readings indicated they were inside a vast, hollow space, definitely man-made—or at least made by something sentient and very good with tools. The ceiling was so far up as to not register on their equipment.

"Spread out," Tamerlane ordered. "Scan for any signs of that power source."

"I don't like this place very much," Singh observed. He moved the black cube off to one side and switched off the function that had caused it to follow him. "Something about it gives me the creeps."

"Me too," Dalton added.

"That's why we're going to find what we're looking for and get out of here," Tamerlane stated. "Now get going."

The five of them walked slowly around the pitch-black cave, not bothering with lights and frankly somewhat concerned of what they might disturb if they turned one on. The interior looked particularly bizarre in the over-saturated colors of infrared and sensor scan; clearly nothing natural had carved out the big open space, given the regularity of its dimensions, but the walls had a sort of half-melted look that sent chills up the spines of more than one of them.

For a time no one spoke, and a sort of coldness-that-wasn't-cold descended, despite their high-tech shielding. Each cranked up the warmth generated by their environmental energy spheres. The electromagnetic fields that surrounded each of them and provided a breathable atmosphere were not visible to the naked eye, but a very faint luminescence shimmered in the air just beyond as they moved. Tamerlane ascribed it to the fields interacting with something in the cave's own atmosphere.

After a few minutes Singh called out, "Major—I'm detecting an energy spike here."

Tamerlane and the others hurried over. Each of them switched through a variety of sensor modes, as they all tried to gather what data they could.

30

"I'm sensing…*something*," Tamerlane noted, frowning as he ratcheted up the sensitivity of his scanner. "But—"

The cavern lit up like a flashbulb.

"Whoa!" exclaimed Tamerlane, stumbling backwards. The others were holding their arms and hands up before their faces to block the sudden blinding light.

An instant later, there came a sound—low, deep, rumbling—as though the entire mountain had transformed into a volcano and was about to erupt. But the sound was not natural; it had a regularity, an artificiality to it. Like an alarm claxon, Tamerlane realized—but one that had been slowed drastically down.

Several seconds—long, awful, blinding and deafening seconds—and then the glare faded to a manageable level. The five soldiers blinked furiously and squinted until they could see again, then looked around, seeing the interior of the cavern in visible light for the first time. It revealed an even more disturbing tableau than they'd first thought: the half-melted walls gave the impression that they represented the inside of some giant's digestive system. The faintly blue radiance that revealed all of this to them had no obvious source; it was as if the air itself glowed, and glowed most strongly only a short distance in front of them. It cast harsh shadows on the nearly-black walls and floor.

The low rumbling claxon ceased. The resounding silence it left behind was somehow even more deafening.

Tamerlane turned and was about to ask for opinions from his team when a bizarre voice echoed out, again coming from no obvious source, filling the cave with loud but unintelligible words.

He turned back in the direction of the light source just in time to witness three big humanoid shapes forming out of nothingness. He gawked for a moment, then reached for his pistol.

Seeing this, one of the troopers behind him whispered, "They're not real, sir!"

Tamerlane's eyes never left the apparitions. "What?"

"Holograms, sir," Singh replied. "Look at their feet!"

The major did this and saw that the giants' feet faded out into static near the ground. They weren't solid—not enemy warriors somehow teleporting in or stepping through a dimensional portal—but were instead simply some sort of projected images.

Tamerlane removed his hand from his gun and made sure his recording devices were all switched on. He studied the apparitions more closely.

Before them now stood three very distinctly humanoid beings, each at least twelve feet tall, each rendered in exquisite detail. Their heads were bald, their skin pale, their faces impassive. They wore dark gray suits of what looked like high-tech armor, or perhaps pressure suits. Or both. The design was so alien that it was hard to tell. They stood in a triangle formation, all gazing steadily ahead.

"Anybody recognize these guys?" Tamerlane asked, not taking his eyes off of them.

The one at the front began to speak. The words were like nothing the major had ever heard before; deep and powerful, like the claxon had been.

"Or that language?"

No one answered in the affirmative.

After nearly a minute of talk, the lead being raised first one hand and then the other up to chest level, palm outward. The gesture could be taken as either a sign of greeting or a warning to stay away—and the blank facial expressions offered no contextual clues.

The giant spoke one final phrase, its voice so low and rumbling that it seemed to vibrate the cavern floor, and then lowered its arms. The hologram flared brightly again and faded.

For several seconds the five soldiers simply stared at the empty spot that the aliens had occupied. Then they turned toward one another, all looking extremely puzzled.

"So..." Tamerlane croaked, discovering that his throat was very dry. He swallowed. "So—anybody make any sense out of that?"

Grunts and head-shakes in the negative.

"Looked like a pretty clear 'stay away' to me," Westerfeld observed.

"I'm not sure I agree," Dalton stated. "They didn't shout—didn't wave any weapons around. Maybe it was their way of saying, 'Hello.'"

Reilly snorted at this. "Anybody else here get the feeling what we just witnessed was some kind of *warm welcome?*" he asked. No one answered.

Tamerlane nodded. "Okay, then let's—"

Another light, this one far less intense. It shimmered into existence just beyond where the giants had stood. This time the light took the form of a rectangle about fifteen feet to a side, its edges wavering all around, floating just above the ground, looking like a window into some other world.

"Nobody move," Tamerlane ordered. The others complied but they all had recording devices aimed at it.

As he stared at the rectangle of light, the major suddenly thought he could make out shapes within it. He felt as if he were looking though a sort of translucent glass, seeing color and movement but no real details.

"What do you make of that?" he asked the others.

"It's a portal," Dalton responded immediately. "A natural one!"

Tamerlane's eyes widened. Naturally-occurring dimensional portals were legendary, bordering on mythological. Supposedly those beings centuries earlier that man had considered "gods" had been able to open and close portals at will, and even lead others through them— but no human ever could. *At least, not naturally*, he thought, as he glanced over at the big black box Singh had dragged along behind him from the ship. *Well. This could certainly make my job here a bit easier...*

"Westerfeld," he barked, "send a probe toward it. Quick!"

The soldier Tamerlane addressed had already taken a small silver sphere, about the size of a golf ball, from a pouch on his uniform. He held it up and activated it via the Aether link, then released it. The little ball hovered in midair for a moment, then shot forward, directly at the rectangle of light.

It passed through and curved around the other side, as if the rectangle was but a ghost-shape—like it wasn't even there.

Tamerlane cursed. "Okay—we're humans, not gods, so it's not going to let us just walk through. But clearly we've come to a very interesting and unusual place."

Dalton nodded, rubbing her hands together. "The dimensional walls are extremely thin here. Maybe the source of the energy spike was on the other side of one of those portals. That might explain why the readings have been so inconstant."

"Let's find out," Tamerlane said. He motioned to Singh. "Alright, everyone—let's help the lieutenant set up the scanning equipment. Let's get going."

"No help needed," Sing replied with a smile. He grasped the floating black box he'd shepherded all the way over from the ship and positioned it very close to the shimmering square of light. He sent a signal to it via the Aether and it gently lowered itself to the ground. At the same time, the lights along its side switched from red to green. Immediately the box began to unfold itself, pieces sliding out and rotating into different positions. In less than a minute it had transformed itself into a black rectangle about ten feet tall.

"Very good, Lieutenant," Tamerlane noted.

Singh didn't reply. He knelt down beside the base of the rectangle and began fiddling with something.

Dalton and the others were staring, puzzled, at the device Singh had activated.

"Major," Dalton said, "What kind of scanner is this supposed to be? It looks more like—"

"Like a doorway," Reilly finished for her. "Minus the door."

"It's what we need," Tamerlane replied, staring up at it, "to accomplish the job we've been sent to do." He turned to face Dalton directly. "Now, I think—"

He paused as a signal came in over the Aether. It was Radikov, back on their ship. He held up a hand to Dalton— *one moment, please*—and then turned away from her and the others.

"Tamerlane here, Captain," he sent back.

"Major, we've received a message for you from Central Command."

"Send it over."

A second later, thanks to Tamerlane's Aether connection with the ship, a voice—the voice of his commanding general, Nakamura—resounded in his head: "Ezekial, I need you back here immediately." A pause. "And by that I mean *immediately*, not 'after you finish whatever fool's errand the Eccleisarchy has you on this time.' I've complained loudly and long enough that they've given in— you've been reassigned to me again. Captain Radikov has been ordered to grant you use of the *Donbas's* shuttle, so you can depart without disrupting their current mission. And—you'll be happy to hear—I've gotten your rank restored, too—*Colonel* Tamerlane. So come on home."

The message ended abruptly.

Tamerlane reeled.

I'm a colonel again? And—I'm no longer in the doghouse with the military?

He couldn't quite process this at first.

Bless you, General. You've never let me down yet.

35

The others had stopped what they were doing and were all looking at him. He realized he must be acting rather strange. He smiled at them and somewhat modestly revealed the news.

"So—you're *Colonel* Tamerlane again. Congratulations, sir," said Reilly, grinning. The others joined in, shaking his hand and clapping him on the back.

"Alright, that's enough," he told them after a few seconds. "There's been a change of plans. I've been recalled to base."

Westerfeld blinked. "You've been *what*?"

"I've been ordered back to General Nakamura's central command, effective immediately. Just me—not the rest of you," he added quickly.

"You have to go, sir?" Dalton exclaimed. She gestured at the cave around them, clearly encompassing everything they'd experienced in the past few minutes. "They're pulling you out of here *now*?"

Tamerlane laughed. "Great timing, huh? Gotta love the military."

Despite his outward good humor, though, Tamerlane realized he wasn't entirely happy. As much as he'd inwardly complained about being sent on this mission, he found he sort of liked his teammates and was even starting to become somewhat engrossed in what they were doing, now that it had become a bit more interesting than he'd expected—now that they actually were getting somewhere. He hated to have to leave them now, perhaps right on the cusp of discovery.

Still, if there was one thing he'd learned in his years of service to Nakamura, it was that the man expected you to jump the second he said, "Jump." And he had gotten Tamerlane's rank restored. In truth, his debt to the general was growing larger seemingly every day.

Dalton clasped his hand again. "We wish you the best, Major. I mean, Colonel."

Westerfeld and Reilly did likewise. Singh appeared engrossed in something he was working on at the base of the machine and didn't look up.

Tamerlane disengaged from the others and opened a direct, private Aether link to Singh.

"Sir?" came the other man's mental reply.

"You know what to do, right, Lieutenant? You can handle it on your own?"

"I'll take care of it, sir. I'll have the portal open in a few minutes. After that, it's just a matter of timing."

Tamerlane nodded.

"Are you going to explain it to the others, before you go, or—?"

"I've been holding off just in case the machine doesn't work," Tamerlane answered. "No point revealing state secrets needlessly. Once you're sure the machine works— once you actually have a portal open—send them out of the cave, so they don't see exactly what you're doing."

"I understand, Colonel."

"Very well. We will speak about it further once it's done."

Tamerlane closed the private connection and addressed the entire group. "I'm heading out. Lieutenant Singh is in charge for now. He will report to me on how things are going, until a new officer is assigned to this mission."

The others nodded.

"It was a pleasure, people. I'll look forward to hearing how this all works out." He paused. "Curious about those big gray guys, too. I'll let General Nakamura know about them as soon as I get there." He spared Singh one more glance; the man had turned away and was at work on the big machine again. He'd slid a long, narrow box out of a compartment in the device's base and was fiddling with it. That seemed somewhat premature to Tamerlane, seeing as how he knew what was in that box, and he started to say something. Then again, he didn't want to undermine

Singh's new authority with the others by questioning his actions already. So he shrugged and turned back to the others.

"Take care, Colonel," Dalton said, saluting. Westerfeld and Reilly did likewise.

Tamerlane returned their salute. Then, activating his flight pack, he lofted into the air and shot out of the cavern. His Aether link directed him quickly back to the ship, the barren landscape sliding by in a blur beneath him. Within a matter of only a couple of minutes he was back aboard the *Donbas*.

"You're welcome to the shuttle, sir," Captain Radikov said, leading him down to the small hangar bay. He gripped Tamerlane's hand warmly. "We'll miss you. Good flying back home."

"Thank you, Captain," the Colonel replied, climbing into the tiny ship. "It's been a pleasure."

The hatch slid closed as Radikov turned away, and Tamerlane activated the singleship's engines. Gently it lofted through the open hangar doorway atop the larger vessel and then spun about, angling upwards. Tamerlane moved the accelerator forward and he shot like lightning up through the atmosphere, rocketing toward space.

He'd scarcely been airborne fifteen seconds when Radikov called him, the signal relayed from ship to ship and then directly to his Aether link.

"Colonel, I thought you'd like to know—we're reading another energy spike, this time right there in the cavern where your team is working. I've informed them."

Tamerlane frowned. Another spike? Could it be a new portal opening by itself—or perhaps some other warning system, or intruder defense system, or... The possibilities tugged at his brain.

Or maybe Singh has already opened that box, he thought.

He was too far away now for a direct link to his old crew. Instead, he addressed Radikov. "Captain, could you patch me through via relay to—" He started to say "Singh," then paused, considered, and changed his mind. "—to Dalton?"

"Will do."

Two seconds of silence, and then, "Dalton here, Colonel. You're really missing out, sir."

"What's happening, Lieutenant? I hear you've got an energy spike."

"Yes, sir. It started when Singh had us position the scanner machine directly in front of the dimensional portal area. The portal's gotten a lot brighter, a lot more vivid, I guess you could say."

Tamerlane mulled this over for a second. Then, "Lieutenant," he said, "you deserve to know—and, understand, what I'm about to tell you is top secret—that's not just a scanning machine. It actually was designed to enhance existing dimensional portals—to magnify them—so that, we hope, a real doorway can be opened into the Above."

Dalton said nothing for a couple of seconds.

"Lieutenant? Are you there?"

"Yes—yes, sir. I'm here. Yes—what you said makes sense. The machine *looks* like a doorway. I can see how it would work that way, to—" She paused, then, "Sir—it's gotten a lot brighter now. I think it's working!"

Tamerlane smiled. "I wish I could be there with you guys. I hate missing this."

"It's pretty intense, sir."

Tamerlane remembered his private orders to Singh, and added, "Lieutenant, at any moment now, Singh is going to order the rest of you out of the chamber. Do as he says. There are even more top secret things still to come, and the less you all know about it, the better, I suspect."

"Umm... Understood, Colonel," Dalton replied. "I think."

Tamerlane chuckled at this.

"Okay," Dalton went on a few seconds later. "The portal is really swirling now. All kinds of colors and shapes and whatnot. Singh's got a device and is measuring something, right in front of the opening. I don't know—I assume he knows what he's doing."

"He should," Tamerlane replied. "The rest of you might want to go ahead and step out for a bit, just to be safe, and come back later when the readings have settled down—"

"Leave now? Aw, c'mon, Colonel," she whined. "This is really amazing. The portal is shining like the sun now. And Singh hasn't ordered us out yet, so I have to assume that whatever he's going to do, he's not ready to do yet."

Tamerlane took this in and felt himself growing ever so slightly concerned. Shouldn't Singh have already booted the others out? He'd thought the man had clearly understood his orders. Frowning, he eased back on his ship's accelerator. "Maybe I should come back," he told Dalton.

"I'm sorry, Colonel," Dalton quickly replied. "If you're ordering us out, I'll get us out right now."

Tamerlane started to agree with this, but then he hesitated. He was starting to get a bad feeling, and he had no clear idea why. "No, no," he said, "stay there for now. Tell me what's happening."

"Singh's done with whatever he was measuring," Dalton reported, clearly enjoying her new role as play-by-play announcer. "Now he's back down by the base, working on something. The rest of us are just standing around, enjoying the ambiance of the place. It's so nice," she snorted. "Maybe I should build a house here someday."

Tamerlane laughed. He was coming to like Dalton. To like her a great deal, and more every minute.

"Hey, what's that?" Dalton was saying. Tamerlane snapped back to reality, hearing the surprise in her voice.

"Something wrong, Lieutenant?" he asked over the relayed link.

Dalton didn't reply. She was obviously addressing Singh. "Hey—where did you get—*hey*, that… is that really what I *think* it is?"

"What's going on?" Tamerlane demanded, growing slightly concerned—and frustrated by his inability to see what was transpiring in the cave. He didn't like surprises, particularly at sensitive points in a mission, and particularly from his own team.

A pause, and then Dalton finally answered. Her voice was full of puzzlement and wonder. "Singh just pulled a sword—a *golden sword*—out of a box he had here."

"In front of you all?" Tamerlane snapped, surprised.

"You—you *knew* about it, sir?"

"Just a minute," he told Dalton. Accessing the Aether link, he recalibrated for Singh.

"Lieutenant," he called. "What are you doing? You weren't supposed to let the others see the sword!"

No reply. The link felt dead.

"Singh! Can you hear me? Are you receiving?"

Nothing.

Frustrated, Tamerlane switched back over to Dalton.

"What's happening there, Lieutenant? What's Singh doing?"

"I—I have no idea, sir," she answered. "He won't talk to us. He's moving all robotically, and he's got the sword, and—" She hesitated, then, "No, Reilly—stay back from him. I don't like this. Something is wrong!"

Tamerlane was growing increasingly frustrated. "Dalton, what—?"

She screamed. Even piped across the relayed Aether link, it was blood-curdling.

That was enough. Tamerlane spun his ship around and pointed it right back where he'd come from.

"Colonel," Dalton said, her voice shredded by horror, "Singh just killed Reilly."

"What?"

For a second she apparently couldn't speak at all. Then, "Cut him down with the sword, right here in front of us!"

Tamerlane's mind reeled.

"Colonel—it's like he's possessed!"

Tamerlane was at a loss for words. All Singh was supposed to do was use the machinery to fully open any naturally-existing portal they could locate, and then throw the sword through it. As strange as that sounded—and it struck Tamerlane as very strange indeed—those were the orders handed down directly to Tamerlane from the highest levels of the Imperial government, following his successful theft of the sword from the vault on Candis. It was all top secret, of course; nobody outside of Tamerlane and Singh, aside from the Emperor himself and his closest advisors, even knew the sword's whereabouts at all. And so the other soldiers present on this mission were not supposed to see anything. But Tamerlane had taken that to mean, "Shield them from seeing the sword and what becomes of it." There had been nothing in the orders about actually *eliminating* any possible witnesses.

Another thought struck Tamerlane then. Was Singh trying to steal the sword for himself? Could that be possible? Where would he go with it? How could he get it off the planet? Was someone else in it with him?

Panic began to grip Tamerlane's heart. He shoved the accelerator of his shuttle almost all the way forward. "Shoot him, Dalton!" he barked. "Just shoot him!"

"We're trying, sir! Nobody's pistol is working! By the gods—" Silence again, enough to make Tamerlane want to scream. Silence that extended for several more excruciating seconds. Then, "Westerfeld rushed him and now he's dead, too," she murmured, her voice sounding softer now and very far away. Tamerlane suspected she was going into shock.

He slammed his fist down on the console.

"Dalton," he called, "get out of there. Now! That's an order!"

"He's doing something, sir," she replied, apparently ignoring the colonel's words. "He's standing in front of the portal. He's got the sword—sir, I think it really is the Sword of Baranak. I think he had it all the time! Is he the one that stole it? How? None of this makes any sense to me."

"Dalton, don't worry about that now. You've got to get away from him. I'll be there in a minute—I'll deal with him. Get back to the ship!"

Dalton ignored him, if she was even hearing him anymore. "Now he's raising the sword, holding it up over his head. And now—what's he doing? He's throwing it through! Sir—he just threw the sword through the portal, into whatever dimension lies on the other side." Her voice grew stronger, louder, as she called to the man. "Why did you do that, Singh? What are you—?"

Tamerlane's singleship had just passed over the horizon to the point that he could see the mountain and cliff face. Lightning was flaring out from the cave. The larger *Donbas* was a tiny silver sparkle resting nearby, illuminated by the horrific discharge.

"Dalton!"

A flash, blindingly bright.

The explosion ripped the top off the mountain, sent Tamerlane spinning nearly out of control, and annihilated the *Donbas* and everything else in a two-mile radius.

2

Major Niobe Arani slipped from shadow to shadow in the night, her target never leaving her sight. The man she followed wore a black cloak and hood, and he hurried along through the deserted backstreets of the ruined city with a definite purpose—a purpose Arani suspected she knew very well. She adjusted her night vision implants while trying to ignore the reeking smell of smoke and death all around. As soon as the target rounded a corner, she rushed across the street to the next point of concealment, keeping her target always in view. Her slender, lithe figure was almost invisible in the gloom, her silky black hair blending into the darkness along with the rest of her.

Along the way she had to sidestep chunks of rubble and debris that filled the street. The bombing, followed by the long ground campaign, had ultimately pacified this rebellious city on a fringe planet—*Trezibond*, she thought it was called, but wasn't sure—in an insignificant corner of the Anatolian Empire, but at tremendous cost to its infrastructure. In short, it had been bombed nearly back to the Stone Age. And even after that, General Nakamura still believed elements of the enemy's forces remained in place—though mostly gone to ground.

That was where she came in. Niobe Arani was a Special Forces agent with the First Legion, highly trained and highly skilled at surveillance and covert action. Where an army had perhaps failed to clean up all the bad elements of this world, it was hoped agents like Arani could root the worst of them out on an individual basis.

So she hurried along, keeping to the darkest corners, at least one eye always on the target. And after nearly half an hour of tailing him, she was finally rewarded for her skills and her persistence: the target seemed to reach his destination.

The man in the black robes stood before a narrow door set into a nondescript gray concrete wall. It appeared to be the side entrance to a warehouse complex of some sort. Arani suspected it was much more than that.

The door slid silently open and the man passed inside. It closed behind him.

Arani transmitted her current position and situation to her commanders via an encrypted Aether link, just in case the automatic tracking wasn't working or was being somehow blocked—as unlikely as that was. Having done so, she held her position and waited for confirmation from the higher-ups.

Two minutes later, she was still waiting.

Arani frowned. While it had been understood up front that Aether communications were to be kept to a minimum, just in case the enemy had some way of listening in, they should have at least acknowledged her transmission, if only with a single tone at the prearranged frequency. But— nothing.

Normally—ideally—her job would be over now. Having tracked her quarry to his destination, which she hoped was a high-value target as well, she should have been able to sit back and watch as the army came rushing in, armed to the teeth, to capture all the bad guys in this cultist cell and drag them all away for interrogation and incarceration.

Instead, she found herself all alone in this crater of a city, swimming in darkness, with likely very dangerous individuals only a short distance away. Dangerous individuals who might well be blocking her communications with the rest of the team this very moment, she realized. Who might well know she—or at least someone—was observing them.

The mission parameters had been exceeded, she understood then. Nobody had ordered her, on her own, to go up against a dangerous cell of terrorist cultists. Time to go. She would make her way back out of this section of the city and look for the first army patrol she could find—she'd tell them where her target had holed up, and then try to figure out why her link to the rest of her unit had been cut off.

She never got the chance to do any of that.

When she turned to head back up the street, she ran headlong into two figures in black who were lurking just there. They had been sneaking up behind her but apparently had not expected her to move so suddenly, and they both stumbled backward a step.

Shocked for an instant, Arani recovered quickly and sprang into action. She leapt up and delivered a sharp kick to the chin of the nearest figure, then turned her landing motion into a tuck-and-roll that caused the second figure's punch to miss over her head. Swinging around, she kicked out and took that one's legs out from under him.

Springing back to her feet, she immediately started to sprint away from the two attackers—but another shape suddenly appeared in her path. It was too late to stop; she tried to dodge to her right but the new figure moved like lightning. It shot out a hand from within dark robes and grasped her in an iron grip, nearly yanking her off her feet. Before she could counterattack, the first two caught up and took her one by each arm, pulling her back, as the third figure released her.

She struggled but couldn't break their grip. Angrily she glared up at the big shape as it turned to regard her.

"You'd better let me go," she hissed. "I'm with the First Legion—and they're on their way now."

"I'm counting on it."

"What?"

The larger figure reached up with rugged, powerful hands, and now she could see under the hood.

A silvery mask glinted there; a mask inscribed with incredibly complex, sweeping black lines and blasphemous shapes. His voice was distorted to the point that it scarcely sounded human.

Arani's eyes widened slowly. Her legs grew weak. She gasped.

It was the mask of a high priest of the death cult of Vorthan.

The masked man laughed softly, then motioned toward the door. He started that way, and the two goons in black dragged Arani along behind him.

"As you can doubtlessly imagine, I am well aware that the First Legion is in this city," the silver-masked man told her in his highly-distorted voice as the other two set her up on the rough stone altar at the center of the room and began to tie her down flat upon it with smooth, synthetic ropes. "And I have every confidence that we are mere moments away from your fellow soldiers crashing our party. They are quite welcome."

Arani was taken aback by this. She had no idea how to respond. These terrorists were looking forward to the Legion breaking in and arresting them? How could that be?

Her eyes flashed beyond the robed and hooded figures that loomed over her; quickly she absorbed what she could see of the room they all occupied. It stretched for twenty meters in every direction and the ceiling was so far above them that she could barely make it out in the dimness. A haze of smoke or fog hung over everything, as well, obscuring her view.

What her eyes settled on next sent chills through her.

The big figure—the leader—saw where she was looking, and saw her reaction. He laughed softly. "So—you recognize the symbol of our lord, then?"

An iconic image about two meters wide and slightly taller hung on the wall directly in front of her as she was presently oriented. Its border gleamed gold; its interior was a swirl of red and black. A flame seemed to dance, hologram-like, across its face.

"Vorthan," she hissed.

The big man laughed again. "Yes. Our Lord Vorthan. The god who died and will live again."

"Not likely," Arani spat. "He was dissolved—dispersed by the powers of Heaven. The Lord Lucian—"

"The criminal Lucian is long gone," the masked man snapped. "That treacherous monster will never again work his deviltry on humanity."

Arani couldn't help but gasp in incredulity at this. "*Lucian* was the treacherous monster? Are you serious? You—a Vorthan cultist—have the gall to—"

The other raised one hand to halt her. "Clearly we have differing views. That is to be expected. But this is probably not the best time or place for a theological debate." He gestured all around. "Your opinions aside, the master *is* returning. And *you* will be a small part of making that happen."

"What do you mean? I'm not doing anything to help you."

"Oh, indeed you will." He stepped back, and his grin was visible through the mask's open mouth. "For you see, we believe that an offering of blood and death will effect our lord Vorthan's return to this universe."

Arani blanched. "Blood and death?" She looked down at herself, lying prone on a rough-hewn altar, and began to understand. Panic flirted with the edges of her mind. She took a couple of seconds to compose herself, to settle her thoughts. "So," she asked, "just how much of that 'blood and death' to you believe it will take to bring him back?"

"We have no idea," the masked man answered, his grin still evident. "So we will simply continue to try—to create plenty of both—until we finally succeed. However long it takes."

Arani tried to swallow and found she could not.

"So," she croaked, "what are you planning to do? Drive a ceremonial dagger into my chest? Does it matter if I'm a virgin or something?"

The three all laughed. "Blood is blood," the masked man replied. "Death is death."

Arani balled up her fists in frustration.

The leader looked away for a second, likely hearing something over a closed network, since Arani found the Aether still blocked from access. He nodded, spoke a few words very softly, such that Arani couldn't hear them, and then looked back down at her. "The army has arrived," he said, appearing well pleased. "Time for my associates and me to get clear."

Arani processed this. "Get clear? What do you mean?"

The other two turned and darted out of the room, vanishing through a shadowy doorway. The masked man started to follow them, then stopped and regarded her one last time.

"Blood and death," he said. He turned so that his back was to her, reached up, removed the mask, and tossed it aside. And then he was gone.

And Arani understood.

Desperately she tugged at the ropes that bound her to the altar. She redoubled her efforts to access the Aether link, cursing meanwhile her decision not to carry a standard communicator with her. The Aether being jammed, she had absolutely no way to contact the rest of her team.

Seconds ticked by. She grew increasingly frantic—not just for herself but for all of them. She had to get loose. She—

The ropes. She strained to raise her head and shoulders far enough to see her arms, and when she did she saw something that gave her at least a sliver of hope. The ropes were synthetic smart ropes—and military-issue, which made sense, given what she'd witnessed thus far.

Quickly she issued a mental order to her Aether link to override the external repeating signal she'd been attempting to send to the Legion—that was hopelessly jammed—and switch to internal systems. That granted her access to a very limited range of tools she could command mentally, but one of them was a subsystem that lined the sleeves of her black uniform: the system allowing her to manipulate military-issue smart rope.

A second later the order she gave had been relayed through her uniform and directly to the ropes where the two touched. The ropes obeyed; they instantly expanded, releasing her.

Arani sprang to her feet and leapt from the altar, then sprinted across the room to the door the cultists had used moments earlier. As she went, she couldn't help but laugh defiantly: their plan would've succeeded if only they'd bothered to roll up her sleeves!

As she passed through the doorway and down a hall that led back out onto the street, she switched her Aether link back to external communications. This time she saw that the other members of her unit were close enough that the connection could overcome the jamming signal. She practically screamed over it, "Arani to Unit One! Danger! Do not approach the building! Pull back! Pull back!"

She smashed her way through the outer door and stumbled out into the darkened, rubble-filled street. There she ran headlong into a dozen black-clad soldiers coming from the opposite direction, converging on the building.

"Major," the nearest one—a sergeant—greeted her. "That was you just now, on the Aether? What's going on?"

"It's a trap," she hollered. "Everyone pull back!"

The sergeant blinked once, twice, and then whirled about and began shouting orders at the troops surrounding them. "Everyone back! Back to position three! *Now!*"

Arani was turning in a circle, looking all around, trying to see past the soldiers.

"Major," the sergeant said, trying to get her attention again. "You need to come, too." He frowned. "What are you looking for?"

She saw them. "There!" She pointed frantically.

The sergeant followed her gesture. He saw what she was pointing at: three figures in black robes rounding a corner further down the street.

Arani was already sprinting that way. The sergeant hesitated, then issued orders to the nearest group of troopers. "Come on!"

They all ran after Arani.

A second later, the building exploded.

Arani rounded the corner and what she saw there forced her to come to a sudden halt: The three black-robed men were standing there, as if they were waiting for her. The big one drew a blast pistol from his robes. Arani started to leap to the side, to try to avoid the shot that was surely coming, when the explosion hit, nearly knocking her off her feet.

Her head spinning, she struggled back to her feet. Her first thought was for the sergeant and his men, behind her—had they survived? But that thought quickly took second place as she remembered that she was about to be shot by the cultists. Dropping into a fighting stance, she looked up, her eyes trying with difficulty to focus on what lay ahead of her. She gasped.

Two of the cultists lay unmoving on the ground. Standing over them was a third figure—but it was no longer a robed and hooded terrorist. It was an officer in the First Legion. He was tall and slender, with very tan skin and dark hair. His nose was long and narrow and his eyes dark. He held a blast pistol and was gazing down at the two men he had obviously just shot.

Arani approached slowly, carefully. She looked from the officer to the two cultists and back to the officer. She started as she realized just who he was.

"Colonel! Colonel Barmakid. What—?"

The man looked up at Arani and nodded.

"These two attacked me as I was approaching," he informed her. "Cultists, trying to escape, obviously."

A shiver ran through Arani then. She'd never spoken directly with Colonel Barmakid, the adjutant to General Nakamura, before. His voice gave her the chills, though at first she couldn't have said why.

"They're dead?" she asked.

The colonel snorted a sharp laugh. "When I'm attacked, Major—particularly by lunatic terrorists—I don't hesitate to defend myself to the maximum."

"Of course, sir," she said with a nod. Then she frowned. "Two?" She looked around. "You didn't see a third?"

"Third?" Barmakid regarded her sidelong. "I saw no third cultist, Major. No." He looked around, then pointed toward an alleyway nearby. "Perhaps he ran that way, before I saw them."

"But he was at the rear," Arani murmured, frowning, looking around as well.

"What was that, Major?"

At that moment the sergeant and his squad rounded the corner and approached. They appeared soot-stained, bruised, and dazed, but were generally intact. Arani saw them and felt enormous relief that they were still alive.

The sergeant saw Barmakid and hastily snapped a salute, then addressed Arani. "Major," he said, "thank you for the warning." He pointed back toward the building where she had been held captive; it was now a pile of blazing rubble. "We were going *in* there…!"

Arani nodded, glancing at his name tag. "Glad you're still alive, Sergeant Garner."

"Sergeant," Colonel Barmakid said, from where he was kneeling down over the two bodies. He had stripped the black robes off both of them and set them aside in a pile, and was patting down the remaining clothing they wore. "Have these two carried back to headquarters." He stood and backed away to allow the soldiers to move in. "I want every inch of them and their clothing gone over, down to the molecular level. Whatever can be found out about them, I want it found."

The sergeant saluted again. "Yes, sir." He motioned for his men to move up.

"Wait," Arani said.

The sergeant and his men hesitated. Colonel Barmakid frowned.

"What's the trouble, Major?" Barmakid asked.

Arani squeezed past the soldiers and knelt where Barmakid had been crouching a few seconds earlier. She studied the two figures who lay dead on the street; they seemed the right size for the two that had attacked her. She looked up at the colonel. Then she looked at the pile of robes. She reached out for it.

"What are you doing, Major?" Barmakid asked, a sharp and suddenly hostile tone to his voice.

Arani turned to Sergeant Garner. "Sergeant, arrest Colonel Barmakid."

Garner opened and closed his mouth soundlessly but otherwise made no sound.

"Have you lost your mind, Major?" Barmakid asked, speaking almost casually now.

"I think I almost did, for a minute there," she answered. "But I can see much more clearly now."

"And what is that supposed to mean, Major?"

By way of response, Arani lifted the pile of robes. She let one drop to the pavement, then another.

She was still holding a third. *A third.*

"Arrest Colonel Barmakid!"

It took Sergeant Garner another second or two to grasp the significance of what he was seeing. Then, eyes widening in astonishment, he directed his weapon at the colonel.

Barmakid already had his gun leveled.

No one moved. No one breathed.

Seconds ticked past. The tension was unbearable.

Then finally Barmakid smiled and relaxed. He turned his pistol around and offered it to the sergeant. Garner, surprised yet again, reached out and took it from him.

The colonel regarded Arani with what looked to her like an odd combination of respect and contempt.

"Well done, Major," he said. "You might have quite a career ahead of you." He laughed. "At least, until my lord Vorthan returns, frees me, and consumes you in fire and death."

As the soldiers led him away, he laughed again, long and hard.

Arani watched him until he vanished around the corner. Then she exhaled slowly and dropped to a sitting position on the street. She stared up at the smoke-occluded stars high above and shook her head in wonder.

"Barmakid," she whispered. "Colonel Barmakid—the general's own adjutant—a traitor and a cultist. Has it come to that? Are we that far gone?"

She breathed in and out slowly, the air acrid with smoke and gunpowder and ozone from energy weapons fire, trying to reacquire her bearings.

"Major Arani," came a voice over the Aether a few seconds later. At least the jamming had apparently ceased. "Major Arani. Come in."

"Arani here," she answered wearily.

"Report to rendezvous point delta immediately for new assignment."

Arani bit her tongue, balled up her fists, and then sent back, "Acknowledged."

Climbing slowly to her feet, she dusted herself off, consulted the Aether for her present location, and started walking toward point delta.

Around her, a city—a city whose name she hadn't even bothered to learn—continued to burn.

3

I apologize for my outburst, General," Tamerlane sent over the Aether connection after regaining control of his emotions, "but—with all due respect to the Emperor and his advisors, who doubtlessly labor day and night in the service of the realm—have they all lost their minds?"

This was actually a question the colonel had asked himself on numerous occasions in the past six months. It was the first time, however, that he'd expressed the sentiment aloud, and to his longtime commanding officer. But he couldn't help it; here they were—Tamerlane and his commanding general—caught in the middle of a firefight on a mostly insignificant planet. And the reason they'd been ordered there in the first place remained for the most part obscured.

General Hideo Nakamura started to reply, but Tamerlane would never know if the response would have contained the general's truthful feelings about such orders, or a simple admonition against questioning the priorities of their political leaders. For, even as the general tapped the Aether link to send his message, a blizzard of energy bolts perforated the air—and the wall just above and behind him and his troops. As they all instinctively ducked, shards of masonry and clouds of dust descended on Nakamura and his staff of support officers.

From his position a relatively short distance away, Tamerlane could see what was happening. The enemy forces had broken through the lines almost directly ahead, and the First Legion's defenses were collapsing. What had started out as a simple scouting maneuver had become something infinitely worse, and their position had become the front line of the invaders' assault.

"Pull back!" the gray-haired general ordered over the link to his forces. "Ezekial—get them back!"

Tamerlane acknowledged the order, though he wasn't exactly certain how to go about such a thing, and stuck his head up again to get a sense of their current tactical situation. The words "rapidly deteriorating" came to mind. Another volley of energy blasts also nearly came to his mind—and the rest of his head—as well, and he quickly ducked back behind the remains of the stonework where he'd found refuge.

He and Nakamura had landed on this planet—Kampong, an outpost along the fringes of the Anatolian Empire, which they both served—to investigate rumors of new incursions from Riyahad, the neighboring empire in that galactic quadrant. Oddly enough, it lay in the same general sector as the barren NM-156 where Tamerlane had headed up the portal expedition. No sooner had boots touched the ground here than a wave of Riyahadan forces had launched a full assault on their landing grounds. With Nakamura's support fleet in orbit caught up in an engagement far overhead, the soldiers under his command on the ground were left to fend for themselves.

Tamerlane tried to peek out again but the level of enemy fire coming at him and the others was simply too much. They were all pinned down, here in the outskirts of a bombed-out city that contained nothing of value. Even the intelligence reports that had drawn them here with promises of double-agents and secret information had been wrong. Now there was nothing left to do but get as many members of First Legion out alive as possible.

"Aren't you glad now that I managed to get you recalled back onto my force?" Nakamura called from his own hiding place. "You could've missed out on all of this!"

"Thank you," Tamerlane replied back, deadpan. "Thank you so much, General." He looked around as best he could without revealing himself, taking in the tactical environment. It wasn't good. He and the general and another dozen or so troops were scattered within the shattered front of a large concrete building. The main street ran past just beyond them. Enemy soldiers were advancing from the left as Tamerlane could see them. They wore the thin, loose-fitting robes of Ryahadi soldier-fanatics, and each of them carried both an energy rifle and a dagger. They all had murder in their eyes. The Anatolian Empire and the Riyahadi Empire had never been close—politically, socially, or even religiously—as the long string of wars between them over the centuries attested to. These guys, Tamerlane knew, meant to kill them quickly—but to be captured alive by them would be even worse.

He started to issue the set of orders he'd just formulated for a hasty but careful retreat, when a blood-curdling cry of bloodlust arose from the Riyahadi forces. They charged, a headlong sprint forward, guns firing into the fronts of all the buildings along their side of the street.

Tamerlane cursed. His idea for an orderly withdrawal had been stillborn. There was simply no way his small band of fighters could hold off a well-armed Riyahadi mob for very long, while the bulk of Nakamura's army slipped away. Their only chance now was simply to flee—to flee this battleground as quickly as humanly possible, and by any means possible.

He gave the word—"Retreat! Back to the shuttles if you can!"—and then leapt out of concealment, rolling and dodging, blasts flashing and roaring all around him, to get to Nakamura. Somehow he survived long enough to make it.

"Come on, General," he shouted, grasping the older man by the shoulder. "We have to get you out of here."

The general pulled himself up from his shooter's stance—he'd taken out a half-dozen of the attackers already—and hurried after Tamerlane. The colonel motioned to two troopers he spied off to their right to come over and join them, but the men never made it even halfway. In a flash of green, two of the Riyahadi soldier-fanatics leapt over the rubble and landed just in front of them. The two First Legion men were caught completely flat-footed. Blades flashed and the soldiers fell.

Tamerlane instantly moved around in front of Nakamura, positioning himself between the somewhat short, stocky general and the Riyahadis. His energy pistol was in his hand, at the ready, and he fired as the first of the attackers rushed forward. His first shot missed slightly wide and the blade came up. Now Tamerlane could see the man's face: the lower half was obscured by a scarf-like cloth, but dark eyes blazed just above. Surprisingly, the man didn't utter a sound as he leapt, dagger flashing—and he made no sound when Tamerlane's second shot caught him in the face and brought him down hard and unmoving on the dusty floor.

Tamerlane heard scuffling sounds even as he turned around to check on the general. To his shock, he realized that the second Riyahadi had somehow slipped past him in the brief moment that he'd fought the first one, and the savage killer was now struggling with Nakamura. The general had managed to block the first dagger swing and was grasping the man's left forearm with both hands, holding the dagger at bay. The right hand, however, was rising, preparing to swing around and club the general in the head. Tamerlane didn't hesitate—he fired, from only a few meters away. The Riyahadi's right hand exploded.

The soldier-fanatic screamed and whirled around, waving his bleeding stump, his scarf falling away to reveal his entire face. His dark features were lined with pain and hatred, and his eyes locked onto those of Tamerlane and burned with fire and murder. He started forward.

Nakamura clubbed him in the back of the head with his rifle butt.

Tamerlane was on him before he hit the ground. He seized the man and rolled him over, face up, holding him by the collar—only to see that the Riyahadi had bitten into a poison capsule and was already dead.

The colonel looked up at the general. Nakamura shrugged. "There was nothing of any use we could've learned from him," he said.

Tamerlane let the body slump back down to the ground and glared at it. "You're right," he said. "It's the higher-ups in our own military that I have questions for," he replied, angry.

Together the two men hurried through the ruined building and out the back. After a quick look around, checking for the safest path back to their ships, they jogged north. They could see other members of Legion I similarly slipping from one point of cover to another, evacuating as ordered. The enemy seemed to be confining itself to the street in front of the buildings, at least for the moment. That was good; it meant most of the unit might be able to get away. Even so, Tamerlane had the distinct feeling, honed from years of operations against the Empire's enemies, that a major assault was coming at any moment.

As soon as the transport ships came into view, Nakamura motioned for them to halt. He nodded toward a shattered wall to his right. "We can set up a perimeter defense here," he stated. Accessing the Aether, he issued orders to his troops, attempting to sculpt order out of chaos again.

Tamerlane did likewise, issuing specific replies to questions coming in from the various sub-commanders.

As soon as he was done, Nakamura switched off the link and cursed violently. "I hate retreating," he spat. "I hate it, Ezekial. I want to go back and fight those people."

"I know you do, sir—and so do I," Tamerlane replied. "But we both know the first priority is pulling the First out intact. Our tactical situation here is just too shaky to do anything more. At least for now." He gazed out at the rubble- and ruined-building-filled space between their position and the seemingly-now-halted enemy line, and could make out the other First Legion soldiers hurrying back in their direction. "They're not pressing their advantage at the moment, for whatever reason. Nothing we can do for now but sit tight here, and wait for everyone to get regrouped at the ships. And hope they don't suddenly realize they could overwhelm us all pretty easily if they launched a full-scale attack."

Nakamura scowled but nodded. Then he looked more closely, more intensely, at Tamerlane. "I heard what you said about questioning the higher-ups. Believe me, I have some questions for them, too. But—Ezekial—you mustn't say that in front of anyone else."

"Somebody needs to say it." Tamerlane gestured around at the ruins of the city. "For starters—who thought *this* was a good idea? Sending us down here, into this mess?"

"You're right, of course. But—do you have any idea how difficult it was for me to get you reinstated? To get you your rank back? Do you want me to have to go through that all over again?"

Tamerlane couldn't speak for a moment. Finally he managed, "I'm very grateful for all that you did, General."

"I know. I know you are. But my point is—" He reached out and patted Tamerlane on the shoulder. "—You are far too valuable an asset to lose. And I certainly don't need you self-destructing. So—keep your mouth shut with regard to the insane orders we received today. Understood?"

"Understood, sir," Tamerlane answered quickly and crisply. He considered for a moment, then ventured, "Might I speak freely, sir?"

The general eyed him warily. He shook his head with a sigh. "You just can't let things go, can you, Ezekial?"

"Sir, with all due respect—and that's a very, very *great* deal of respect—you don't know the half of it."

Nakamura frowned at this. He pursed his lips, studied Tamerlane's face, then nodded once. "Speak, then."

"With pleasure." Tamerlane quickly launched into an extremely abbreviated version of recent events. He began with the Emperor's order for him to break into the Imperial vault on Candis and steal the Sword of Baranak from the Emperor's own holdings.

Nakamura interrupted him immediately. "You cannot be serious."

"I'm dead serious."

"That was you? *You* stole it?" He scoffed. "Ezekial— please. I find that extremely hard to believe—for several different reasons."

"Oh, it gets much better."

Nakamura offered him a strange expression and motioned for him to continue, but more quietly. To either side of them, their troops were filing past, withdrawing from the debacle their current mission had become.

Tamerlane reminded the general how his success at this covert and rather bizarre mission had of course resulted in his public demotion from colonel to major—seeing as how Tamerlane himself had been in charge of security—and his reassignment to the exploratory team aboard the *Donbas* at NM-156.

"I fought that tooth and nail," the general interjected.

"I know, sir—and I appreciate it."

"Nobody could have anticipated it," the older man went on. "Someone being able to break into the Candis vault and steal the Sword of—wait," Nakamura stopped himself, growing confused. "But—you're saying *you* stole it. So you *could* have anticipated that someone—um—that *you*—um—"

Tamerlane snorted. "I know. It's insane. But it gets even crazier." He continued with his tale: No sooner had he taken up his new position than the Emperor's representatives had come to him and assigned him an even stranger mission.

"They gave me the sword," he told Nakamura. "They had recovered it from Candis after I had left it there in a prearranged hidden drop location. They told me the Emperor himself wanted it thrown away."

Nakamura gaped. "Th—thrown away?" he stammered. "The most priceless object in creation—the weapon that allegedly belonged to the great golden god of battle himself, Baranak—and the Emperor wanted it *thrown out*?"

"Thrown away in a very specific place," Tamerlane explained. He told the general of their instructions: to take charge of the team headed to the barren frontier planet, NM-156. To pretend they were investigating a mysterious energy spike there. The truth was far different: An earlier Imperial team had discovered a strange cavern on that world where the walls separating the various levels of reality were extremely thin. It looked as though ancient alien visitors there had already built some sort of equipment to open a portal into the Above. But the previous team had been unable to get the dimensional portal itself to manifest sufficiently for a human being to pass through it. Tamerlane was given a set of equipment that it was hoped would boost the portal's coherence enough to open a doorway into the realms beyond our own. His chief lieutenant on the mission, Singh, was in on the secret: They were to take the sword with them to the cave, open the portal, and throw the Sword of Baranak through.

"And that's exactly what I did, at NM-156," Tamerlane concluded. "Or rather, what Lt. Singh did. I had already been recalled to join you, so I left it to him to finish the job, and I believe he did. And..."

Tamerlane trailed off. Nakamura, who had been listening to all of this with an incredulous expression, finished for him. "The explosion."

"Yes, sir. As best as I can put it together, the moment Singh threw the sword through the portal, the entire mountain blew up." He paused, then, "And my entire squad was killed."

Nakamura stared at him in silence for several long seconds. Then he looked away, gazing off at the horizon.

"I know this is all hard to process, General," Tamerlane began after a few seconds.

"That's putting it mildly, Ezekial. And yet..." He frowned, closed his eyes, shook his head slowly, and then finally turned to face the other man. "If it were anyone other than you telling me this ludicrous story, Ezekial," he said, "I would have them tossed out of the Legion—and up on charges—in a nanosecond."

Tamerlane could only nod.

"It's all true, then? Yes," he answered himself immediately. "I know it is. I *know* it." He inhaled deeply and exhaled. Around them, the last of the troops were passing by, headed for the shuttles. "And you don't know *why*? Why the Emperor desired *any* of this to be done? Why he chose *you*—why he *used* you like an instrument, from beginning to end?"

Tamerlane shook his head. "No idea, sir. But I did as I was commanded. Every bit of it."

"Yes," Nakamura replied. "Yes, you did. No one can fault you there." He gazed out at the ruined city, but he was obviously deep in thought. "This occurs to me," he said after a minute. "If the Emperor intended all along to have the sword thrown into the Above, he would've had to have it stolen for that purpose beforehand."

"Sir?"

"Think about it, Ezekial. He couldn't very well have openly gone to the vaults on Candis and demanded it be handed over to him, so that he could just toss it through some cosmic doorway. The Imperial Senate, among others, would've balked. He'd have been deposed, at the very least—or found to be mentally unstable and removed from power for medical reasons."

"Yes," Tamerlane nodded. "It had to look like it had been stolen—taken off the grid entirely. At that point, he could do whatever he wanted with it, and no one could stop him. No one would *know*."

"No one but you," Nakamura pointed out.

"And Singh," Tamerlane said—then winced. "But he's dead."

"And you're the only one left—or were, until you told me."

"And here we are," Tamerlane added after a second, "having been sent unprepared into the middle of a death trap."

Nakamura raised a hand. "Hold on there, Ezekial. Let's not stretch the conspiracy aspect of this too far. We don't know—we can't begin to say—that the Emperor and his top advisors would send our entire unit into a firefight for the sole purpose of having you—and, by extension, the rest of us—killed."

"We can't *say* that, no, General," the colonel replied. "But it's hardly the strangest aspect of all of this. It's a lot less strange than being ordered to steal the Emperor's own sword and throw it away."

Nakamura took this in, frowned even more deeply, but didn't reply.

Before Tamerlane could say anything further, the general jerked his head up sharply—a movement recognizable to anyone in the service as indicating he was receiving a signal over the Aether.

Nakamura engaged in silent conversation for a few seconds, then turned to the colonel and motioned toward the shuttles parked nearby. "Our ships in orbit are safe," he reported with very visible relief. "We're clear to evacuate the surface."

Tamerlane nodded at this. Maybe they would live—maybe everyone in this detachment of the Legion had a chance at survival now. He couldn't help but wonder if that fact might disappoint someone higher up the chain of command.

After another few seconds of brief conversation, Nakamura's eyes widened. He broke the connection and looked at the colonel, seeming at a loss for words.

"It's the Emperor," the older man managed to blurt after Tamerlane finally had to ask what had so disconcerted him. "He's on his way into this sector."

Tamerlane frowned at that. "This sector? But—" He'd started to point out that there was a war going on here, but figured the general was already perfectly aware of that fact.

Nakamura was already hiking rapidly toward the shuttles. Tamerlane hurried to catch up.

"We have to intercept him," Nakamura said in a low voice as the colonel moved up alongside him. "He's young; impetuous. Anxious to be involved. He means well, but he could get himself killed out here. We have to persuade him of that fact, and send him packing back to the palace."

"He nearly got *us* killed out here," Tamerlane couldn't help but point out.

Nakamura's eyes flashed up, met his. "We'll go into *that* later," he stated in a low but firm voice.

The two men boarded the nearest shuttle and settled into the cushioned acceleration couches in the passenger cabin.

After making sure there would be more than enough space left in the other vehicles for their evacuating troops, Nakamura ordered immediate liftoff.

Once the shuttle was airborne and streaking upward in the direction of the support fleet in orbit, Nakamura turned to Tamerlane. "I'm naming you my adjutant," he told him.

Tamerlane was taken aback by this. He'd only risen to the rank of colonel a year before Nakamura had reassigned him to Imperial security—and then, of course, he'd lost that rank. To be the top assistant to the top general... Tamerlane's mind was reeling. Then he considered it from Nakamura's point of view and his mood darkened. "Are you certain you want to do that, General?" he asked, frowning. "I wouldn't want my reputation in certain circles of the government to reflect poorly on you."

The general regarded him with a half-smile. "Ezekial, if you have indeed done the things you say you've done at the behest of the Emperor, then—conspiracy theories aside—he can only respect and honor you for that, privately if not publicly. And that means everyone else should, too." Nakamura offered his old friend a tight smile. "You won't reflect poorly on me, my old friend. Quite the opposite."

Tamerlane argued a bit more before at last yielding and accepting the appointment. For a few moments afterward he said nothing, merely considering his sudden change of fortunes. Then he thought about the man who had been his predecessor as adjutant; a man he had scarcely known at all, and that only briefly. "General, what's become of Colonel Barmakid?"

Nakamura reddened. He rubbed at his chin for a second before answering. "Barmakid has been...*removed* from First Legion. From the military. From any connection with the government."

Tamerlane reacted to this with a start. He hadn't heard about any of it. "Why?"

The general squirmed uncomfortably in his seat. "Hard as it is to imagine, evidence was discovered linking him to a cult. A *Vorthan* cult."

Tamerlane blinked, completely taken aback. "You have to be kidding. *Sir*," he added quickly.

Nakamura shook his head. "It was the most remarkable thing. When interrogated by the Imperial Inquisition, he utterly broke down and started... *raving*."

"Raving?"

"About how everything will be different soon... about how some new savior is coming to shake up the galaxy—to pave the way for Vorthan's return."

Tamerlane shook his head in astonishment. "Barmakid? I can't imagine it. He was always intense, of course, but not like *that*...!"

"You never know," Nakamura replied. "It's funny—in our society, there are many gods, both living and dead, that one can worship. But there are a few that, if you're caught worshipping them, your career will be over. Vorthan, obviously, is one."

"Even though he's been dead for centuries."

"Living or dead doesn't matter, Ezekial. Gods are gods. The cults surrounding some of the dead ones are bigger than any of the living."

Tamerlane thought about the pantheon of gods—or at least semi-immortal, godlike beings—that their Empire held in highest regard. The golden sword that had so prominently figured in his activities of late had belonged to one of them—to Baranak, the golden god of battle, dead these many centuries. It had passed to the Emperor's family many years later, through circumstances that always varied depending on who was telling the story.

"So, Barmakid turned out to be a secret cultist," Tamerlane marveled. "And now I have his job. Hmm. Never thought my career path would depend on something like that."

Nakamura chuckled. "You're exactly where you need to be, Ezekial," he said. "Right where—" He broke off as a message came through the Aether link. "The Emperor's ship will arrive at NM-156 ahead of schedule," he reported after listening. "And likely ahead of us. We have to hurry. When we get back to the ship, get into your dress uniform as quickly as you can and be ready to move."

Tamerlane nodded. Then he frowned and looked at the general. "Sir—are we *supposed* to be joining the Emperor there? Do we have orders—or even *permission*? Does he even know we're coming?"

Nakamura looked away for a second, then turned back and regarded Tamerlane with his trademark half-smile. "I've never let something like that stop me before, have I?"

As a sense of dread fell over Tamerlane, the shuttle moved into position for its rendezvous with Nakamura's mothership. It slid inside the hangar bay and the doors closed behind it. The instant the hatch opened, Nakamura was on his feet and hustling away. Tamerlane fought his way out of the seatbelts and hurried after him, his sense of gathering danger not diminishing at all.

4

Out onto the wide balcony of the palace at the heart of Anakh strode the planetary governor, Amon Rameses. A tall, stout man in his early forties, he wore the full ceremonial robes afforded to the ruler of the planet Ahknaton—strongly Egyptian in motif, complete with headdress, shimmering blue and gold robes, gilded sword and hooked staff—along with the eight-pointed-star emblem of office of the Imperial court. His skin was deeply tanned, his dark eyes rimmed with black in the local tradition. He stood alone for a moment at the center of the balcony, gazing down at the open square some seventy meters below, and the throng of people gathered there. Seeing him, they cheered; in response, he brought one hand up and offered a very slight wave, as if only grudgingly acknowledging their presence.

A moment later, he was joined on the balcony by another figure—a man wearing a very different outfit. He was clad in the heavy black livery of an officer in the Second Legion of the Empire, with silver metal trim and insignia here and there. His collar was high and his jaw strong. How he stood wearing such clothes in the blazing heat of midday in Anakh was beyond Rameses' understanding.

"Shall we tend to this last bit of business, Governor?" the man asked, his voice deep and resonant.

Rameses didn't bother to turn. Truthfully, he found the man's company distasteful and was anxious for him and his soldiers to depart Ahknaton as soon as possible.

"Certainly," he replied, placing his hands on the railing and looking down the sloping surface of the pyramid-shaped palace. "Again you have my thanks for the fine work your army has performed on my world, rooting out the cultists that had infested it. I am hopeful that this sector, at the very least, has now seen the end of this fighting for good."

The other man said nothing; he merely moved alongside the governor and laced his fingers behind his back. His expression was cold and hard; his eyes stared fixedly out at the horizon. After a few seconds of silence, he looked up, touched his index finger on his right hand to his right ear, and nodded. "Thank you, Major," he sent over the Aether connection. Then he turned to Rameses. "The prisoners are here. My men are bringing them out now."

Rameses nodded absently. He couldn't ignore the fact that his skin seemed to crawl whenever the other man was near him. He wasn't insubordinate; not overtly, at any rate. Could it be entirely psychological on his part? "I don't know," he muttered—but didn't realize he'd said it out loud until the other looked at him suddenly.

"What was that, Governor?"

"Nothing," Rameses replied, setting his jaw firmly. Now he cast a quick look at the other, assessing him once again, as he had already done at least a half a dozen times since he and his army had arrived on Ahknaton, allegedly at the direct order of the Emperor to settle matters permanently. There was no question that the man exuded the air of someone who *enjoyed* settling matters permanently.

Colonel Ioan Iapetus appeared to be in his late thirties, with rough features that looked to have resulted from a lifetime of fistfights. Given the man's personality and his nickname within the Second Legion—"the Unyielding"— Rameses didn't find such a possibility all that unlikely. The crisp, well-tailored black uniform lent him an air of sophistication belied by his physical appearance. In short, he looked to Rameses to be a mere street thug dressed up in fancy army clothes.

Seeing Iapetus's eyes narrow, Rameses turned back to look down into the courtyard. There, soldiers in black carrying gleaming silver blast rifles were herding a group of approximately two dozen men and women through the open archway at one end and out into the open center of the space. The soldiers were not being the least bit gentle with these people, who were quite obviously their prisoners. Seeing the violence exhibited by the troopers, the crowd hurriedly parted to let them all through.

"That's all of them?" Rameses asked, puzzled.

"It is," Iapetus replied. "All that are left."

"I was expecting a much larger group," Rameses said, looking from the huddled mass of prisoners back to Iapetus. "A terrorist cell—dangerous cultists."

Iapetus nodded. "Just so."

Rameses frowned even more deeply. He studied the faces and demeanors of several of the accused, then shook his head slowly. "These would appear to be very average citizens. You mean to tell me they are—"

"Cultists," Iapetus said flatly, his eyes never once moving away from the circle of prisoners down in the courtyard.

"And their guilt is beyond question?"

Iapetus didn't bother to reply to this. Perhaps, Rameses thought, he felt such a question was beneath him. This only served to anger the governor. He already didn't care for the man on a visceral level—now he was making himself an open annoyance.

Rameses turned to face Iapetus, starting to ask another question, determined to gain more of an understanding of the crimes the people below. Before he could speak, however, Iapetus raised a hand to his ear and spoke a command that was inaudible to Rameses.

The stiflingly hot air of the courtyard cracked suddenly with the sound of gunfire, followed immediately by cries and screams from the prisoners and from the bystanders.

Rameses lurched reflexively to the handrail and stared down in shock.

The soldiers had opened fire, executing every one of the prisoners.

The crowd that had a mere moment earlier surrounded the scene below was now fleeing *en masse*, through the arches and back out into the Heliopolis complex of Anakh that surrounded the pyramid. Only the soldiers of the Second Imperial Legion remained alive in the courtyard, some twenty-four dead bodies sprawled before them.

Rameses took this all in, swallowed hard, and whirled on Iapetus. The colonel was cool as ever; he had taken a pack of cigarettes from his jacket pocket and was lighting one as he gazed down evenly at the scene.

Rameses wanted to shout, wanted to vent his raw anger at the man, but he quickly reined himself in. He knew from long experience that he had to calm himself and gather his thoughts before saying a word, or he would dissolve into sputtering anger and frustration and merely embarrass himself instead of putting the fear of Imperial wrath into the colonel.

Iapetus dragged on the cigarette and then blew a thin stream out in the other direction. As Rameses started to speak to him, he raised a hand between them in a "just a moment" gesture, clearly receiving a private communication via the Aether link. He nodded to himself and said aloud, "That's fine, Major—excellent work. You men head back to the camp at the landing site—I'm sure the governor will be happy to dispose of the waste for us."

Rameses blanched and felt his anger rising all over again. Who was this man—this lowly colonel—to make assumptions and to issue orders on his behalf, without checking with him first? What monstrous arrogance could possibly—

Iapetus had severed the link and now faced Rameses directly for the first time—something that once again broke Rameses' train of thought.

"I trust you are satisfied with how this was handled," the colonel said, blowing smoke off to the side.

Rameses felt his face darkening. "I—*no*, Colonel, I cannot say I am satisfied."

"Oh?" Iapetus did not seem concerned by this news.

"You simply ordered an execution," Rameses barked. "Ordered it yourself!"

Iapetus regarded him coolly, as if visually appraising him for the first time. "You wanted to do it? You wanted to be the one to issue the order?"

Rameses scowled. "No—that's not what I'm saying at all. Not that I *wanted* to." He paused for a moment, gathering himself again. "I mean that, in *legal* terms, if it had to be done—and I'm not convinced that it should have—*I* should have been the one to—"

"I acted within my authority," Iapetus interrupted smoothly, "as ranking Imperial military officer on-site, present at the express order of His Majesty himself."

"Well, but—" Rameses stammered, then, "You had not yet persuaded me of their guilt."

"I didn't need to."

"There was no trial—"

"I had already issued my judgment."

Involuntarily, Rameses tightened his grip on the crooked Egyptian-style staff he held in his left hand. He felt his blood boiling over and had to restrain himself from actual violence.

A second later, the doors on the far side of the room opened and four more soldiers of the Second Legion entered, marching smoothly and swiftly across to the balcony, their boots resounding as they struck the marble floor. There they took up positions behind Iapetus and stood at attention. Their weapons were slung or holstered but clearly they were at the ready, and the threat and potential of violence hung like heavy smoke in the air.

He had called them, Rameses understood then. He had signaled for them to come, over the Aether link, while the two of them had been talking.

What is this man up to? Just what is he capable of?

But then, as if in direct counterpoint to the show of force, Iapetus raised a hand in a placating gesture toward the governor and his heretofore hard expression softened somewhat. Rameses watched it happen and couldn't immediately decide if it was an act or sincere.

"Governor," the man in black said, his voice now gentle, "I apologize if I have acted in a manner contrary to your wishes or expectations. That was not my intent."

I seriously doubt that, Rameses thought to himself—but he did find himself somewhat mollified by the words and the apparent conviction behind them. Then he glanced at the four armed soldiers standing like statues behind the colonel and for the first time he wondered where his own guards had gone off to.

"Rest assured that you have witnessed the lawful execution of known terrorists and cultists," Iapetus was saying. "This is a good day for the Empire, and the cooperation of your forces in their capture is much appreciated."

Rameses almost reluctantly nodded in acknowledgement. "They were cultists—that much is certain?"

"Most assuredly," Iapetus replied, dropping his cigarette on the marble tile and crushing it with a black boot.

Rameses considered this and nodded. "Then you did well to kill them. Being rid of worshippers of the foul god Vorthan is something any citizen of the Empire can rightfully accept and appreciate—no matter how it was carried out. They are simply too dangerous to—"

"They were not Vorthan cultists," Iapetus said.

"What?" Rameses blinked, meeting the colonel's eyes. "But then, who—?"

Iapetus shrugged—a miniscule, almost undetectable motion—and looked to one of his soldiers. The man spoke up: "They were followers of Korvak."

"There you are," Iapetus said with a nod to the soldier.

"Korvak?" Rameses was taken aback. "Korvak has never had cultists—he has some few devotees scattered about the Outer Worlds, but nothing like—"

"The new Korvak. The false god."

"What?"

"Someone—a *man*—claiming to be Korvak has recently begun popping up on worlds along the fringe of the Empire," Iapetus explained, making it clear from his tone that he felt extremely put-upon to have to present this news to a mere planetary governor. "This *man*—" and he strongly emphasized the word *man* again— "is a liar, a deceiver. He lures victims into his cult with wild promises and claims of godhood." Iapetus snickered. "We will see just how much of a god he truly is, when I capture him and fire a pulse-blast into the side of his head."

Rameses started at this.

Iapetus's lips twisted slightly with distaste. "Any of the gods could become a threat, but I worry far more about those who pretend to their status—and to the poor unfortunates, like these—" He motioned toward the bodies lying lifeless in the courtyard below. "—who place stock in them—in their lies, their deceptions."

"Whether Korvak is a god or a man," Rameses argued, trying to hold his returning anger in check, "his followers have never caused problems for the Empire—have never acted as terrorists." He rounded fully on the colonel. "When you came here, when you told me what your mission entailed, I naturally assumed you were pursuing the twisted devotees of Vorthan the godslayer."

"I will not abide cultists, or rebels, or terrorists of any stripe, Governor," Iapetus snapped. "Whether Korvak is a god or a man, he is usurping the power of the Empire, subverting its citizens and destabilizing its society." He moved in close to Rameses and his eyes burned bright. "I will not have that. I will crush it out wherever I find it. Without mercy."

Rameses was filled with wrath and tried to respond but found that he could not.

"*Those people* were cultists," Iapetus said with finality. "Terrorists and rebels. Now they've been eliminated. And I will do it again—over and over again, if I have to—to protect this Empire."

Before Rameses could formulate a response—or unleash an uncalculated and emotional one—Colonel Iapetus gestured sharply to his soldiers and they spun in unison on their heels. The five men in black crossed the chamber rapidly and exited the far doors.

Rameses hurried after them, wishing to summon his own guards but unable to locate any of them. As he reached the open double-doors on the far side—the doors through which Iapetus and his retinue had just passed—and moved out into the broad hallway beyond, he saw his own Sand Kings elite troopers, resplendent in their fancy dress blue-and-gold uniforms, standing against the wall, disarmed, hands raised, as a veritable battalion of Second Legion soldiers held their silver guns on them. Once Iapetus was past, his men lowered their weapons and followed him out.

The Sand Kings looked up at Rameses in shock and humiliation.

"Rearm yourselves, fools!" the governor shouted, waving his crooked staff at them to emphasize the point.

The guards quickly snatched up the pistols they had been forced to cast aside. The commander stepped forward and offered the arms-crossed-over-chest salute of the Sand Kings. "Shall we follow them out, Governor?" he asked, anger and resentment clearly dueling with embarrassment on his dark face. "Should we arrest them?"

Rameses started to agree to the suggestion, then hesitated. He considered things carefully.

"No, Commander," he said after a few seconds. "Let them go."

The commander clearly wished to object, but knew better than to openly challenge the governor's orders. He swallowed with some visible difficulty and waited.

"Get your men back to their normal positions," Rameses said at last. "And leave me alone."

The commander saluted again and issued sharp orders to his men. Within a few seconds, the Sand Kings had all hurried from the hall.

Rameses inhaled deeply and exhaled slowly, then turned and walked back across to the balcony. There he stood again, this time gazing upward. As expected, a few moments later, he saw the transport ship and fighter escorts of Iapetus's retinue rising into the sky. Seconds later, they had streaked away, gone from visibility, on their way back to their ship riding high in orbit over Ahknaton.

"This is for the best," Rameses whispered softly to himself. "All I wanted was that madman and his soldiers gone from my planet, as swiftly as possible. If I had sought to detain him, whether to have him arrested or simply to debate with him any longer, there would have almost certainly been violence, with who knows how many dead on both sides. And he would still be here." He gritted his teeth. "And who knows which side the Emperor would've taken in this? Who can predict how that man will react to anything?"

He leaned his staff against the side wall and rested both hands on the railing, gripping it so tightly he idly wondered if he might actually crack the masonry.

"But what happened here today can never be allowed to happen again. Never again."

He inhaled again, then looked down and saw the cigarette butt where Iapetus had stepped on it. Quickly, reflexively, he kicked at it, knocking it over the side and down into the courtyard; the same courtyard where some two dozen citizens of his planet lay dead. Dead because they had kept alive the memory of one of the gods. One of the decent ones.

"I must never lose control of the situation—of my own capital, my own palace, my own quarters, my own men—again," he whispered. "Whatever it takes, this must never happen again."

A trio of Sand Kings had emerged from the archway to the right and were taking it upon themselves to begin dragging the bodies away, one by one. Rameses watched them work for a time, thoughts and plans rapidly racing through his mind.

"I must never again allow my men to be shoved aside or intimidated by outsiders," he growled, his teeth grinding. "Whatever it takes, from this point forward, I must be in control In absolute, unquestionable control."

He gazed up at the sky, where Iapetus's ship had passed a few moments earlier.

"And I will not forget you, Colonel," he added. "There will be a reckoning between us, one day. Have no doubt about that."

He looked back down. The bodies were nearly all gone now. One of the Sand Kings looked up, saw him on the balcony, and saluted. Rameses returned the gesture.

"Never again," he repeated to himself. "Never again."

5

Tamerlane leaned against the smooth metal bulkhead of the Imperial starship *Edo* and gazed out through the thick layer of molecularly-altered transparent alloy at the darkness of space that lay beyond. The stars he could see felt unfamiliar, alien to him, even though he'd just been here only weeks earlier. In his two-plus decades of service to the Imperium of Janus IV Rahkmanov, he'd traveled across vast swathes of the galaxy, but nowhere else had quite creeped him out as much as this region. Something about it just didn't feel right. His experiences with the crew of *Donbas* had increased that uneasiness exponentially.

"What are we doing here?" he whispered, while the vast bulk of the Imperial battle cruiser *Monrovia* came into view as three linked silver cylinders gleaming in the void. "What foolishness could bring the entire royal court to the middle of nowhere?"

"That's what I aim to find out, Ezekial," came the smooth, steely voice from behind him. "And you'd better not let anyone else hear that kind of talk."

Tamerlane turned about quickly and saluted as General Hideo Nakamura strode onto the observation deck.

"Absolutely, General," he replied, somewhat abashed. "My apologies." Subconsciously he smoothed at his dark red dress uniform as he nodded at the man's words.

"You know you haven't offended *me*," the general told him with a mild snort. "But, just remember—we're about to be thrust into an entirely different environment than the one you've been used to lately. A, shall we say, highly-charged, *political* environment. If one of His Majesty's fancy sparkledy Guardsmen heard you say something like that, you'd find yourself put head-first out the nearest airlock."

"I understand, sir."

General Nakamura continued to stare at him with hard, flinty eyes for another few seconds before moving past him to take up the same position he'd just occupied at the viewport.

"The *Monrovia*. Well. It's not every day you see one of the Emperor's precious yachts this far out along the fringe." The general pursed his lips as he watched the massive vessel grow larger and larger as they drew nearer, quickly filling the entirety of the view.

Tamerlane considered saying something, then bit it back. He trusted the general implicitly and knew that Nakamura in turn liked and trusted him. But, that aside, he hadn't achieved his present rank by flagrantly questioning the orders of his superiors—and certainly not those of the Emperor himself.

It was too late. Nakamura had already turned away from the port and was regarding him fully, seeming to size him up, even though the two of them had known one another and served together in the Imperial military for more than two decades.

"What is it, Ezekial?" the general asked at last. "I can tell you're simply dying to say something." He hesitated, then allowed the thinnest hint of a smile to play across his lips.

"And if it's sedition, far better to bring it up now, before we rendezvous with the royal yacht."

Now it was Tamerlane's turn to smile. "You mean you don't mind sedition, sir?"

Nakamura shrugged, then pointed to his sidearm. "I figured I could simply execute you for it here, cleanly, and avoid having to involve a full hearing before the Inquisition. Not to mention troubling the Emperor himself." His smile had spread into a grin. "The gods know I've heard enough of it from you lately, anyhow."

Tamerlane cringed and rubbed at his eyes and the bridge of his nose. "You don't exactly create the most open and accepting of environments for frank discussion, if you don't mind my saying so, General."

Now Nakamura actually laughed. "When have I ever held that reputation?"

After a moment Tamerlane finally relaxed a bit and started to speak. Even so, he found himself leaning in close and using a soft tone.

"Why exactly is the Emperor coming all the way out here?" He motioned toward the viewport, and toward those strange, alien stars. "What does he want out here in the middle of nowhere? At, interestingly enough, the same planet where I was recently commanded *by him* to secretly throw the Sword of Baranak through a dimensional portal?" He hesitated, then, "And why didn't he tell *you*, of all people, that he was coming?"

The general didn't speak for a long moment. His dark eyes met Tamerlane's and held them. Then, "You have many questions, Ezekial," he stated.

"And answers haven't exactly been forthcoming, have they?" the colonel responded. He was making no effort to break the other man's stare. "General, you know as well as I do that something very, very strange is going on."

It was Nakamura who finally looked away, staring down at the dull gray metal deck plating. "I know," he said softly.

"And I wish I knew what to tell you. But I don't. I'm a loyal officer in the Emperor's First Legion. If he gives an order, I follow it. No matter how strange it might seem to me."

"That's right," Tamerlane replied. "I know all about following strange orders. I've carried out quite a few lately."

Nakamura looked at him sharply, then exhaled and nodded. "And suffered the consequences, yes, I know." He rubbed at his chin for a moment, then, "As best as I am able, Ezekial, and without bringing down the full brunt of the Emperor's wrath upon us, I intend to find out exactly what's going on. Believe me."

Tamerlane considered this in silence for several seconds. His frown deepened by the moment. At last he looked away, gazing back out at the big royal yacht as a docking tube slid smoothly out of the surface of its central cylinder section. It waited to connect with their ship. Tamerlane suppressed a gasp. He'd never seen it up close before, and he had to admit the vessel was truly spectacular—far larger even than he had been led to believe by first impressions from a distance. Battleship-sized. A sweeping sculpture wrought all in silver and gold.

As the two ships docked, Tamerlane turned back to Nakamura, leaned in close, and whispered his final thoughts on the subject: "I'm not sure which is more troubling, General. The fact that the Emperor and all the rest of us are out here, in the middle of nowhere—or the fact that no one has explained why, even to *you*."

Nakamura led the way through the airlock tunnel and into a broad, high-ceilinged reception area so vast that it seemed out of place on anything other than an Imperial carrier. Behind him came his top military staff of senior officers from Legion I, led by his new adjutant, Colonel Tamerlane, and Major Konstans Belisarius. A large congregation made up of special ops forces and support staff followed behind them. All wore the dark red dress uniforms of Nakamura's First Legion.

Tamerlane motioned for the others to stay back, behind him, as Nakamura separated from them and moved quickly across the space separating them from the Emperor's party. He moved quickly to the front of the formation that already half-surrounded the Emperor, and snapped a precise salute.

"Well, well. Hideo," the Emperor said, gazing at the general with an expression that was impossible to read. "So—you came, anyway."

"I came because I serve you, sire, and my primary duty is to protect you, along with your Empire."

Janus IV Rahkmanov, Emperor of Anatolia, largest of the four empires of mankind, turned to face Nakamura fully and returned the salute. Only in his late thirties, the Emperor kept in good physical condition, as his visible muscles demonstrated. His hair was dark, wavy, and a bit long, his nose angular and narrow, and his eyes a deep brown. He wore a military uniform quite similar to Nakamura's, though of a dark shade of purple with gold trim—the Rahkmanov colors—rather than red. A variety of dubiously-won medals were displayed across his chest. Behind him, almost ludicrously attempting to blend into the crowd, stood the six members of the Emperor's Guard—six giants in gleaming armor fashioned from synthetically-grown crystal and mineral. The bulk of their bodies occupied as much space as two or three normal men and their faces were entirely obscured by multifaceted helmets of the same substance as their armor.

"I know that to be true, Hideo—and your fine career of unsurpassed service to me and to my family is why I permit you these indiscretions."

"Indiscretions, sire?" Nakamura asked, feigning surprise. "You mean you did not wish for me to be here? In a sector of the Empire still recovering from the recent hostilities? I had assumed the message calling me to your side was disrupted in transmission."

The Emperor smiled flatly and laughed once. "You never cease to entertain me, Hideo," he said. "Truth be told, I'm pleased you're here."

"I'm very glad to hear that, sire."

The Emperor nodded toward the person who stood to his right. "I believe you are already acquainted with Ecclesiarch Zoric?"

Nakamura blinked, then recovered quickly and greeted the older man. He'd scarcely recognized him. In their previous encounters, the Ecclesiarch had always been adorned in the sumptuous golden robes of the Church; now he wore merely a priest's simple working outfit of slacks and tunic, both in off-white. The elaborate formal headgear he normally wore had been traded for a matching, lightly filigreed cap.

"General," the man murmured, bowing his head ever so slightly. Nakamura did likewise.

As the general turned his attention from the Ecclesiarch back to the Emperor, Janus IV smiled and made a show of looking past him to the crowd of immaculately-dressed officers in red who surrounded Tamerlane. "I see your entire retinue is with you. Including my erstwhile security chief." He turned back to glance at the civilian technicians who stood at a sort of respectful half-attention across the room. "I trust all will go well, and we won't be needing our entire First Legion today—including the ones who have failed me before," he added. "But I appreciate your bringing them along, just in case."

Tamerlane bristled at the remark, as utterly unfair as it was, but managed to keep any reaction off his face. Nakamura, who knew the truth of it, did the same.

"We were already together, sire, returning from a mission against the Riyahadi," he replied, having to force a somewhat convincing smile onto his face as he remembered the circumstances of his team's withdrawal.

"Yes, well," Janus said, "let's hope your present force amounts to substantial overkill."

The Emperor turned and began to walk through the crowd, which hastily parted for him as he advanced. The Ecclesiarch moved easily alongside him. The shorter Nakamura hastened to keep up with them. Tamerlane looked on, uncertain of what to do.

"To be honest, sire," Nakamura was saying as they passed out of the reception area and into a short, broad tunnel leading to another chamber, "I was uncertain of exactly what level of force might be needed here. I haven't been made aware of the precise purpose of this mission."

Frowning deeply, Tamerlane made his decision—he started after the Emperor's party, motioning for the others to follow him.

"So, what am I doing out here, then, you mean to ask me?" The Emperor looked back at Nakamura with a half-smile.

"It is your realm, sire," the general quickly answered. "You will move about it as you please." He paused as they emerged into an even larger chamber of the station. Then, "I merely wish to have as much information as possible so as to provide the most secure environment for you and your—"

"Patience, General," the Emperor interrupted, waving a hand at him. "I've purposefully kept all information about this mission a top-level secret from the beginning."

Nakamura nodded. Listening in from behind them, meanwhile, Tamerlane found it extremely curious that the head of First Legion and the ranking officer in the entire military somehow hadn't qualified for a "top-level secret."

Nakamura gazed expectantly at the Emperor, waiting. Finally, he blurted, "But you're going to tell me now, yes, sire?"

The Emperor laughed.

"Hideo, you worry like an old woman. Are we not secure here? Particularly with your entire team now present." He gestured toward a broad viewport that curved across the surface of the far wall, covering some fifty yards in width and twenty in height. "How many in the galaxy are even aware of the significance of this region of space—and of that number, how many would guess that I am present here, now?"

Nakamura swallowed uneasily and nodded.

"Very true, sire. Even so—"

"Even so, you wish to know everything. Isn't that true, Hideo?"

"Always. The more I know, the safer you will be, majesty."

The Emperor gazed back at him, unflinchingly, for several seconds. Then he smiled again and nodded.

"You're right, my friend," he said to the general, softening. "And I know that everything you do, you do with the safety and welfare of the empire—and of myself— firmly in mind. I should not tease you so, nor keep you in the dark."

This time, Nakamura merely returned his gaze evenly, waiting.

After several seconds of this, with neither man speaking or even moving, the Emperor finally laughed and reached out to clap his general on the shoulder.

"Now that is the legendary Nakamura patience I was expecting," he said. "Very well—you have worn your Emperor down, my friend. I will tell you."

As the Ecclesiarch looked on, beaming like a proud parent, Janus IV leaned in close, whispering in the general's ear. While he spoke, he gestured toward a particular bank of equipment that covered a large portion of the chamber they currently occupied. A swarm of technicians moved across it, checking this and adjusting that. At that moment, they finished snapping together a number of components and raised the entire affair up on its side. It was a tall, rectangular frame of black metal covered in wires and cables and glowing crystals. It looked for all the world like the frame of some massive doorway. An open doorway.

Tamerlane recognized it at once. He nearly screamed. It was a very near duplicate of the machine he and Singh had been ordered to assemble on NM-156—the machine that enhanced and opened the dimensional portal in the cave. The machine that, Tamerlane was convinced, had exploded and killed his entire team.

He started forward, but Belisarius shot out a hand and grasped him by the upper arm, restraining him. Tamerlane stared down at the hand and then up at Belisarius, his eyes filled with anger.

"My apologies but, whatever you were about to do, Colonel," the major whispered, "you probably ought to think about it a little more first."

Tamerlane gritted his teeth and by sheer willpower forced himself to calm down, to not wrench himself free of the man's grasp, to not be angry with Belisarius. *How ironic,* he thought as he nodded once to the major, *that his nickname is "the Belligerent" and yet* he's *settling* me *down.*

Belisarius released him. "Again, my apologies, Colonel," he said quietly.

"No—you did the right thing," Tamerlane whispered back. He turned to listen in on the general's conversation with the Emperor again.

Nakamura's eyes were wide. When the Emperor reached the final portion of his statement, the general clearly balked, stepping back a step. He looked up at his ruler with unabashed shock and slowly shook his head. Before he could speak, however, a dark-haired woman in an immaculate dark green suit entered the chamber and approached the Emperor respectfully, bowing as she neared. Tamerlane didn't recognize her at all.

"Majesty," the woman said, still looking down at the metal flooring, "I am Leona Dharva, chief administrator of this project. It is time for you to take your place within the observation chamber." She gestured timidly toward a broad, gleaming window set into the far wall that appeared to be at least six inches thick. "If you would?"

"I would not," the Emperor replied testily. "I have made my intentions in coming here perfectly clear, and they do not include mere *observation*."

The administrator blinked, her mouth opening and closing. She looked wide-eyed from the Emperor to the other scientists. No one stepped up to support her.

"Majesty," she said, "as administrator, I am responsible for your safety while you are present—and therefore must insist that, for that very safety's sake, you accompany me inside the viewing chamber. I assure you, not only will you be able to witness everything that happens from very close by, but you will have access to all of our electronic data— you will see everything pertinent to the experiment as it happens."

The Emperor glared at the woman. As the others looked on, many of them would have sworn the administrator actually appeared to be melting away into thin air.

"You presume to tell me what I can and cannot do, administrator?"

The woman was taken utterly aback and said nothing for a long second. Then she opened her mouth to respond, but instead seemed to be choking on something.

Tamerlane watched the events transpiring with no real degree of surprise. He had known of this Emperor's reputation and personality his entire life, seeing as how they were both of similar ages. He also wasn't surprised to see Nakamura step forward, a respectful smile bolted onto his face as he approached the Emperor.

"Sire, the scientists here seem to believe it would not be safe for you to be here in the chamber when the device is activated—let alone to actually travel through it."

The Emperor's eyes flashed as he turned to Nakamura, but then his expression softened somewhat.

"I understand that, Hideo," he replied, sighing heavily. "But the Ecclesiarch believes I will receive a tremendous blessing from such a pilgrimage. And if I should be so fortunate—so blessed—as to actually *find* it…"

Find it? That perked Tamerlane's ears up even more. *Find what? Surely he couldn't mean…*

"Indeed," the older man stated, smiling beatifically at Nakamura. "And through him, the entire *Empire* will be blessed and will prosper."

Janus IV was nodding at this. "And, in the end, Hideo, it's up to me—my choice, my decision. I am the Emperor, after all."

Tamerlane knew that Nakamura recognized the expression that was settling onto his ruler's face. He'd surely seen it many times before. He knew then that no further argument would be brooked. Even so, Nakamura couldn't simply stand aside without a word and allow the ruler of a quarter of all mankind to so flagrantly risk his life. "Perhaps, Majesty," the general ventured, ever so carefully, "we should step into the administrator's offices and discuss it further." He cast a quick glance at the Ecclesiarch. "The scientific aspects of it, I mean. With all of the experts present—"

The Emperor's expression soured instantly. "I grow tired of my subordinates instructing me constantly in what I can and cannot do," he growled—and everyone in the big room instantly noted the chill that descended. "I am the Emperor. I do as I please. The rest of you make accommodations for that."

"Of course, sire," Nakamura responded quickly. "But—"

"Always a *but*! As if all of you know better!" The Emperor glared at him, all traces of good humor having evaporated. "Well—this time *I* know better. *I know!*" He swept his arm wide to indicate virtually everyone in the room. "All of you know *nothing*! Only *I* know!"

Tamerlane was growing concerned not just for the Emperor's safety but for his mental stability in general. And for Nakamura's continued health—and survival.

Janus raised his right hand and snapped his fingers. Instantly the Emperor's Guard in their gleaming crystalline armor of red and green and sapphire and turquoise and garnet stepped forward, surrounding their master protectively. Their heavy quad rifles were already unslung from their backs; long, rugged, black and silver affairs, far too heavy to be carried by an average soldier not wearing high-tech armor, they featured twin energy-weapon and particle-beam barrels up top and matching high-speed, high-capacity projectile-throwers at the bottom. While the Guardsmen weren't precisely aiming them at anyone at the moment, there was an undeniable sense of extreme menace in the air.

"The next words out of your mouth, Hideo, had better be, 'As you wish, Majesty,'" the Emperor growled, "or I will find a new general for your division."

Nakamura reddened, but he did not blink. His dark eyes remained focused intently on those of the Emperor even as every other pair of eyes in the chamber stared intently at him, and when he finally spoke it was in a strong, clear voice: "As you wish, Majesty."

A second passed, and then another, moving at glacial speed. Then the Emperor's scowl dissolved and his usual half-smile returned. He reached out, between two of his imposing Guards, and grasped Nakamura by the shoulder.

"Old friend, you worry too much. All will be fine."

And with that, the icy tension vanished and the Emperor whirled about, striding toward the equipment and the technicians and that strange, rectangular framework. The administrator, meanwhile, appeared to grow only more troubled and afraid. She shuffled quickly away.

Tamerlane rushed forward and caught up with Nakamura. He leaned in and whispered, "What was that all about? What does he want to do?"

Nakamura shook his head wearily and pointed at the black rectangle. His reply was almost too soft for his colonel to hear. "That thing's supposed to be some kind of doorway to another dimension. To the Above, if you can believe it."

Tamerlane looked from the general to the big rectangle. "Alright. And?"

"And he wants to travel through it when they open it. In fact, he wants to lead the way," Nakamura hissed.

"He *what*?"

Tamerlane's startled exclamation was much louder than he would ever have intended. All eyes once again turned their way. Nakamura wanted to sink down through the metal floor, and ice ran through his veins as he waited for the Emperor to react—to turn back and order the colonel's execution, most likely, given his current mercurial mood.

To the immense relief of both men, either the Emperor hadn't heard Tamerlane's reaction or simply chose to ignore him. Either way, Janus continued across the room to where the team of scientists and techs were gathered, hard at work on the massive banks of electronics that filled this entire side of the chamber.

"He says," Nakamura went on, speaking very quietly, "his agents have discovered that the terrorists who stole the Sword of Baranak—"

Tamerlane gawked at this.

"—carried or tossed it through a dimensional doorway, in this local region of space."

Tamerlane reddened but managed not to exclaim anything. Barely.

"And he plans to go and get it back."

Tamerlane forced himself to swallow. He looked off to the side for a couple of seconds, at nothing in particular, as he struggled to regulate his pounding heartbeat. Then he leaned in closer to the general.

"That…is…insane. There's scarcely a word of truth to any of it."

Nakamura shrugged. "It's the word of the Emperor."

"I—I simply don't know what to say," Tamerlane stammered. "I—"

The Emperor was on the move again, and Nakamura had to rush off to keep up with him. Tamerlane waited a few seconds before following along, keeping a respectful distance. Inside, his mind was in turmoil.

Nakamura caught up to the Emperor again as he was looking the enigmatic machinery over and managed to catch his attention.

"Majesty—if I may ask one more thing?

The Emperor favored Nakamura with a warm smile. "Another question, Hideo?"

"Just one, sire, before you embark on your glorious expedition."

The Emperor visibly warmed to this. "By all means, then—proceed."

"If I may ask, sire," he all but stammered, "How—or where—did you get the idea—the inspiration, I mean—to go on the mission yourself? And to be the *first* through this portal? And that you might find the Sword on the other side?"

Janus IV gazed back at him, surprised, as if this was not the question he had anticipated. A warm smile finally rekindled on his face.

"It all came to me, Hideo," he said, his voice now soft as silk, "in a *dream*…"

The dream—if dream it was—had come upon Janus Rahkmanov several months earlier with the force of religious revelation. And the voice that spoke to him in it... well, the voice sounded to him like a multi-part harmony of every good and pleasing sound he had ever heard in his life. And it said:

"With me by your side, conquer."

Janus's eyes opened—or his eyes within the dream opened. He was not at all certain. Was he awake? Asleep? Some state in between?

"What?" he whispered to the night and the darkness.

"With me by your side, conquer," the voice repeated, its tone warm and friendly yet filled with a distinct sense of power.

Janus sat up and looked around, almost frantic at the thought of someone sneaking into his royal bedchamber. Despite the pleasing tone of the voice, its mere presence was more than enough to set his heart racing and cold sweat beading on his forehead.

"Lisbeth?" he whispered frantically, knowing full well that his wife, the Imperial consort, had not spoken the words. Indeed, as he looked and felt to either side of him in their huge bed, he knew he would find no sign of her, and he did not.

"Who are you?" he asked, his voice louder now. "I can't see you."

"I am not here. I am… *elsewhere*. You must open the way for me."

Janus frowned. As Emperor of Anatolia, one of the four great kingdoms of mankind, he was not accustomed to being told what to do, or to being denied instant gratification of his desires.

"Where are you, then?" he managed after a few seconds of consternation.

Another pause, and then the voice came again, full and masculine yet somehow incredibly alluring.

"A heartbeat away. A universe away from your tiny corner of reality."

Janus tried to comprehend this and failed.

"I—I don't understand," he muttered, as much to himself as to the strange, disembodied presence that had dared to invade his bedroom and disturb his slumber. "A universe away...? What realm is there beyond this one? My empire has expanded into the most remote reaches of this sector of the galaxy. All is known that can be known."

The voice laughed—softly, but with enough of a mocking tone to nearly enrage the Emperor.

"Foolish man. Your empire floats as a bubble on a pond and you believe you comprehend the ocean."

This Janus quickly understood, and to it he took the gravest offense.

"My empire is vast and mighty," he growled into the darkness. "Largest of the four realms of mankind. How dare you—"

"Would that you ceased your arrogant objections and simply listened," the voice interjected, growing harsh now, "you would find yourself on the path to true power, true

95

knowledge, true mastery of your kind." It paused, and then repeated, "*All* of your kind."

Janus blinked, processing this. What the voice was offering certainly sounded attractive: Nothing less than the conquest of the other three rival empires—of all of humanity, if he understood it correctly. Then he frowned.

"*My* kind, you say? Are *you* not of my kind, then? What are you?"

"I am beyond your understanding, but I come to you with this opportunity, this offer. I will not ask again."

Anger, resentment and defiance all flared to brighter life within Janus's heart and mind. And yet, having served in his role as Emperor for more than a dozen years already, and despite all natural inclination to the contrary, he had managed to learn a bit of subtlety, guile and diplomacy along the way. Calming himself, he nodded solemnly.

"Very well. You wish for me to open a way for you. How do I do this?"

"You possess an object of incalculable value."

"I am the emperor—I possess many objects of such value.

"The value is not in wealth but in power. It is a bauble to you. But it is vital to me. Give it to me and all you desire will be yours. A dominion greater than this miserable collection of planets you presently rule."

Janus's resentment at such talk had already faded and been forgotten. For a reason he could not fully comprehend, he now found the words utterly believable and compelling. He was nearly breathless when he managed to ask, "This *bauble*—what is it, exactly?"

"The sword."

"Sword?"

"You know of what I speak."

Janus was taken aback. "You desire the Sword of Baranak? One of the crown jewels of my empire? How could *that* help you—"

"Have it brought to the appointed place at the appointed hour. You will know. When the time is right, it must be handed over."

"But—but neither the Imperial Council nor the Senate would allow anyone—not even *me*—to remove the Sword of Baranak from the place where it is kept—much less *give it away*. It is one of the most important artifacts in all of human history!"

"You are the emperor. It is your destiny to unify the galaxy under your rule. You will not allow a minor technicality such as that to deter you. You will find a way."

Janus struggled to follow the words. "Yes," he said after a few moments. "Very well."

"One thing more: You must not be present when it is handed over. Be certain you are far away."

"What? But—"

"There is nothing more to say, O man. Follow my instructions and all will be as I have described."

"I—alright. When should I do this?"

"You will know. Beyond all doubt, you will know." A pause. "They will try to prevent you from coming. Those who claim to love you best. They will warn you of the dangers. Ignore them. You are the ruler of this empire, and soon the master of all mankind. Power beyond your wildest imaginings awaits you. Let no one deny you what is rightfully yours. Let nothing stand in your way."

"Yes," answered Janus IV. "Yes—it will be as you say."

Silence.

"Are you there?"

Silence.

Janus brought his hands to his eyes and rubbed. When he moved them away, he realized he was sitting up in bed. His wife, the royal consort Lisbeth Salome Rahkmanov, lay beside him, sleeping soundly. The bedchamber was otherwise empty. The sun was just beginning to creep over the edge of the marble balcony railing. Silence reigned.

"Yes," he whispered to the fading dream that he knew had been no dream at all. "Yes—it will be as you say. The power must be mine. Nothing will stand in my way."

7

A ...*dream*, Majesty?" Nakamura asked, and it was obvious to Tamerlane that he was doing his absolute best to prevent his astonishment, his incredulity, from showing on his face. Tamerlane hoped it wasn't quite so obvious to the Emperor.

Still smiling, the Emperor nodded.

"It was a holy vision, General," the Ecclesiarch interjected, leaning in. "Just as his ancestors received, centuries ago, when they first built this empire from the ruins of the Great War of the Alliance."

The Emperor turned away before Nakamura could react further—an act that might well have saved the general's life, since he was not being terribly successful at projecting a poker face.

Nakamura glanced back at Tamerlane, blanching. The colonel understood very well. Here was the most powerful and important individual in the Empire—the man it was his job to protect, above all others—and he was about to risk his life at the behest of a mere dream!

As the Emperor and his hangers-on moved across the room, Tamerlane drew near. Nakamura leaned in close to him, his expression reflecting more indecision and doubt than it likely ever had in his life, and he whispered almost frantically, "Ezekial—what do I *do*?"

"What *can* you do, General?" Tamerlane shrugged. "You have to let him go."

"But—"

"You have no choice."

Nakamura frowned at this. "But—"

"If you object to him again, he's likely to react in a way none of us would like. He could demote you, dismiss you altogether..." Tamerlane's eyes moved from the general's stricken face to the Emperor, now standing near the portal machinery. "You know how he can get. What he's capable of. And that wouldn't do any of us any good."

Nakamura nodded slowly, resignedly. Then, "Well—it would do Attila or Beyzit some good," he corrected his colonel, "assuming one of them was promoted into my spot."

At the mere mention of the other two generals, Tamerlane groaned. Each of them commanded a mighty army within the empire—the Second and Third, respectively—but both reported within the chain of command to Nakamura. Neither was particularly well-liked or well-regarded within the Imperial military.

"Don't even joke about that idea, General," Tamerlane said. He looked back to Nakamura then. "What is this all about? Why would he go to such trouble to have me steal the sword and throw it through the portal on NM-156, only to go and fetch it back himself? To make himself a hero to the masses? He's already the Emperor—what more does he need? And—if he simply wants to be known as the Emperor who retrieved Baranak's Sword after it was taken—why all the business with the Above, in the first place?"

Nakamura merely shook his head. "I don't know, Ezekial," he said. "I simply don't know." He breathed deeply in and out several times, as if steeling himself for a bold leap. "But, whether I anger him or not, it is my duty to find out."

Before Tamerlane could object, or even reply, Nakamura turned and walked away, stalking over toward the Emperor and the scientists surrounding him.

Working his way alongside the little group of technicians gathered around one section of the machinery, he stood silently for a few seconds, listening and absorbing the conversation. Then he leaned in. "If I may ask," he said to the lead tech, "how exactly will this work? What will this equipment actually *do*?"

The lab-coated man blinked as he realized that everyone—including the Emperor—was looking at him. He quickly straightened and replied, as if reciting the words from a text, "This machine will open a passageway from our universe into a heretofore-unexplored region of the Above."

"Tell him why we're doing it *here*, on this ship, at this specific location," the Emperor urged, grinning as he looked from Nakamura to the lead tech.

"For safety, I assume," the general stated.

"Safety?" The Emperor scoffed. "That scarcely entered into it. This is all perfectly safe—is it not?" he asked the technician expectantly.

"We believe it is entirely safe, yes, your majesty," the tech replied, sweat trailing down the side of his face. "The doorway is being opened *here* mainly because *here* is the only place it *can* be opened."

Nakamura shook his head, puzzled. "What do you mean?"

"He means," the Emperor interjected, moving to stand directly in front of the general, "that this planetary system—this one location in all the galaxy, that we have found thus far—is the only spot where the wall separating our universe from the target location in the Above is thin enough that, with the proper machinery, we can simply punch a hole and step through. That would be *this* machinery, of course," he added, gesturing toward the wall of equipment and the black rectangle nearby.

"Ah," Nakamura said, nodding slowly. "I see." He paused, as if thinking carefully, and then went to the question he'd held in mind all along. "And—as the commander of your military forces, and chief among your protectors, I feel it is my duty to ask this—what sort of menaces might one expect to find, on the other side of this *doorway?*"

No one spoke for several seconds. Then, "We…cannot be entirely certain," the lead technician began.

The Emperor cut him off. "Menaces?" He regarded Nakamura with surprise and no small degree of scorn. "It's not as if we are traveling into the Below, where the demons dwell. We will be venturing into the Above, Hideo. The *Above!* That's where we believe the Sword rests, awaiting us. There are no menaces there—only wonders!"

The lead tech frowned. "Well, your majesty, we of course believe that to be true, but—"

"What dangers could there possibly be?" the Emperor snapped. "The Above is Heaven itself! Home to Those Who Remain!"

"It was home to Vorthan," one of the technicians muttered, saying aloud the very thing that Nakamura and Tamerlane and virtually everyone else in the group was thinking.

The Emperor glared at the young man, thunderclouds gathering about his brows. The technician grew deathly pale and his mouth opened and closed soundlessly. For several seconds no one spoke, and few even breathed. The entire chamber was utterly silent. Then the Emperor turned to the Ecclesiarch and nodded once.

"Vorthan," the Ecclesiarch hissed, "was an aberration. The serpent in the garden. And he was cast down for his crimes, long ago. Utterly annihilated." He made a gesture of warding with one hand. "Even now, the Emperor's forces act to destroy the last remaining cells of his vile cult, out among the fringe worlds."

Still no one else said a word, or even dared to move. The poor young technician seemed to be melting into the deck, both from embarrassment and out of a desire to escape. The towering, imposing figures of the Emperor's Guard in their glittering armor were extremely obvious in their presence, their swords and quad-rifles an obvious threat. For another long second, no one breathed.

Then the Emperor turned away from the young man and faced the lead technician.

"How soon until we are ready to proceed?"

Everyone in the group exhaled—though very quietly.

"Only a few more moments, Majesty."

The Emperor nodded. "Good. The Ecclesiarch and I are quite anxious to be on our way."

"He's going, too?" Nakamura whispered to no one, even as the technicians scrambled to prepare for an extra traveler.

The Emperor moved through the crowd and past them, stopping only when he was directly in front of the rectangular doorway. There he stood, hands on hips, gazing up at it, a look of serene happiness on his face.

Tamerlane approached the general again, speaking softly. "Well then," he said, shaking his head slowly. "Now I'm wondering if we brought *enough* soldiers."

Nakamura didn't reply. Instead he flashed a quick series of silent signals via the Aether to his red-clad troops across the big room, instructing them on precisely where to stand and how to react to several different potential eventualities. Meanwhile, the elite Emperor's Guard warriors in their multi-colored crystal armor took up positions on either side of the portal machinery. Lastly, a team of some dozen figures in sealed yellow environment suits entered the chamber. One carried a pair of extra suits, neatly folded, and approached the Emperor with them.

"Majesty," the man said, bowing, as he held one of the suits—a pale yellow one—out before him.

The Emperor took his suit and handed it to Nakamura. The general in turn handed it to Tamerlane. "Ezekial," he said quietly, "assist the Emperor into his environment suit."

Tamerlane nodded once, sharply. Then he motioned to a pair of his own men and they stepped up, saluting. Together the three of them helped the Emperor into his suit. At the same time, the techs were getting the Ecclesiarch suited up in a blue version.

A few moments later, the Emperor of Anatolia had been transformed into a trans-dimensional explorer, his clear faceplate fogging slightly as he breathed. He gave a thumbs-up that his in-helmet indicator lights were all green and everything felt fine. Then he activated the comm link.

"Ladies and gentlemen," he said, eagerness quite evident in his voice as it boomed over the room's speakers, "I believe I am quite ready to lead this little expedition into the heavenly realms."

The crowd of scientists in their own suits started forward.

The administrator swallowed, after some small amount of difficulty in doing so, and leaned in close to General Nakamura. "For the sake of Those Who Remain," she whispered sharply, "at least make sure someone else is standing in front of him as he passes through! We have no idea what to expect on the other side."

Nakamura nodded.

"Wait!" said the Emperor, and everyone froze.

The lead tech rushed forward, hoping against hope that his liege lord had changed his mind. Alas, no.

"My Guard will be accompanying me," he informed the man. "And the Ecclesiarch, of course. No one else. This is to be a divine mission—a holy crusade. I will have nothing that sullies or detracts from that. Scientific inquiry can come afterward."

The administrator and other officials looked around at one another, but by this time their resistance had entirely crumbled and they simply nodded.

Gesturing toward his own protective suit, the Emperor stated, "My Guard will need whatever of this equipment is necessary to survive in the Above, as well."

The techs looked the eight members of the Guard over quickly but carefully, studying their organic crystal armor. They conferred for a few moments and then the leader addressed the Emperor.

"Their armor should be suitable for that environment, sire. They will, however, need shield generators and tethers…"

At the lead tech's direction, the Emperor and his elite Guard attached small silver disks to their belts. The disks generated an additional layer of protection, projecting a defensive aura—an electromagnetic field of considerable strength—around each individual that would serve to ward off harmful particles and rays. No one had any idea what sorts of dangers they might encounter on the other side of the portal, but the technicians felt confident that—if he insisted on going through first, as he did—those two defenses would be enough to prevent the Emperor from coming to harm.

They could not have been more wrong.

Thin wires were run out from massive spools mounted on the opposite bulkhead, and the ends were attached to the belts of each member of the party. Though extremely flexible, the lines were nearly an eighth of an inch thick—but they needn't have been so large; given the tensile strength of the composite material they were composed of, they could have been thinner than a single thread and remained just as strong. The fear, of course, was that at such a narrow size, they might actually slice through the torsos or extremities of members of the group. Thus they were manufactured to the diameter of very small ropes.

An attendant tried to fuss over the Emperor's protective gear but Janus shooed the little man away and motioned to his assembled Guard.

"We are ready," he announced grandly, his eyes sweeping across the crowd. "No more delays. Osman! Zayid! Up here with me." He turned to the lead tech. "Open the way!"

The beleaguered chief scientist signaled to the Emperor that all was in readiness.

The Emperor nodded back, saluted Nakamura, and turned to face the black rectangle.

Nakamura motioned for his men to move into standard defensive positions.

The two nearest of the Emperor's Guard warriors tramped forward at their master's call. Their heavy boots rang loudly on the deck flooring. No one present could help but stare at them; their armor dazzled the eye in spectacular fashion.

In place of the smartfabric-based protective gear worn by Nakamura's men and the other troopers milling about the portal room, the Guard warriors were clad in bulky, intimidating Elite-class plate armor with multi-faceted, gemlike helmets. Guardsman Zayid sparkled a brilliant red from head to toe, the main components of his suit having been shaped from a single massive synthetic ruby. Likewise, Guardsman Osman's emerald armor shaded the light all around him a vivid green.

From the moment they had first entered the chamber, Tamerlane had become aware of a low humming sound that moved just into and out of his hearing. Now it increased, subtly at first, until it was just enough to set his teeth on edge. He became convinced that he could feel the metal deck beneath his boots vibrating. At the same time, lights on the doorway-shaped black frame ahead of them began to blink on and off, faster and faster, until the entire apparatus virtually shimmered with rainbows of color. The rhythmic oscillation of the lights and the grinding sound of vibration merged until Tamerlane felt the two were one and the same—as if the room itself had come to life and he was hearing its heartbeat and feeling its pulse.

When the shimmering of the lights reached a point that the individual flashes were no longer visibly discernible and had instead achieved a sort of uniform soft glow, an order was barked from one of the technicians and controls were activated across the range of consoles spread around the room. In response, a moment later, the interior of the rectangular frame itself filled with a soft white light.

Tamerlane watched this phenomenon with particular interest and no small degree of puzzlement. The light seemed to float, in spherical form, at the center of the rectangle, with no visible source. It was as if a ball of lightning had been caught in an invisible trap and now floated there, slowly expanding, forking tendrils of energy snaking out from it occasionally to strike the frame and then vanish.

"What is that?" Tamerlane asked Belisarius, who stood next to him, leaning closer to whisper the question.

"I have no idea," replied the major, his own eyes widening. "But I can't say I like the Emperor being this close to it, whatever it is."

Nakamura, his hearing acute as ever, looked back over his shoulder at them. The meaning of his expression was clear: "Shut up."

They shut up.

The lead technician meanwhile spoke up: "Majesty," he said, bowing, "the gateway is open."

Indeed, the entire interior space of the black-framed doorway was now filled with a nearly blinding white light. Nakamura wasn't thrilled with this; it meant that any menaces that might possibly emerge from—from *whatever* lay on the other side, *wherever* it was—would be extremely difficult to detect beforehand. Without thinking, his hand moved down such that his fingertips brushed across the grip of his blast pistol.

The Ecclesiarch's own hand moved in a gesture of blessing. Then the Emperor nodded to the technician, his features forming an almost childlike excited grin. He started toward the black framework, the thin line trailing from where it was attached at his waist. The seven members of his Guard tromped along beside and behind him. He halted again only at the very threshold, turned and waved at the two hovering spheres that were recording this occasion.

"I, Janus IV, am proud to be the first man to traverse this new doorway into the Above, created by the brilliant scientists of our empire. When I return in a short time, it will be with word—and perhaps visuals, if the technology permits there—of this new realm of the heavens, and whatever we find there. Including, if all goes well, the Sword of Baranak."

As the assemblage of technicians applauded, Nakamura leaned in toward the Emperor and whispered something. The Emperor frowned slightly but then nodded once before turning away. He stood facing the shimmering doorway, his hands on his hips as he regarded it, as the Guard waited patiently behind him.

"What was that?" whispered Tamerlane as the general moved back over to where he was standing.

"I told him that if we haven't heard from him in an hour, I'd come looking for him."

After seemingly contemplating the coruscating light of the doorway for several seconds, the Emperor faced the crowd of scientists and soldiers and smiled broadly. He tossed off a jaunty salute, turned back, and stepped into the white light. He vanished. An instant later, the Ecclesiarch and the seven members of the Emperor's Guard followed him through, their crystal armor gleaming as the white light flooded around them.

Within five seconds, all nine of them had passed through and were gone.

Tamerlane put a hand on Nakamura's back, simply to remind him that he was needed here and not to do anything crazy like go charging along after them. He didn't *truly* think the general would do that, but still, it didn't hurt to be sure.

The nine cables were slowly spooling out and, stretched taut, ran across the room to the gateway, where they vanished into the light. More of their slack played out into the portal every second, at a slow but steady rate, presumably as the Emperor and his retinue advanced into the Above.

Tamerlane laughed inwardly; Major Belisarius appeared wholly unconcerned, while Nakamura wore his stress and tension on his sleeve. He assumed he registered somewhere between those two extremes. Still, he understood the general's concern. It wasn't every day one's head of state, the man you were most responsible for protecting, disappeared from the universe right in front of you—and on purpose.

Nakamura roused himself from his seeming daze and barked, "Start the clock," and on one of the large displays to the left of the gateway frame, "00:00:01" appeared.

The general inhaled deeply and exhaled slowly. "And now we wait," he said.

Tamerlane nodded.

"But only for a little while," Nakamura added. "A *very* little while."

No communications. Terrific," Tamerlane muttered. He stood just behind Nakamura where the general was seated at one of the command consoles, absorbing what little telemetry they were receiving from the other side. The Emperor and his Guard had been away now for over half an hour.

"As expected," pointed out Major Belisarius. "The Above is an entirely different universe. Even time itself runs differently there."

"Slower, yes," Tamerlane said. He had never much cared for Belisarius—"the Belligerent" indeed—and didn't feel the need to be lectured on the workings of alternate dimensions by him right now. He straightened and surveyed the big room, observing its many and diverse occupants; a remarkable collection of scientists and soldiers and government officials.

"So you can't expect to talk with the Emperor while he's there," Belisarius went on, "as if he's simply a star system away here in our universe."

Tamerlane ignored him. When he spoke again it was to Nakamura. "Did you really tell the Emperor that you were giving him an hour before you came and got him?"

The general shrugged. "I told—" He paused, pursed his lips as he likely reconsidered that choice of words, and started over. "I asked—I *politely requested*—that he not be gone too terribly long, as we his loyal subjects would worry for his welfare. And I added that, had he not returned in an hour, as we measure time here in this dimension, we might take that as a sign that he needed reinforcements or assistance."

Tamerlane suppressed a laugh. "Well played."

Nakamura could only shrug in reply. Then he stood and paced away, back across the chamber to where the lead technicians were congregating. He began to question them yet again about the Emperor's physical condition, based on the poor telemetry coming in via the cable link.

"He worries like a mother hen," Belisarius muttered, his voice very soft, as he leaned in again.

Tamerlane started to reply but was stopped by another voice speaking out—one he hadn't expected to hear.

"He has to. The Emperor's safety is, ultimately, his responsibility. And we must all live up to our responsibilities."

Tamerlane turned and saw who the speaker had been: a rough, stocky man in a dark green dress uniform, his head smooth and barren as the surface of the moon. He recognized him as Major Vostok, called "The Cold," an officer of the Third Legion, under General Beyzit's command. Next to him, Tamerlane recognized the tall, muscular, fair-haired Colonel Agrippa, "The Golden," whose youthful and healthy appearance contrasted sharply with that of the rough colonel.

They were called "The Cold and the Gold," though rarely to their faces, and they made for a remarkable contrast in their positions near the top of Legion III.

Tamerlane could see that Belisarius was considering retorting to Vostok's remark, but the major decided instead to let it go with a gracious nod. That was probably wise.

Their presence puzzled Tamerlane. If they were part of Beyzit's Third Legion, what were they doing here, now?

That question was answered moments later as their army's commander himself, General Abdul-Rashid Beyzit, strode regally into the room. Not a particularly imposing man, physically, "The Thunderbolt" nonetheless carried himself with a sort of swaggering self-confidence that conveyed the impression of massive and barely-contained power. His skin was deeply tanned and his face was a web of creases, his eyes small and very dark within shadowed recesses. A dark green long coat flared around him, the gleaming lightning insignia of his Third Legion prominent.

Tamerlane found himself quite taken aback. Two generals—here? Why? Even with the Emperor himself in attendance, this seemed like extreme overkill.

If Beyzit's presence shocked him, however, the next development nearly bowled him over. General Esteban Attila passed through the hatch just behind Beyzit, his own retinue in their dark blue Second Legion uniforms accompanying him.

Tamerlane unabashedly gawked. That was the reaction Attila "The Bold" usually provoked. A big, powerful man, he filled out his uniform in impressive fashion, muscles bulging under the blue smartcloth. His expression, legendary among the troops, was perpetually that of an attack dog.

Behind Attila was the almost equally infamous Colonel Ioan Iapetus, a man regarded more for his cruelty and intolerance than for any particular military genius. He'd won his share of battles, yes—but the stories that leaked out afterward, invariably denied by the men of Second Legion, chilled the blood. He wore not the dress blues of Legion II but his customary black—and no one seemed inclined to call him on it.

Tamerlane's eyes flicked from Attila to Beyzit to Nakamura. He couldn't quite fathom it. Three generals? The three top generals in the entire empire? Here, together?

And Nakamura, deep in conversation with the technicians monitoring the progress of the Emperor's party, still hadn't become aware of these new arrivals.

Tamerlane shook his head, bewildered. His feet were already moving him with great haste toward Nakamura. Before he could reach him, however, the general happened to look up. His eyes flickered across the suddenly much more crowded room and Tamerlane nearly laughed at his shocked expression.

So Nakamura hadn't known, hadn't expected these other two generals to appear. Interesting.

The three men came together near the center of the big room, and it was immediately obvious to Tamerlane as he hurried over to take his position behind his general that Nakamura was not at all pleased to have the other two men present. The conversation—a somewhat unpleasant one, in fact—had hardly begun, however, when the doorway that led into the chamber snapped open and booted feet resounded from the metal deck. Tamerlane frowned at this unexpected intrusion and looked in that direction—and thereby beheld the one element that could bring all three generals together in firm solidarity.

Before them stood three figures in jet black, broad cloaks flaring around each of them as they came to a halt directly in front of the generals, practically glaring at them in scarcely contained anger. Tamerlane recognized the three instantly and suppressed a groan. Who else would it have been? Who else would have the temerity, the gall, to behave in such a manner? To stalk right up to the three highest-ranking military men in the entire empire and glare at them as if they were misbehaving toddlers?

Nakamura moved to the forefront of the generals. He nodded his head ever so slightly to the tall, slender man who had assumed the forward position of his own group's triangular formation. Taken together, the two groups resembled two spear tips pointed directly at each other. The latent aggression inherent in such a formation was no accident, Tamerlane knew.

"Inquisitor Stanishur," Nakamura said by way of greeting.

"General Nakamura," came the faint, almost inaudible response from scarcely-moving lips.

The man was pale; deathly pale and gaunt, with stringy white hair dangling from a pasty skull. His eyes lay within deep, almost black recesses. His elaborate uniform, all in black but comprised of layers of buckles and vests and straps, served at least to fill out his form somewhat.

Behind Stanishur stood two shorter and much younger-looking figures dressed in similar fashion. One of them was a woman. Nakamura's eyes momentarily flicked over the two of them, one after the other, and Tamerlane couldn't help but be impressed with his general's memory for the names and faces of potentially troublesome people with whom he rarely dealt. "Inquisitors Chopra and Delain." And his ability to lie to their faces, as he did next. "A pleasure to see you again."

The two offered nothing by way of greeting, so Nakamura returned his attention to Stanishur, the chief. The man was already speaking.

"We have no time for pleasantries, General," came the hissing voice from the cadaverous figure. "The Inquisition has only just learned of the Emperor's presence here, and we have been dispatched to...*persuade* him... not to go through with this."

Nakamura's face adopted a look of disappointment and regret as he replied, "Then I'm sorry to inform you, Inquisitor, but the Emperor has already embarked on his journey."

At this news the gaunt man's expression at last cracked. His eyes widened to the point that Tamerlane, now standing just behind the second row of generals, could actually see them within their shadowy recesses. His mouth opened and closed once before he was able to gather himself.

"That...is most... *unwelcome*... news," he managed to sputter. Then, as he regained his composure, "How in the name of the holy gods—of Those Who Remain—could you allow His Majesty to do such a thing?"

Nakamura offered the Inquisitor a slightly exaggerated puzzled look. "*Allow* His Majesty? Inquisitor—think what you are asking. How could we *deny* His Majesty...*anything*?"

"For his own safety, of course!" Stanishur's voice was quite audible now, that exclamation echoing all around the big chamber and seemingly startling even his two unflappable assistants. "And in the best interests of the Empire," he added, his voice under control again. "Those are the arguments that you should have employed, obviously."

"Your concern for the safety of His Majesty is touching, Inquisitor. Inspiring."

Stanishur's pale features darkened as he leaned forward, glaring directly at Nakamura. When he spoke this time, only the general and the men immediately behind him could hear his words. "My concern, as you well know, General, is for the Holy Faith. For the sanctity of the Above. For its purity. I will not allow anyone in our empire—in our universe!—to besmirch it. Likewise," he added, his voice growing even softer but even more intense, "I will not allow anyone—*anyone!*—from this universe to defile its sacred soil, its firmament." He leaned in closer, such that he was nearly nose to nose with the general, and he emphasized each of the next four words he spoke with jabs of his bony finger to Nakamura's chest: *"Not. Even. The. Emperor."*

Then Stanishur's voice grew louder again, so that everyone in the chamber could hear him. "If any harm should come to the Emperor, General Nakamura," he barked, "know that you as the party here most responsible for his safety will bear the brunt of the blame." He stepped back, turning slowly so that he could look and appeal to everyone in the chamber, before ending up facing the general again. "So you must retrieve him now, by any means necessary, before any harm befalls him—" His voice dropped to near-inaudibility one more time. "—or, much more importantly, any harm is done *to the Above itself!*"

Despite the skeletal Inquisitor's efforts, Tamerlane, standing just behind and to one side of Nakamura, had managed to hear everything. Now anger welled up inside him. He looked to the general to see what response might be forthcoming—what Nakamura would say that would slap this haughty inquisitor down and teach him some humility.

Alas, no one there would ever know. For at that moment, a cry came from several of the technicians standing near the gateway. "The cables are retracting! They're coming back!"

Smiles broke out among the gathering, but Tamerlane cast his gaze at the big spools and frowned. They were indeed spinning backwards now, reeling the cable back in—but at a highly accelerated rate, much too fast for a human being on the other end to be keeping up.

"General," he said, leaning close toward Nakamura, "this is not good."

The spools abruptly stopped spinning. A second later, the technicians near the portal were exclaiming in horror, with half of them dashing about here and there between equipment banks. The other half merely stood in a semicircle before the big rectangle of the gateway machine. They were staring down at something on the floor.

Nakamura barked orders for everyone to get out of the way and let him pass. Tamerlane hurried after him. Shoving their way through the crowd of lab-coated men and women, they were at last able to gaze down and see what had everyone there in such a state of agitation and shock. When they saw it, they understood.

There at their feet lay all nine of the tether cables, each of them cleanly severed and lying flaccid on the floor just before the gateway.

make ready!" shouted Nakamura, turning his back momentarily on the gateway rectangle and the gaggle of scientists who flanked it, in order to address his troops. "We depart immediately!"

Everyone in the chamber looked up at Nakamura in shock. The members of First Legion, however, instantly went to work, checking their weapons and ammunition and testing their Aether connections. Quickly they began to congregate around Tamerlane as he motioned them over.

Suddenly the Inquisitors were there again, directly in front of Nakamura. Stanishur glared at the general with an awful intensity.

"Departing?" the cadaverous man bellowed with a voice that belied his slender frame. "You cannot be serious! You are simply *leaving*?" His eyes burned with a palpable wrath as he leaned in, his two assistants both visibly outraged behind him. "Where in the name of the Above and the Below do you think you're going?"

Nakamura regarded the man with a thinly-veiled contempt. He jerked a thumb in the direction of the gateway rectangle—the path taken nearly an hour earlier by the Emperor and his honor guard.

"Through there," he said.

The Inquisitor froze. He blinked, his mouth opening and closing once. When he spoke again, his tone was much softer, his demeanor vastly more restrained.

"You—you're going through the portal? You're going after them?"

"Of course," Nakamura replied, and Tamerlane could only laugh to himself as he watched the confrontation out of the corner of his eye. He knew precisely what the general would ask next—though the reply he received was not exactly what he expected.

"You'll be joining us, of course," Nakamura added. "Won't you?"

The Inquisitor blinked again. He half-turned away, as if to consult with his two assistants, but then apparently thought better of it and halted, turning back to face the general. Standing up straight to his full stature—a height that all but dwarfed Nakamura—he replied, "Yes. Yes, we will be joining you."

Nakamura must have been surprised by this; Tamerlane certainly was.

"We have no choice," the gaunt man went on. "The Emperor has dared to set foot into the realm of the gods themselves—a realm we of the Holy Inquisition are charged with defending and preserving and keeping sacrosanct. He appears to be suffering the consequences of that brash act. We have no choice but to see this folly through to its conclusion."

Namura pursed his lips at this, then nodded once. He looked to Tamerlane and his men. "We've wasted quite enough time already," he barked. "The Emperor may be in the gravest danger. I want my team through that portal in the next sixty seconds!"

Tamerlane acknowledged the order, then reacted with surprise as a deep voice addressed him from behind, rumbling, "Colonel."

He turned and found himself staring up—very definitely *up*—at the features of his counterpart in the Third Legion, Beyzit's adjutant. "Colonel Agrippa," he said, offering a grim but sincere smile. "What can I do for you?"

The big, muscular man returned the smile, also in grim fashion. "I imagine you and General Nakamura intend for this expedition to be comprised of First Legion personnel only," he rumbled. "That's Nakamura's right. But I'd like to volunteer, anyway. I believe I could be of some assistance—"

Tamerlane's smile grew warmer. He'd always liked Agrippa, and thought highly of him as a soldier. This act only added to the regard he felt.

"That is appreciated," he replied, "and I'll pass the word to the general. But I'm sure it won't be necessary."

Agrippa nodded, clearly understanding that he was being turned down. "I respect that," he said. "It's Nakamura's call. And yours." He reached out with one big hand, and Tamerlane grasped it. They shook. "Good luck, Colonel," the blond giant said. "And good hunting. Bring him back alive."

"Thank you, Colonel. Will do."

The two men parted and Agrippa moved back across the room to stand with his Third Legion compatriots. Tamerlane meanwhile huddled with the technicians, discussing the tactical aspects of the mission. After a rapid-fire discussion, they concluded that the severed ends of the tether cables could be attached to the belts of the new expedition personnel. It wouldn't be as dependable as before—they would have to be attached in a makeshift manner, given the time constraints—but it was probably better than not having lifelines at all.

Seconds later, Tamerlane and Nakamura, along with four of their specialists of lieutenant rank and the three Inquisitors, had all been outfitted with the silver discs that provided energy shielding around their bodies. The tether cables were crudely tied onto their belts, while one of the lieutenants, by the name of Keefe, accepted a small device that the techs promised could track the Emperor through whatever environment they found themselves in. Nakamura, meanwhile, refused the atmospheric suits offered by the techs.

"Won't we be needing those?" Stanishur asked, somewhat taken aback.

"They're constricting, they'll slow us down, and there's no evidence they're necessary in the Above," Nakamura said with finality.

"But—the Emperor wore one," Inquisitor Delain protested, having watched a recording of the Emperor's departure.

"No one here was going to take any chances with him," Nakamura said. "Beyond the gigantic chance he was already taking."

The Inquisitors didn't appear happy about that, but they accepted it in silence.

Nakamura motioned to General Attila and the big, bald, muscle-bound man approached.

"Esteban, you are in charge here until we return."

The Second Legion general's small, dark eyes glinted under heavy brows. "Understood."

A second later and the six soldiers and three Inquisitors had taken position just before the black-framed doorway. The lights on it were shimmering again, the white swirl at its center growing in intensity.

"Any last concerns before we go through?" Nakamura asked, his blast pistol out of its holster and held at the ready.

The others shook their heads.

"I have to admit I'm curious to see what could have defeated an entire squad of elite Emperor's Guard," Tamerlane noted with a wry smile. He cradled a quad-rifle in both arms. "And how it will fare against us."

The two younger Inquisitors exchanged nervous glances, but Stanishur's expression only hardened. "Let us proceed," he hissed.

"By all means," Nakamura agreed. He stepped forward, into the white light. Tamerlane followed immediately on his heels, the others pushing forward behind them.

The universe they knew dissolved into nothingness at their backs, and an entirely new one swallowed them whole.

10

They were floating.

Tamerlane fought to retain his equilibrium as his inner ears went mad.

He became aware very quickly that his feet were not touching the floor. He looked down and understood why: There *was* no floor.

Below him, emptiness extended forever. Not the deep, dark depths of space; simply a blankness, a void.

His head spun even worse. He thought he might be sick, but fought back and got his stomach under control.

A gagging sound from nearby revealed that someone else was not so lucky. He turned his head to his left in the direction of the sound and saw that it was one of the two younger Inquisitors—the boy—who was throwing up.

Turning back the other way, he found that his entire body was slowly rotating, for now the rest of the group was moving into view. They were drifting about, arms and legs moving in slow motion as if they were attempting to swim, or to catch themselves from falling.

Tamerlane inhaled deeply and found that the substance they floated in wasn't precisely air, but it wasn't a liquid, either—he could definitely breathe it. That was a plus, anyway. He tried calling out, but his voice sounded weak and filled with echoes. It didn't seem to be carrying at all.

"Test," he said, both aloud and internally, accessing the Aether—the mental subspace data and communications link that all Imperial soldiers shared. Essentially a telepathic link, under normal circumstances it could cover great distances instantaneously. These were, however, not normal circumstances. "This is Tamerlane," he sent across the network. "Testing."

A crackle that sounded not so much in his ears as in his head caused him to wince, and then, "I hear you, Colonel," said Nakamura, "speaking" across the link from only a short distance away. "We appear to have extremely limited local Aether connections."

"Limited is better than nothing, sir," Tamerlane replied. "Everyone sound off."

The other four soldiers—Lieutenants Torval, Keefe, Ling, and Landau—reported in, their voices scratchy and overlaid with static.

"What about those three?" Ling asked, pointing toward the three Inquisitors who floated nearby.

"The Inquisition isn't part of our Aether network," Tamerlane said—but he'd barely gotten the words out, or rather gotten them sent, when a somewhat familiar insignia popped up in the corner of his vision. It was an identifier mark, being transmitted into his virtual-reality view. He looked at it and recognized it and frowned. Then he twisted around so he could see the Inquisitors where they floated nearby. They were staring back, waiting.

"General, are you seeing this?" Tamerlane asked.

There was no question that Nakamura knew exactly what he was referring to: a narrow black rectangle, which might also double as the capital letter "I."

"Indeed," the general said. "Go ahead and accept the link."

Tamerlane focused on the Inquisition symbol and ordered the Aether to make the link with it, then instructed the lieutenants to do likewise.

"How about that?" they heard Nakamura saying as the connection was made. "You have your own network—and can link into ours."

"Of course," Stanishur stated. "We could scarcely function as an effective arm of the Imperium without it."

Tamerlane noted that three little black icons had joined the five red ones along the edge of his VR-vision. Like it or not, the Inquisitors were now an integrated part of their expedition and not just tagalongs.

"That's fine, then," Nakamura said. "In this environment, anything that helps us to communicate is a plus." He realized he was drifting again and slowly spinning to face away from the others, and gyrated his arms and legs to fight against it; it would have looked ridiculous if not for the fact that several of the others were having to do the same. "Obviously," he added, "we now need to figure out how to move. And quickly!"

"I'm working on that," Tamerlane reported. "The techs were trying to explain it to me but there wasn't time for me to fully grasp it or test it out." He was holding his arms out from his body and angling his knees and elbows, like a parachutist. Slowly—very slowly at first, but with gathering speed—he started to move forward. He looked back at the others and grinned.

"How are you doing that, Colonel?" called one of the lieutenants.

"Show us all," Nakamura added.

"It's simple." Tamerlane explained that if they focused via the Aether on the silver disks they'd been given, they could access the controls and reshape the electromagnetic fields it projected around them, such that they could create a sort of propulsive effect. "It's like skydiving, sort of," he noted. "You just form the field so that it's at an angle, and then you slide through the air—or whatever we're in—like a wedge."

Within moments, the others were doing it; some taking to it quite naturally, others somewhat clumsily.

"That's good enough," Nakamura declared after a couple of minutes of everyone testing it out. "Let's get going." He spun around and looked to Keefe. "Lieutenant, you were given the tracker, yes?"

"Yes, General," the blond woman—the only other female member of the expedition—replied. She was holding the small, square device the scientists on the station had given her. "It's tuned to pick up on the unique energy signature of the Guard's crystal armor." Tamerlane watched as she stared down at it for a couple of seconds, doubtlessly using the Aether to connect with it in similar fashion to the way they'd accessed the silver disks. Then she pointed ahead. "The readings are very weak, but—*that* way."

They angled their fields—some figured it out more quickly than others—and the entire group slid forward, slowly at first but with gathering momentum.

Time passed, though in this strange no-universe its passage seemed oddly disjointed. Tamerlane soon had lost all sense of how long they'd been moving. He checked the chronometer in his VR vision but the numbers there seemed random, skipping forward and backward, fast and slow— they made no sense at all.

Keefe had them change direction three times in fairly quick succession, and she seemed somewhat bewildered by the readings she was getting. Tamerlane meanwhile kept glancing back at their tether cables. He had no intention of losing the way back out, while everyone else was focused on what lay ahead.

"Could they have really gone this far?" asked Ling after a timeless time.

"How far is *this* far?" Landau countered. "I can't tell if we've covered much distance at all."

It was true, Tamerlane had to agree. The seemingly endless depths of pale light all around them made a mockery of any attempts to judge distances.

And then, quite suddenly, that entire situation changed.

"Are you men feeling that?" asked Tamerlane. He frowned as, against all of his efforts, he began to sink below the others. Keefe, who had been out front with the tracker, was dropping even faster.

"It's almost like... *gravity*," Ling said as he started down just behind them.

"Try to stay together, everyone," Nakamura barked. "Keefe—are we being pulled off the trail?"

"No, General," the blonde lieutenant called back and up to her commander. "The Emperor's party seems to have gone this way, too."

"Fine, then. Stay sharp."

Tamerlane spared a look back over his shoulder and saw the others following along behind Keefe and him in a ragged line, the Inquisitors at the tail.

"There's something ahead," Keefe called back to them.

In the zero-gee environment, Tamerlane had fastened the big quad-rifle he'd been carrying to his back, allowing it to be towed along easily behind him. Now, as the sense of gravity increased, he reached back and grabbed it, holding it at the ready. It was a massive weapon, and he held it awkwardly; it was better suited for someone big and strong and wearing combat armor, like the guys in Agrippa's Golden Phalanx, than for a man in nothing but smartcloth. But, in an environment like this, he'd wanted whatever advantage he could gain. He simply hoped the gravity wouldn't increase to the point that he could no longer effectively carry or use it.

Some sort of fog was creeping around them as they continued along, and visibility dropped. The light dimmed;

the depths of the strange environment darkened as though a thunderstorm were rolling in.

"Tighten up the formation," Nakamura ordered. "Let's don't lose sight of one another."

"Detecting some odd radiation readings," noted Landau. "Straight ahead. No—wait. All around us now."

"We can't worry about that right now," Nakamura said. "Trust the disks to protect us from anything too harmful, and keep going."

Tamerlane spared a quick glance down at the silver device clipped to his belt and offered a quick prayer to whichever of Those Who Remain might be watching him now to keep that little machine working.

A few moments later, the fog beneath Tamerlane had thickened to the point that it could have hidden an imperial battle cruiser just ten meters away from him with him being none the wiser. And then, as he was noting that fact, something even more surprising than a battle cruiser was revealed beneath his feet: the ground.

Keefe was already impacting the surface—such as it was—and tumbling over to one side, like a skydiver landing in slow motion. Tamerlane had only an instant to call a warning out to those above and behind him before he, too, made contact with what was definitely a hard surface. He tucked and rolled, protecting his weapon as he went.

Grunts and exclamations erupted from the others in rapid succession as they landed, a couple of them getting slightly tangled in their lines. Tamerlane climbed back onto his feet and hurried toward Keefe. He found the surface was relatively easy to move across; slightly spongy, which had probably prevented the entire expedition from suffering multiple broken bones, but firm enough to hold his weight easily.

"I'm alright, Colonel," Keefe reported as she accepted his help in getting up. She still clutched the tracking device in her right hand, and offered him a wry smile when she realized that was what he was most concerned about. "It's safe and sound, sir."

Nakamura ordered everyone to report in and gather around. No one had been injured, including even the almost elderly Stanishur—a fact that somewhat surprised Tamerlane, who had feared they'd be carrying him on a makeshift stretcher.

"Which way now?" the general asked Keefe.

She turned slowly and then pointed into the ever-thickening fog. "That way, sir."

The party had scarcely taken ten steps in the direction indicated when they all abruptly halted and stared at what had been revealed as they advanced into the fog.

It took them aback at first. One of the Inquisitors—the boy—even cried out. Tamerlane felt his mouth go dry as a sort of instinctual, almost primordial fear crept up from the depths of his stomach. *"What in—?"* he whispered.

What they saw a few steps before them, wreathed in the fog, most of them first took to be a gigantic *eye*—a cat's eye, complete with the long, narrow, vertical pupil—staring back at them out of the darkness.

Landau stumbled back a step. Keefe put her hand over her mouth, either to stifle her reaction or to try to keep from throwing up, or both. The others looked from the strange vision that lay ahead, of them to Nakamura and back, unease apparent on all of their faces.

"General," Keefe asked, her voice low, "what in the name of all that's holy *is* that thing?"

Inquisitor Stanishur stepped forward, pushing rudely past the soldiers, and stood with his hands on his hips, gazing up at the gargantuan eye.

More than ten meters tall, it was blood red around the edges, like an infected wound. Darkness swirled all through it and while the pupil was utterly black, a sort of sickly light emanated from it.

"I smell something," Ling noted.

"Something rotten, yeah," Keefe agreed, wrinkling her nose.

Stanishur continued to stare up at it and nodded slowly. "I have heard rumors of such things, though I have never seen one with my own eyes." He hesitated, still staring directly at it, as if the eye had hypnotized him somehow. "It is a rip, a permanent tear, in the very fabric of the Above," he continued after a few seconds, and venom dripped from every word. "It is a blight on the multiverse, and an affront to the gods themselves." He turned and looked at the others then, his expression sour. "It is a blasphemy."

The lieutenants looked at one another nervously. Nakamura seemed to be searching for the right words to say; words that would overcome the religious concerns of his soldiers. He didn't appear to be having much luck with that.

Keefe leaned in and murmured something to Tamerlane. The colonel nodded after hearing it and turned to Stanishur. "Then I'm afraid I have some bad news, Inquisitor," he stated, gazing up at what now was slightly more discernible as a hole punched through the very air in front of them, opening onto some other layer of reality.

The tall, dour man almost reluctantly turned away from the eye. His expression changed only slightly, questioningly, inviting the colonel to finish the thought.

"I'm afraid," Tamerlane told him, "the Emperor's trail leads directly through there."

11

The entire party stood only a short distance away from the eye, that great gash sliced into the fabric of reality, and stared up at it with a mixture of awe and trepidation. Beyond just its disturbing appearance, it seemed to radiate an almost palpable sense of danger, of menace—like the eye of some horrific predator, waiting to pounce. It gave even a hardened soldier like Tamerlane the chills. He tried to look away from it, but found it kept drawing his attention back to it. In this universe of swirling fog and dim, pale light, there was nowhere else to look.

"Through there?" the Inquisitor asked, his bloodshot eyes flashing toward Tamerlane. "You're saying the Emperor passed through that—that *blasphemy*?" He didn't seem to truly believe it.

Tamerlane motioned again to Keefe, who held the small tracking device up before her face and turned in a slow circle. Once she'd completed a single rotation, she lowered it again and nodded to the colonel.

"If His Majesty found the level of the Above we're in now not exciting enough—and how could he not, since all this gray fog is so exciting—then I could very easily see him continuing on to a different level," the colonel stated, "regardless of whatever assurances he made."

"The Emperor is quite...*headstrong*, yes," Stanishur reluctantly agreed. "But, even so—" His gaze returned to the eye before them and he shuddered. His two assistants exchanged troubled glances.

"The walls of our universe were determined to be thinnest at the location where the Emperor's yacht was stationed—above NM-156," Nakamura explained. "It follows that the walls between this part of the Above and those levels even higher would also be thinner here."

"That they might even be torn in places," Tamerlane added, nodding toward the eye.

The Inquisitor blinked, taking this information in, then looked back at the eye, his expression still conveying great dislike and distrust of the phenomenon.

"So the Emperor hadn't found the sword yet, maybe, and he got bored with all the fog here, and simply kept going—right through *there*," Tamerlane concluded. "It's either that, or else someone... or some*thing*... came along and gave him no choice in the matter."

"Let's hold off on idle speculation for now, Colonel," Nakamura interjected. He was already walking toward the eye. "Come on, everyone. We know what we have to do. Let's keep moving."

Somewhat reluctantly, or at least with less enthusiasm than up until now, the rest of the party followed him. The three Inquisitors came last, and their discomfort was obvious and profound.

When he reached the threshold of the eye, Nakamura turned back and addressed the team.

"I don't plan on traveling too far on the other side, wherever it might be," he said, his calm and even voice in stark contrast to the malignant red swirl of the eye.

Tamerlane and the others nodded readily at that.

"Alright," the general said, his jaw firm and his expression one of resolved determination, "here we go."

He stepped into the black pupil of the eye, and the darkness swallowed him up. Less than a second later, he was gone.

Tamerlane repressed a shudder, then started to follow after him.

Nakamura's tether wire dropped to the ground, cleanly severed.

Tamerlane shouted a profanity and rushed forward. Before he could cover the three additional steps between himself and the eye, however, a shape formed within the black and separated itself, moving out into the pale light.

It was Nakamura. His face was drenched in sweat, and he was not happy.

"What happened?" he demanded, before Tamerlane could ask the same of him. "Who cut my cable? And what's been keeping you?"

Tamerlane was taken aback. He glanced quickly at the others, then down at the severed end of the cable on the ground, then back at Nakamura, who was fuming.

"General—what do you mean? You only just—"

"I waited for more than a minute, but no one else came through, so I started back—but the opening on the other side is different," he said, his voice strained and angry. "The eye there—it's not an eye. Just a kind of doorway. And it drifts around. With my cable cut, I had to chase it. And the sounds…" He shuddered.

Tamerlane paled. This was not like Nakamura—not like the virtually fearless soldier that Tamerlane had sworn his allegiance to as a young boy. Nakamura had been all but a father to him for the better part of his life, and never once in that time had he seen the man so unnerved.

"The time differential," Ling interjected. "Time must move faster on the other side."

"No," Keefe argued, shaking her head. "We're in the Above. Time moves slower. Passing into an even higher level should only make time slow down even further—not speed up, as the general experienced."

Tamerlane scratched at his chin, considering what they were saying. He looked at Nakamura again, and was relieved to see that the man had calmed himself somewhat.

"I take it there was no sign of the Emperor and his party," Inquisitor Stanishur stated as he and his two assistants moved up alongside the others.

"No," Nakamura answered, "but I didn't have the tracker with me."

"Then what do we do now, sir?" Keefe asked.

Nakamura breathed deeply of the strange not-air through which they all moved, then nodded toward the eye. "We go through," he said. "Together. All at once."

The three Inquisitors made holy signs with their hands.

"What about your wire, General?" Tamerlane asked, nodding toward the few inches of severed end dangling from Nakamura's belt.

"Since I assume no one here cut it," Nakamura replied, "I'm guessing the eye did it. I'd guess that's what happened with the Emperor's wires, too."

"We should detach them," Tamerlane suggested. "Leave them on this side."

No one objected audibly, but the looks exchanged by more than one of the others clearly displayed their feelings about such an idea.

"No, no," Nakamura said quickly, seeing the discontent brewing within his team. "The colonel is quite right. We would lose them anyway. Better to leave them here, anchored somehow, so that we will have them when we return."

As the others somewhat reluctantly began to disconnect their wires and passed the ends to Tamerlane, who was using a tie cable to bind them together neatly, Nakamura stopped Torval from detaching his from his belt. "You remain here with the wires," he said to the lieutenant. "We're going to need you to maintain the connection and show us the way back out."

If there were objections to that plan, no one voiced them. Thus, moments later, the entire group—minus Torval—was gathered tightly together, directly in front of the black tear in reality.

"Hold hands," the general ordered. "Everyone."

Each member of the group awkwardly reached out and clasped the hand of the person on either side. Once that was accomplished, Nakamura gave the order and they all walked into the darkness.

Disorientation; disconnect. A sense of falling. Equilibrium gone. Stumbling into one other. The world turned upside down.

Through. Out the other side.

Darkness.

Tamerlane felt the person to his right—Keefe—going down to her knees, wobbly, and pulled her back up. The human chain never broke.

He looked up then, at their utterly different surroundings, and more disorientation followed. He reeled; the gray fog of the previous environment had been replaced by a nightmare vista of bold colors, all swirling about madly. He felt as if he'd been dropped into a bucket of paint—a bucket where all the different shades were being mixed together slowly. The very atmosphere around them felt wet; not wet with simple humidity, but thick and dense as if actually comprised of water. Their movements were sluggish, too, as though they were deep under the sea. And the sounds— like hundreds or thousands of voices, echoing endlessly, forming no understandable words yet conveying an overwhelming sense of bleak uneasiness.

Nakamura had already turned around and was pointing back in the direction from which they'd come. Tamerlane looked and, sure enough, on this side of the tear there was no eye. Instead he was looking at a solid black rectangle, perhaps five meters high and three wide. It didn't stay in one place but seemed to shift about, ever so subtly, as though drifting in the currents of some dark ocean.

Nakamura grasped Ling by the arm and pointed at the doorway. "Your job now is to keep that thing in sight at all times," he growled. "Do you understand?"

Ling nodded. "Absolutely, General."

Approaching Keefe, Nakamura demanded, "What does it tell you now?"

The young woman already had the square tracking device held up and was turning slowly. "That way," she said, pointing into the nightmare swirl of colors. "The signal is much stronger now."

"Good." He motioned to the others. "Let's move."

With Torval waiting back on the other side of the eye and Ling remaining behind on their side of it, the party was now reduced to seven: Nakamura and Tamerlane, Keefe and Landau, and the three Inquisitors. With Keefe in the lead, the tracker held up where she could keep one eye on it, they marched into the depths.

"Radiation levels are much higher here, General," reported Landau after only a few steps, his voice filled with concern. "And the kinds I'm picking up—I have no idea if our shields are able to protect us from it."

"Not our main problem at the moment, Lieutenant."

"But, sir—this could kill us within a few hours!"

"Then that's a matter for a few hours. Our concern at the moment is locating the Emperor and bringing him back." He motioned ahead. "Keep going!"

They walked on for several minutes in silence, with only those awful disembodied voices to keep them company. Tamerlane was looking around in wonder, his eyes repeatedly drawn to the swirling, cascading layers of color that they were passing through—and that he wasn't entirely convinced wasn't passing through *them*, too. Something about it bothered him on a deep, instinctual level. It was as if the entire environment had been poisoned by some foul and alien presence. The longer his eyes dwelt on the swirling colors around them, the more he felt he could perceive faces within, staring back out at him. Staring with malevolent intent. It made no sense on a rational level, but a powerful feeling of hostility directed at him and the rest of the party grew stronger within his mind with every step they took.

"Are you alright, Ezekial?" Nakamura asked, after glancing back at him and seeing the extreme discomfort reflected on his face.

"Yes, General," he replied, sobering. "There's just something about this place—"

"I know," Nakamura said. "It's hot, for one thing." Sweat was again trailing down the sides of his face.

Tamerlane nodded. The heat had built slowly, from the moment they'd crossed over, and now it was starting to get to him, too. "But, beyond that, there's something…"

"This is no part of the Above I've ever heard about," Landau observed, frowning deeply.

Tamerlane couldn't have agreed more. He looked back at Stanishur and his two young assistants. "What about you, Inquisitor? Does scripture speak of this place?"

The cadaverous man was looking all around, his expression more dour than usual. "I—I cannot say," he reported finally. "Certainly it does not match my own understanding of the nature of the Above, but I am only a mere mortal, and cannot—"

"Let's stay focused," Nakamura interrupted. "We find the Emperor and the Guard, and we drag them all back out of here. That's it. We can leave the theological implications of bad weather in the Above to the Ecclesiarchy to sort out at a later date."

"There is another possible explanation," Stanishur intoned from behind them. "Though it is not one I truly care to consider."

The soldiers all turned to face him.

The gaunt figure in black gestured toward the eye. "Taken along with the time flow problem—time should move slower here than outside, not faster—I am beginning to suspect that we are no longer in the Above at all."

The others all frowned, some of them glancing at one another.

"What?" Keefe asked, puzzled.

"Then where else could we be?" Landau chimed in.

"Of course," Tamerlane said, nodding slowly. "I think I've known it all along." He turned to Nakamura then. "And I think you have, too."

The general only nodded. "It doesn't matter, though," he growled. "We have a job to do. For the Emperor. So we keep going until we find him."

"Wait," Keefe said, her eyes widening and panic creeping into her voice. "You—you're saying this isn't the Above? Then—you're saying we're in the *Below*?"

Stanishur reached out with a bony hand and laid it on her arm; it was a surprisingly tender gesture from the dour Inquisitor.

"That is correct," he said. "That eye through which we passed—it was no tear in the layers of the Above. I was right in calling it a blasphemy, but it was something much, much worse than that." He faced the others, his eyes burning and his teeth gritted. "It was the gateway to Hell."

Someone groaned. Others unholstered their weapons.

"General," Landau said, his voice frantic, "we've got to get out of here!"

"Have you forgotten that your Emperor is down here somewhere?" Nakamura barked back. "We can't leave him. We have to find him—before something else does."

Keefe screamed. Tamerlane whirled about, looking to where she was pointing.

Something was coming through the swirl of colors, emerging into the open where they all could see it.

Keefe's gun was in her hand. She fired.

"Wait!" shouted Nakamura, surely wanting to be cautious—but, an instant later, they could all see that the time for caution was past. More shapes were emerging all around them, closing in.

Hideous shapes.

The first one solidified into a snake-form, almost transparent and glowing from multiple eerie light sources deep inside its repulsive body. It moved forward rapidly, closing on Keefe. Whatever it was, her shots didn't seem to bother it—and now it had formed teeth. Many teeth.

Screaming, Keefe fired again, while next to her Tamerlane raised his heavy quad-rifle and opened fire as well, using two of the barrels—one firing high-velocity slugs, the other a particle-beam cannon. The creature roared in anger and perhaps in pain, though the full effect of their efforts was hard to tell, given its amorphous body.

Now the other shapes solidified into monstrous forms and advanced from all around them.

"Demons!" Landau cried, and nobody contradicted him. "Demons of the Below!"

12

The party, recovering quickly from their initial panic and fear, instinctively moved into a defensive circle. Everyone opened fire. Even the Inquisitors turned out to be armed; as they chanted ancient phrases and prayers of warding and protection, they drew from their robes exquisitely-crafted pistols that looked more like antiques but proved to pack quite a punch.

The demons—five of them in all—pressed the attack for several more seconds, though they were beginning to show signs of injury from the sustained fire of the humans. Some of the weapons appeared to have more of an effect than others; the slug-throwers seemed to do them great damage, while the energy-blast and particle beam guns scarcely fazed them.

The snake-thing that had attacked Keefe was the first to fall back, screeching as it went, the sounds not just of bestial anguish but almost resembling words.

Chills raced up the spines of everyone in the group at the unholy noise. They redoubled their efforts at the remaining creatures, seeing the success they'd had with the first one. Within moments they'd driven the others back as well, though none of the monsters looked to have been mortally wounded—if such a term as "mortal" could even be applied here, to such beings.

Guns were hot, bullets were low, and everyone was gasping for breath. At that moment, more shapes appeared and began to emerge from the nightmarish swirl of light and color. Grimacing in anger and fear, Keefe raised her pistol and fired.

The shot deflected off of something solid.

"Wait," shouted Nakamura, reaching out and grasping her arm before she could fire again. "Hold your fire, everyone!"

Two solid colors were separating from the shimmering storm around them, and it was quickly obvious that they were human shapes. One had a hand raised, waving. The colors were red and green.

"The Guard!" shouted Tamerlane, rushing past Keefe and reaching out to the nearest figure. He recognized the ruby armor instantly—there was only one man in the Empire who wore its like. "Zayid," he called, trying to see through the man's crystalline helmet. "Are you alright?"

The Emperor's Guardsman didn't reply. He stumbled past Tamerlane and dropped to one knee, while more of the armored men emerged. Behind them came two more figures, unarmored. These were barely on their feet, remaining upright only by mutually supporting one another. One wore black, and Tamerlane didn't recognize him at all. The other was clad in a pale blue environment suit.

"The Ecclesiarch!" called Keefe. Together she and Tamerlane lifted the older man under the arms, relieving the burden of the person in black. Tamerlane spared this new individual a quick look, wondering who he could be and where he possibly could have come from. He was tall and slender, with dark hair and piercing eyes.

Tamerlane's attention was brought back to the more pressing issue as Nakamura both shouted and sent over the Aether, "The Emperor! Is he with you? Is he alive?"

Five of the Guardsmen had emerged now. Leaving the Ecclesiarch in the care of Keefe, Tamerlane hurried back in the direction from which they'd been coming. Thus he was first to encounter the figure in pale yellow who staggered out into the open and collapsed into his arms.

"Sire! Are you alright? This is Colonel Tamerlane. Are you—?"

Tamerlane became slowly aware that the Emperor was clutching something in his right hand. For some reason, though, he couldn't quite focus his eyes on it. They just kept sliding right off of it, whatever it was. Even thinking about it made his head swim. Finally he forced himself to ignore it—the Emperor's safety, after all, trumped any other considerations—and he found his growing headache eased a bit when he did that. He shook his head to clear the cobwebs that seemed to be growing there, then called out, "I've got him! I have the Emperor!"

"Yes!" cried Nakamura triumphantly. "Get him over here! Center of the circle. Everyone form up, now!"

By the hardest, the general and his team—with the Inquisitors helping as best they could—managed to assist the Emperor, the Ecclesiarch, the stranger, and the heavy, armored Guardsmen into a tight group, where they could be better protected. None of them seemed in particularly good shape. As Nakamura attempted to communicate with the Emperor himself, Tamerlane did a quick count of the Guard. Satisfied that all five were present, he squatted down next to the general.

"Everyone's accounted for, sir," he stated, "plus one new guy."

Nakamura blinked at this, quite justifiably confused. "What?"

Tamerlane pointed.

Nakamura frowned as he stared momentarily at the man in black. "They encountered someone? Rescued him?"

He waved it away. "We can concern ourselves with that once we're back safely."

Tamerlane nodded. He couldn't help but peer down at the Emperor, whose face was obscured by the gleaming synth-resin faceplate of the helmet of his environment suit. Then, over a tight, one-to-one Aether connection with Nakamura, he asked, "How is he, sir?"

"I—can't tell yet, Ezekial. He's not responding." A pause, then, "Let's just get him out of here."

"Yes, sir." Tamerlane stood. "Alright, everyone," he called out, using both his natural voice and the Aether. "We're moving out. Quick as you can, but stay together!"

Once all the members of the group—now swelled to eighteen—were on their feet, Tamerlane led them back the way they'd come while the general hung close to the Emperor, helping him along and attempting to communicate with him.

"Ling," Tamerlane called via the Aether. "Do you read? Lt. Ling, come in."

A voice, static-filled at first but slowly clearing, came back over the link.

"This way," it said. "Straight ahead."

The party pressed forward. The heat was oppressive now, and no one's equilibrium was exactly right. It seemed the longer they spent in this bizarre environment, the more destabilizing it became on their inner ears, their vision, and their other senses in general.

"That's it," the voice said, sounding increasingly hollow somehow even as the signal strengthened. "Yes. Come this way."

Tamerlane frowned.

"Ling?" he called. "Is that you?"

"Come this way," the voice repeated.

"Ling?"

A huge, monstrous shape appeared before them. It was translucent, like the snake they'd fought moments earlier, but much larger. In its form it was somewhat reminiscent of a gorilla, but with much exaggerated features—and four arms, each ending not in hands or paws but in hook-like talons. Flames burned across its head and shoulders and deep within its pitch-black eyes. An awful stench radiated out from it in waves, and that alone was nearly enough to knock Tamerlane off his feet. The creature leered, then lurched towards them.

Keefe screamed, and several of the others cried out. The Inquisitors chanted wards and protection spells again. Tamerlane had his quad-rifle up and firing from the moment it appeared. Learning from the previous encounter, he stuck to using the projectile barrels, firing slugs and explosive rounds.

Under the barrage of fire, the demon faltered momentarily—and then two more identical creatures appeared behind it, charging at the group.

"Stick with bullets," Tamerlane ordered.

"I'm already out," Keefe cried.

"Me, too," came the wail from Landau.

A massive, clawed hand swiped at the edge of the group. Landau grunted as it impacted him near the waist, and he was sent tumbling off to the side. The silver disk he and all the others wore—the disk that provided a defensive electromagnetic field around him—was knocked loose and rolled away in the fog.

"Your disk!" shouted Tamerlane. "Landau!"

The lieutenant got back on his feet and then Tamerlane's warning seemed to hit home. Reaching down, he felt and discovered that the object was missing. He whirled about, looking for it, to no avail. The flames were already sprouting from his hair and his uniform at that point.

The creatures had halted in their advance for a moment, but still held the attention of nearly everyone present. Thus only Tamerlane, who was already looking directly at Landau, saw what became of him.

The flames that licked across his body spread rapidly, their intensity growing. They seemed to be emerging from inside him somehow. He screamed—a horrifying, blood-curdling scream—and now the others were looking. By then, it was too late to see anything but a column of fire.

The flames grew to blinding intensity, then faded. When they were gone entirely, so was Landau. Only a tiny cloud of ashes remained, quickly lost in the fog.

The creatures roared and began to advance again, clawed limbs slashing.

Tamerlane gritted his teeth at the loss to their ranks and kept firing. His quad-rifle was overheating, and it was nearly out of ammo, anyway. Even as he fired, he noted that the Guardsmen hadn't raised so much as a finger in their defense—they were simply standing there like zombies. Nakamura was basically holding the Emperor up on his feet, meanwhile firing away with his sidearm, contributing what he could to the effort. Keefe was holding up the Ecclesiarch, while the man in black sat on the ground alone, seemingly disoriented.

Tamerlane noticed for the first time that the Emperor was holding something in his hand—something large, hanging down at his side, its color matching the shimmering yellow of his suit. How he'd missed seeing it before, he had no idea—but apparently no one else had taken notice of it, either. There was no time to study it further, though, for the creatures were descending upon the group.

Tamerlane fired until his weapon ran dry. A second later, Nakamura's was out. They glanced at one another, recognizing that this was the end.

As the massive talons swept around and down at him, Tamerlane lowered his gun and waited for death.

Death didn't come.

Blinking, he looked up.

The creatures had stopped in their advance and were standing there, staring down at the group—and at one figure in particular, who stood at the forefront, holding an object up over its head. Tamerlane was perplexed for an instant. He couldn't imagine it was actually who he thought it was—the Emperor—or that he was holding what it looked like he was holding—the supposedly lost Sword of Baranak.

He started forward, but found he couldn't move very quickly at all. It was as if he were covered in concrete; some force was slowing him, dulling his thoughts. Meanwhile he could see the Emperor standing there, holding the sword—radiant with golden light—out before him, and speaking in some unknown language as he stared down the creatures.

The monsters swayed back and forth for a few moments, blinking at the glare from the sword, each of them making snuffling noises. Tamerlane got the distinct impression that they were sniffing his team—trying to smell something— though how they could smell anything over their own awful stench was hard to fathom. Then, as one, they turned and shambled back into the swirling colors, vanishing entirely.

Tamerlane gasped for breath and looked around. As far as he could tell, the group was still intact, everyone still alive.

"What happened?" called the general.

"I—don't know," Tamerlane replied. He seemed to remember that someone in the group had done...*something*? Was it...*the Emperor*? But that was impossible, he realized, turning to see the Emperor sitting where he had been before, zombie-like, nearly catatonic.

Hadn't he done something, though? And it had involved an object—one the seemed familiar...

Tamerlane sighed. His head was splitting with one of the worst headaches he'd ever experienced. Tiredly he decided to let it go.

"General? Is that you? Colonel?"

Tamerlane looked up, as did Nakamura.

"Ling?" the colonel called back. "Ling, can you hear me?"

"Yes, sir," came the voice that was very clearly Lt. Ling this time. "I can see you, too. Look to your left."

Tamerlane and Nakamura both turned that way and could just make out the shape of the lieutenant, jumping up and down and waving his arms. Behind him stood the big, black rectangle. The dimensional doorway.

The way out.

"Thank all the gods of the Above," came the voice of the Inquisitor from behind them. He'd seen Ling, too. "Let us give thanks—to all of Those Who Remain—for this deliverance."

"We're not out yet, Inquisitor," Tamerlane noted—but he could already feel a good deal of weight lifting from his shoulders.

"Let's move," Nakamura barked, as no-nonsense as ever. He helped the Emperor up and together the party headed in the direction of the doorway. As they moved, the general at last noticed what the Emperor was carrying, and he halted in mid-step.

"The Sword!

Tamerlane looked back and now he remembered seeing it, too, during the attack. It *had* been the sword. The Emperor had found it! He'd held it up against the demons. Tamerlane squeezed his eyes closed as pain lanced through his head again. Why in the name of the gods hadn't he been able to remember seeing it afterward?

"Majesty," Nakamura said, astonished. "Where—where did you get that?"

The Emperor was still unresponsive.

"Allow me to carry it for you, at least," Nakamura said, reaching for the gleaming weapon. Janus didn't respond— didn't even look up as the general made the effort to take it—but his fingers were locked like iron around the hilt.

At last Nakamura gave up and began moving forward again. Looking on, Tamerlane frowned. The demeanor of the Emperor and all the others they'd come to rescue was beginning to trouble him deeply, but his overwhelming priority at the moment had to be simply getting everyone back out safely.

As they all reached the big black doorway, and a very visibly relieved Lt. Ling, Tamerlane blinked in surprise. The doorway shimmered for an instant, as though passing through discolored water, and when it solidified again it stood at least two meters to the right of its previous position.

"Is this what you meant before, General?" Tamerlane asked, taken aback.

"It moves, yes," Nakamura responded. "Let's get through it quickly."

"We have to hold hands—all go through at once," Tamerlane reminded the others.

Before the doorway could move again, Nakamura and his team joined hands, pulling the Emperor and his party into their circle by the hardest. While none of those who had been lost had yet spoken, they seemed to wake up a bit as they were forced to clasp hands with the others. Tamerlane noticed that the man in black appeared to be the most aware of his surroundings, his dark eyes glittering as they flicked from one soldier to the next. For the third time since they had encountered the Emperor's group, he wanted to ask the stranger a few questions—and for the third time, such desires slipped from his mind immediately after he thought them.

Once everyone was joined hand in hand, Nakamura gave the order and they all stepped forward, forming a "V" formation behind him to either side, like ducks migrating south for winter. He nodded and they all passed through the doorway.

The disorientation was maddening, just as before. It felt as if it would never end. And then it did, and they were all standing in front of the massive, hideous eye again.

Torval was right where they had left him, his own tether wire stretching off into the fog, the other wires neatly bundled on the ground beside him.

"General?" he said, regarding them with puzzlement. "Something wrong?" Then he saw just how much larger the party was than it had been. "You found them!"

"Remember," Tamerlane pointed out as he disengaged himself from the Guardsman he had helped through, "it hasn't been very long for Torval since we left him."

"Very long?" Torval said, eyes wide. "It's only been a few seconds, sir. Where did you find His Majesty?"

Nakamura shook his head. "Debriefing later," he barked. "I want all of us out of there—now!"

With two or even three individuals per wire, they were able to quickly get everyone moving back toward the portal. Those whose belts were actually connected—or reconnected—to the wires sent the signal that caused the wires to begin to retract, and the entire party was slowly pulled back to where they had first entered this bizarre realm.

Tamerlane watched the swirling gray clouds moving past them in every direction. He frowned as he discerned that they were darkening—almost souring, or curdling—as they passed through them. Puzzled, he glanced over at the Inquisitor to his left.

"You see it too, do you not, Colonel?" Stanishur asked softly.

"I do," Tamerlane answered. "All around us—"

"Despoiled," the Inquisitor finished for him. "The Above becomes despoiled as we pass through it."

Tamerlane's frown deepened. This truly disturbed him. "Are we causing it? Just our presence here?"

"There can be little doubt."

"But—why? We didn't cause anything like this before, on the way in."

Stanishur's eyes met his directly, and he nodded once. "That is quite correct."

"But, then—" He looked over to where the Emperor and his entourage were being pulled along by their cables. "It can't be *them*—"

"Our group carries with it the demonic spoor of the Below," Stanishur stated coldly. "Why, I know not. *Yet*."

The wires continued to reel them in. They dangled from them as though being pulled up through a planet's clouds from a hovering vehicle high in the sky.

A beep sounded from one of the devices at Lt. Ling's belt. He checked it, started, and checked again.

"The radiation is building up rapidly," he reported to the others. "It's different from what I was detecting in the Below, but it's still far stronger than we need to be experiencing."

"What does that mean?" Tamerlane asked, spinning around a bit on the wire to face the man.

Ling shrugged. "There is simply no way our little disk shields are coping with this," he observed, voice hollow.

"I can feel it," Torval said, holding his hand up and staring at it, as if it were about to mutate into some sort of amphibian appendage or the like. "I feel it all inside my hands—Hey, I think I can actually *see through* my hand…!"

"That's enough," Nakamura snapped, loudly enough for everyone to hear. "I told you—we worry about getting home first, and then we deal with the other matters."

"Energy is off the scale," Ling muttered, still staring at the device he was carrying. "We're dead." He groaned. "Already dead, and just our bodies walking back out of Hell."

"That's enough," Nakamura repeated—something he almost never had to do under normal circumstances.

The clouds all around them were lit up now as if a miniature suns had taken up residence behind each of them.

"It can't be much farther," groaned Keefe. "Can it?"

"There!" called Torval, who had quit staring at his hand long enough to look up and see a glowing white circle of light just ahead. The others saw it and, relief washing over them, watched as it grew larger and closer. Now they could see the tether cables vanishing through it.

"We made it," Keefe sighed, grinning at Tamerlane.

The white circle swallowed them up and spit them out back on the deck of the *Monrovia*. They all stumbled forward, unsteady on their feet in the different gravitational field.

"I have returned."

Tamerlane smiled, glad to hear the Emperor speaking. He turned and saw then, to his surprise, that it hadn't been the Emperor who had spoken. It had been the stranger in black who had come back from the other side with them. Tamerlane's smile evaporated and he started to go over to the man and demand to know who he was and where he had come from—when suddenly it dawned on him that the army of technicians in the chamber were behaving in a very unusual and unexpected fashion.

Something bad was happening.

Instead of the happy and joyous shouts one would have expected with the rescue and mostly safe return of the party, the lab-coat-wearing men and women were crying out and racing here and there, madly adjusting the various banks of equipment attached to the portal machine.

"What's happening here?" Nakamura was already shouting, having picked up on it as least as quickly as Tamerlane. "What is the crisis?"

"Energy overload," called one of the techs as she ripped the cover off a console and began to attack the wiring inside. "Massive spike just as you all came through. The ship's main systems are being affected. We're overloading the entire grid."

"Dump it," Nakamura yelled. "Discharge it into space! It could take out the reactor, and—"

"That's what we are attempting to do, General," the chief technician stated sharply. "Of course, it would help if we knew *why* this was happening—what was *causing* it."

"I'm certain it is me," said a voice from behind them.

Nakamura and Tamerlane turned simultaneously and, to their astonishment, saw the Emperor apparently awake and aware at last. He was no longer leaning on anyone for support but was standing upright, with the golden sword he had been carrying held out before him. Lighting flashed from it, forking out to strike seemingly every piece of equipment in the chamber.

Tamerlane grimaced as his awful headache flared back to life. A sword? *The* Sword? The Emperor had it *with* him—had brought it back out? How had he not *known* that? Tamerlane shook his head to rid it of the sudden cobwebs that seemed to be filling it. Wait—he *had* known—he'd *seen*—but then he'd...*forgotten*? How was that *possible*?

No one dared speak—no one dared ask the Emperor a question—for at least two seconds. That was ample time for the overload to become critical.

"The Sword of Baranak," cried one of the technicians at that moment. "It's creating an energy loop in the system! You have to throw it back through, or—"

"Far too late for that," said the man in black who stood at the Emperor's side.

Tamerlane's eyes focused on the man, and he realized he had somehow forgotten *him*, too, for the last few moments.

One of the crystal-armored Emperor's Guard—the one in blue, just to Tamerlane's right—raised a quad-rifle and shot the technician precisely between the eyes from twenty meters away.

Tamerlane recoiled at this. As if in slow motion, he watched as each of the technicians, who an instant earlier had been frantically running this way and that, stopped in their tracks and stared in shock at the Guardsman, the Emperor and the sword.

Nobody moved, nobody breathed.

The lighting flared brighter—blindingly brighter.

"Someone *do* something," Keefe cried.

"The reactor is overloading," shouted a tech at the main control station. "I can't—"

The machinery, the room, and the spacecraft itself all exploded.

BOOK TWO

THE SIEGE OF ADRIANOPLE

1

ire.
Fire and blood.
Light and darkness.
        Cold, so cold—the cold of space.
    And something else.   A presence, entirely unseen; a
sentience speaking within a dream, but not a dream.
    Demons. Fire and demons.
    No. The horror! No!
    Too late—it's too late—they're already here.   They're
going to—
    Awake.
    Ezekial Tamerlane sat straight up, his eyes snapping open.
    His thoughts and dreams fled as reality reasserted itself.
One last fleeting sense tugged at him— the sense that
something very important had been revealed to him, in the
moments just before he'd awoken. But what it had been, he
had no idea.
    Reality was back. He was awake.
    He was sitting in a bed—one of many in a long, high-
ceilinged room. The walls and high, curved ceiling were
white. The other beds extended into the distance on either

157

side of him and opposite him. Some held patients, others did not. An army medical facility, then. Had he been hurt?

"Colonel!" came the voice of a woman from off to his right, sounding surprised.

He tried to look up and see who had spoken, but it was difficult at first. His eyes didn't want to quite focus, and they were scratchy and raw. Blinking and rubbing at them, he was able to see well enough to recognize that she was a doctor—a woman of early middle age, with a dark complexion and her hair tied up in a bun.

"At last," she went on, approaching, a smile playing across her face. "We were beginning to think none of you would ever wake up."

"None of us?" Tamerlane frowned at this. He was still groggy, his mind a whirl of confusion. Looking around, it came to him that he was not alone; the beds on either side of him were occupied—several in either direction— by blanketed figures.

"Something happened," he said, making it as much a question as a statement. Then, "None of whom?"

"I'm sorry?"

"You said you thought 'none of you' would wake up. Who else was hurt?"

She regarded him with a mix of concern and pity. "I'm sorry, Colonel—you don't remember what happened?"

Frowning more deeply, he closed his eyes, then rubbed at them with his fists.

"No," he finally said. "No, I don't."

She gazed down at him, concern etched on her face, but said nothing.

"How long was I—*asleep*?"

The doctor started to reply but then seemed to think better of it. She hesitated, looking back over her shoulder, as if a supervisor were lurking, waiting to censor her.

"How long?" he demanded, anger welling up inside him. "I'm a colonel in the Imperial First Legion and I have a right to know!"

Others in the long hall were looking their way now, and the doctor was clearly aware of it. She bit her lip, then leaned in close and said in a low voice, "You were in a coma for seven weeks, standard time."

Tamerlane heard her but couldn't register the words. "What? What did you say?"

"Seven weeks," she repeated, appearing almost ashamed at the news. "I'm sorry, Colonel."

"Seven..." He couldn't quite fathom it. "I was asleep for *seven weeks*?"

"Not just you," the doctor replied. "Your entire team."

Tamerlane stared back at her, astonished. "Who—who else was with me?"

"They're here, in this room," she said. "You're the first to awaken."

Tamerlane sat up higher in the bed, straining to see around him. Other beds stretched off in both directions, but he couldn't see the faces of the people in them. He rubbed at his eyes again, then, "The Emperor," he said, a faraway look coming over him. "I remember... *something*... about him..." He looked at the doctor. "The Emperor was with us—me and my team—and something happened. Right?"

"You will be relieved to know that the Emperor is fine," the doctor replied, not exactly answering the question. "As are his bodyguards." A more somber expression moved across her face. "His Eminence, the Ecclesiarch, passed away soon after you all were rescued—likely from the strain on his heart. I can only imagine there must have been a tremendous amount of...*excitement*." She brightened. "Many of the others, though, survived—and most of them recovered almost immediately. Of those that weren't killed, all have recovered and been released from care—except for your team." She shook her head in wonder. "Given what happened, it's miraculous."

Tamerlane was attempting to process this information. His head throbbed painfully and much of what the woman was saying wasn't clicking for him. He raised a hand. "Hold on. You said, 'Given what happened.' What happened? Who was killed?" He chewed his bottom lip. "I mean—I remember some sort of explosion...?"

"That's right," she said, her brows knitting and lending her the unmistakable air of someone who is discussing something they don't feel entirely comfortable speaking about. Why that should be, Tamerlane had no idea.

"Generals Beyzit and Attila were there, and both survived," the woman added. "In fact, all the military officers pulled through. Their smartcloth uniforms must have protected them just long enough for the support ships to swoop in and rescue them. As I said, they're all fine." She looked down. "The crew members and support techs weren't so lucky. They were all beyond help by the time their bodies were recovered."

"What exploded?" Tamerlane asked—and then quickly supplied his own answer. "The *Monrovia*. The ship itself."

She nodded.

"We were there," Tamerlane recalled, eyes widening, "and somewhere else, too. Yes—we were coming back from our rescue mission, and—"

"It exploded," the doctor told him, her expression darkening. "That's all we know. You are all lucky to be alive. As I said, it's miraculous."

"But—how did it explode? *Why* did it explode?"

She waved away his follow-ups. "I will defer to the experts on that sort of thing, Colonel. It's not really my area of specialty."

Tamerlane felt his anger and frustration growing, and he sought to meet her eyes. "Doctor," he said, "I apologize for my directness, but—why do I sense a degree of evasiveness and hostility from you? Is there something you're not telling me?"

The doctor wouldn't meet his eyes for a long moment, and Tamerlane's sense of alarm only grew. Finally she returned his gaze and said, "Colonel, all I can tell you is that people are concerned."

"People? What people?"

"People in positions of authority," she said. "After all, the others who survived are fine, and have been for weeks, while your group has lain comatose. Some are questioning exactly why you've all been in those comas."

"What's that supposed to mean?"

She shook her head. "I've said all I can say on that score."

As she said that, he noticed the armed guards stationed at the doors. He started to ask her about them, too, but decided there was little point—she wouldn't answer, or she wouldn't tell him the truth. So, "Alright," he said, mainly to end the conversation and get rid of her.

"My job is simply to get you back on your feet as quickly as possible," she added, flashing an uncomfortable smile.

"Speaking of that," Tamerlane said, happy to change the subject. He was already sitting up, and now he turned to his right and swung his legs over the side of the bed. He tried to stand.

"Be careful, Colonel," the doctor warned, hurrying forward to catch him as he stumbled. "Your legs will still be weak, despite the artificial stimulation we've been administering to the muscles all this time."

Chastened and somewhat embarrassed, Tamerlane allowed the doctor to help him back onto the bed. He felt like he could walk if he needed to, but the stiffness in his legs had caught him by surprise.

"Can I leave?" he asked.

"Soon," the doctor replied, not looking at him.

"What is it?" He eyed the guards at the doors again. "What's wrong?"

"Nothing, exactly," she said. "No specific problems..."

"Then what?" he demanded, catching her eyes. "What aren't you telling me?"

"We simply need to keep you under observation, now that you've come out of the coma, to be sure everything is okay." She paused, then went on in a much softer voice, "As I said, we aren't exactly sure why all of you were comatose to begin with. Some people are concerned about it. That's all I can say."

Tamerlane nodded. "Very well. I need to contact General Nakamura." He paused, then, "You did say the officers all survived—yes?"

The doctor motioned toward a bed two down from Tamerlane on the right.

"He's there."

Tamerlane's eyes were clearing, finally. He looked, recognized the inert form of his commanding officer, and nodded. Slowly he struggled to pull himself back off the bed and this time he managed to stand. The doctor moved to stop him but he brushed her back.

"I've got to try to talk to him."

A pause from her, then, "Alright."

He shuffled on increasingly steady legs over to the head of Nakamura's bed and gazed down at the older man. Then he looked back at the doctor. "Alone," he said.

The doctor frowned at this but nodded and strode away.

"General," he whispered, leaning in close over the man's face, noting that despite his coma Nakamura still appeared burdened with every care imaginable. His blunt features were creased with worry. Perhaps, Tamerlane mused silently, his dreams are troubling him.

"General," he repeated, speaking quietly, "I need your help. I suspect something has happened. Something very serious. And the doctor is being evasive."

Nakamura continued to lie there, his face occasionally contorting slightly, eyes moving beneath the lids.

"I'm starting to remember what happened. I don't exactly know why, but I think the Emperor may be in danger." He paused, then, "To be honest, I'm not entirely sure how he's still alive. Or how any of us are."

Still Nakamura lay there. Tamerlane stared down at him, nearly overwhelmed by feelings of concern for his general—this man who had basically raised him, made a man of him, from a punk kid orphan—and frustration for the developing situation.

"Alright, General," he said at last. "Get some more rest. But come back to us soon." He patted the general's hand. " I need your hel—"

A flame sprang to life, covering his hand, then spreading rapidly to the general's.

Tamerlane cried out and snatched his hand away. The flames vanished as instantly as they had appeared.

General Nakamura gasped, and his eyes snapped open.

2

I didn't imagine it," Tamerlane said for the half-dozenth time.

Nakamura was sitting on the edge of his bed as the last of the doctors to look him over finished his work and retreated, as puzzled as the others had been. He smiled at Tamerlane and chuckled. "Whatever happened, Ezekial," he said, "it woke me up. Got me out of that coma. So let's just be grateful and leave it at that for now."

Tamerlane reluctantly nodded.

It had been an hour since Nakamura had suddenly awakened. A battalion of orderlies, nurses, and several doctors had thoroughly examined both men before Nakamura was allowed to rise. Now he climbed down from the bed and tested his muscles as Tamerlane stood ready to help him. As it turned out, the general could stand just fine. Moments later, the two of them were stretching their legs walking the length of the medical hall. Along the way, Nakamura noticed the armed guards standing at all the exits—just as Tamerlane had very quietly pointed out to him a short time earlier. Nakamura pursed his lips at this, clearly concerned about it, but did not address it, and Tamerlane decided to leave it alone for the time being.

Nakamura halted as they passed before the bed of one of the soldiers from the rescue mission, Lt. Keefe. He gazed down at her comatose form, then looked back expectantly at Tamerlane.

The colonel got the message instantly. *Might as well give it a try—see what happens.* As Nakamura looked on, he moved forward, reaching out and clasping the lieutenant's hand.

Nothing happened. No flame, no nothing.

He looked back at the general and shook his head.

Nakamura appeared mildly disappointed. He gestured toward Ling's bed nearby. "Care to try it again?"

"Why not?"

Tamerlane rounded Keefe's bed and moved toward where Ling lay. Just before he got there, Nakamura called out, "Ezekial. Wait."

The colonel turned and looked back. Nakamura was helping Keefe to sit up. She rubbed her eyes. "General? Sir? What happened?"

"How do you feel, lieutenant?" Nakamura asked her.

"Like I'm hung over from the worst drinking binge in my life, sir," she replied groggily. "But I'll pull myself together. Where are we?"

Nakamura held up a hand, motioning for her to wait a moment, then nodded to Tamerlane. "Want to go for three, Colonel?" he asked, pointing toward Ling.

"This is crazy," Tamerlane replied—but, as Nakamura and Keefe looked on, he reached down and touched Ling's hand.

3

"Crazy," Tamerlane repeated. "Have I become a faith healer?"

"It didn't seem to require any faith at all, Ezekial," the general responded. "You simply *did* it."

"I didn't *do anything*, except touch them. And you."

The two of them were moving slowly along the central walkway between the rows of beds. Occasionally they would stop so that Tamerlane could touch another patient, but nothing came of it—it had only worked with the members of their expedition. But with them it had worked every single time.

"It has to be a coincidence. I just woke up, myself. So maybe whatever was causing us to be in comas was—I don't know, wearing off. Maybe it was *due* to wake us all up right now."

"Maybe so," Nakamura replied. He looked back at Ling, Keefe, and Torval, all of whom were now up and moving. A little further past them, Stanishur and the other two Inquisitors were likewise now awake. Tamerlane had touched each of them, and each of them had come to full consciousness mere moments afterward. Of the flame effect that had manifested when he'd touched Nakamura, however, there had been no further signs.

"There's something else I don't get," he told the general. "You and I and the rest of us were out of it for nearly two months, but the Emperor and the others who went through the Eye of Hell with him are all fine and apparently were never even knocked out."

"They say the ship exploded," Nakamura said aloud, as if simply trying to comprehend the basic concept. "The *Monrovia* exploded around us—though I have no recollection of that at all." He turned then and gazed levelly at Tamerlane. "Why aren't we all dead, Ezekial? How could we possibly have survived something like that?"

"The *official* report is oddly free of specifics and details," Tamerlane stated.

Nakamura nodded. "I discovered that, too. I must admit, it makes me wonder."

"It makes me nervous, is what it does to me," Tamerlane replied. "It makes me nervous to think what's being hidden—and by whom."

The general said nothing in response to that.

"But I got a tiny bit out of our doctor," Tamerlane went on, "and I was able to use the Aether to access some unofficial notes left by eyewitnesses from some of the support vessels, not included in the report."

"I'm assuming that by 'access' you mean 'hack,'" Nakamura interjected in a soft voice.

Tamerlane shrugged. "We were floating—drifting free— in space," he said. "Our support ships—the ones that survived the explosion—picked us up."

Nakamura frowned, deep creases visible across his face— though not the deep crevasses, it seemed, that had been there before. To Tamerlane it almost appeared as if the time in the coma had done the general some good—forced him to get some rest, most likely.

"We were floating free?" Nakamura asked, sounding almost bewildered. "In the vacuum? That makes no sense. We weren't wearing suits or helmets."

"The disks might have protected us," Tamerlane suggested. "They generated some kind of field."

"Protected us from the explosion *and* the vacuum?" Nakamura shook his head. "I find that rather hard to believe. Those disks were only supposed to provide a bit of radiation shielding. How could they save us from—" He waved one hand airily. "—from all *that*?"

Tamerlane shook his head. "However it happened," he said, "I'm not complaining."

Nakamura let that statement stand for a few seconds, not contradicting it. Then, "Has there been any word on why the ship exploded? Did you dig up anything official *or* unofficial about that?"

"Nothing." Tamerlane paused, then, "I did find transit records that revealed that General Attila departed the *Monrovia* a short time before we returned. He took his subordinates, Iapetus and Barbarossa, with him, as well as Belisarius and some junior officers."

"Did he now?" Nakamura met Tamerlane's eyes, clearly very interested now. "For what reason?"

Tamerlane shook his head. "I don't know. There was no communication that I could find, calling them off the ship. But at least we know why *they're* still alive."

Nakamura frowned and was mulling this over when a lieutenant approached; he was tall and slender and his insignia indicated he served the Emperor's Guard.

"General," he said, saluting. "Colonel."

"Yes?" Nakamura responded impatiently.

The lieutenant presented him with a red crystal.

"I was ordered to deliver this to you personally, by hand, as soon as you were recovered."

Nakamura took the crystal, held it up, and squinted at it.

"By whom?"

"By the Emperor himself, sir," the lieutenant replied. "It's your new orders."

Nakamura glanced at Tamerlane, a slight smile playing about his lips.

"That didn't take long, did it?"

"Desk duty," Tamerlane said, frowning. "You know it will be."

"That might not be an entirely bad thing, Ezekial," the general replied. "The men have been hurt—laid up unconscious for nearly two months. Some recuperation could do them all good."

Tamerlane shrugged and then watched as Nakamura accessed the data within the crystal via the Aether connection. "So?" he asked as the general finally lowered it. "Where will we be taking our R&R?"

Nakamura's eyes were widening in mild surprise. Then a smile slowly began to emerge.

"We were wrong," the general stated, staring down at the crystal in his left hand as if it were a strange, alien insect that had just landed there. "No R&R for us."

"What do you mean?"

"We are to join the rest of First Legion at Adrianople immediately. It seems they're being attacked, and all available forces are being routed there."

"Attacked?" Tamerlane stared back at his commanding officer. "Attacked by whom?"

Nakamura laughed a sharp, humorless laugh.

"By everybody."

4

Space battles were the part of being a soldier Tamerlane had always hated the most.

In a real, honest firefight on solid ground, he could control his own destiny. He could choose whether to attack or retreat or hold steady; he could change tactics on the fly; he could select his targets and the manner in which they were engaged.

In space, trapped in the passenger area of a vessel, he possessed none of those advantages. Here, aboard the *Lagos*, he was merely cargo, with no power to affect the outcome of the engagement other than that of prayer—beseeching Those Who Remain to see him safely past the foe and onward to his destination.

Lacking much faith in Those Who Remain, Tamerlane was left with a feeling of utter helplessness.

He'd never really put much stock in the gods, he reflected as he leaned against the nearest observation port and stared out at the grandeur of the galaxy revealed. In the orphanage that was the home of his earliest memories, there had been the occasional efforts by various officials there to try to shape his religious upbringing, roughly in line with official Imperial views—in other words, with whatever the

Ecclesiarchy was saying that week. But each of the orphanage's workers had held slightly different views, and held a different god or gods as most significant and worthy of veneration. The staff underwent such regular turnover that the result was Tamerlane getting a religious indoctrination that was the fabled mile wide and inch deep. Some had praised the name and virtues of Malachek, known for his wisdom; some the martial grandeur of Baranak; some the pragmatic resourcefulness of Lucian. There had even been a couple of women among the staff who adhered to the principles of the warrior-goddess Karilyne, and one odd fish who'd praised the water-goddess Vodina. Tamerlane found all of it fascinating but little of it believable and none of it compelling enough to be granted his blind faith and devotion. When the military had taken him from the orphanage in his early teens and essentially handed him over to Nakamura to raise, he had dismissed all of it entirely and had grown up in the service as a practical man beyond all else. The Empire got his devotion; whatever gods they worshipped in the meantime was of no consequence to him.

Legend held that the gods—or whatever they really were—had once involved themselves in the affairs of men; that entire wars had been fought across the mortal realms as two factions squared off and unspeakable beings—presumably like the ones they had encountered during their expedition through the portal—had been unleashed from the Below to run rampant across a hundred worlds. Evidence yet remained that something like that had happened once but, again, it didn't impact Tamerlane's day-to-day work as a colonel in the First Legion, so he didn't overly concern himself with it. All he knew was that the Ecclesiarchy, the Holy Church of the Empire and defender of its faith, held massive power and influence over the Emperor and the rest of the government simply by nurturing and promoting the beliefs of the people. Its enforcement arm, the Inquisition, kept the public largely in a state of fear, should any be known to deviate from the official line. And that occasionally bothered Tamerlane, at least a bit. He generally got along with officials from both institutions, but he found that he never much cared for anyone that worked for either.

He was brought back from his musings by a series of bright flashes erupting from the blackness beyond the viewport. The voices of the First Legion soldiers around him grew louder in reaction; they were indeed encountering a space battle. Or else provoking one.

"The planet's under siege," Nakamura called from a short distance away. "To get down there, we're going to have to fight our way past the enemy's blockade."

"Joy," muttered Tamerlane.

When the soldiers in front of the general realized who he was, they quickly backed off, allowing him a passage to the viewport. He moved next to the colonel and they gazed out at the scene revealed: a swirl of warships streaking this way and that, particle beams slicing here and there, projectiles glinting as they silently shot toward their targets. Beyond it all, the limb of Adrianople glowed a faint blue-green.

"No," Tamerlane said after reflecting on the situation for a few moments. "It's not 'we' who will have to fight past the blockade. It's the ship and the crew. We're just along for the ride."

"You have a point," Nakamura replied sourly, "but it's one I'd have preferred not to think about."

Tamerlane snorted a laugh. "It's about all I can think about right now."

The ship rocked as it changed direction, artificial gravity struggling to keep up with the helmsman's evasive maneuvers. A couple of times the lights went out, causing the crowd in the passenger area to exclaim loudly and one or two to actually scream. There came a violent shudder, and then another; Tamerlane could only assume they'd been struck by an enemy weapon, though thankfully not badly enough to end their journey here and now.

At one point he was able to get a good view of one of the enemy fighter ships as it cruised by, entirely too close for his comfort. It was dark blue streaked with red and white, with a snub nose and four very short wings for operations within a planetary atmosphere. Each of those wings bore a gold star in a white circle. Seeing this, Tamerlane turned to the general in surprise. "That was a Chung ship," he exclaimed. "Here? At Adrianople?"

"You thought I was joking when I said we'd been attacked by *everybody*?"

Tamerlane shook his head in wonder and turned back to the port. "It's just—this is pretty far away for them to travel, just to raid one of our fringe planets."

"It's not a *raid*, Ezekial," the general reminded him with great patience. "Weren't you listening during the briefing?"

"Yeah—I think I just didn't want to believe it."

"This is a full-blown *siege*. The Chung have launched a major incursion into this entire sector, and it looks like they mean to keep any planets they succeed in taking."

The Chung were not known for laying siege to entire worlds, and this revelation took Tamerlane aback. They were much more renowned for their hit-and-run tactics, raiding supply ships, capturing civilian vessels and the like. Their "empire," if the term could even be used when referring to their somewhat meager holdings, amounted mainly to a core of inner worlds that supported most of their population and a few outer worlds where they took their captive ships, to strip them down for cargo and parts, and to ransom off the crew and passengers. For them to be engaged in a full-blown military operation... Something about it all didn't track.

"Why would they do this?" Tamerlane wondered aloud. "They've kept the peace with us for centuries, a few minor border incidents aside. Why a major attack now?"

"From what I've gathered—and it's been remarkably difficult to gather any information about this situation, for whatever reason—I believe *we* attacked *them* first."

"What?" Tamerlane gawked at him.

The general nodded. He leaned in closer, his voice dropping to a whisper. "I didn't say this during the briefing, because First Legion needs to believe it's doing the right thing—coming to the rescue of innocents being menaced by the evil foreign powers. But the truth of the matter is, during the time we were unconscious, the Emperor ordered attacks against *all three of our neighbors at the same time*."

Tamerlane could think of nothing to say to this. For a few seconds, he found he couldn't speak at all. The Emperor had *started* this fight? Had started fights with *everyone* at once? *Why?*

The ship rocked again as explosive projectiles detonated nearby. The lights flickered. Tamerlane found himself much more bothered by those things now—now that the cause he fought for no longer seemed quite so pure, so just. He very easily might get killed here aboard this ship—and for what? In service to what ideal?

As if reading his mind, Nakamura leaned in again. "Stay strong, Ezekial. This is still our Empire, these are still our people under siege on Adrianople, and we're still going to come to their relief. Regardless of why the war is happening. Understood?"

Tamerlane breathed deeply in and out and then nodded to the general. "Understood, sir. Of course." But the fact was that he did feel queasy—and not just about the mission. Something was bothering his stomach and his head. He was dizzy. The ship's compartment was spinning around him. He reached into a pocket of his uniform and fished out a pill, and when he brought his hand up to his mouth to take it, he cried out in shock and fear.

His hand was on fire.

Nakamura looked up from the datapad he was reading a report on and frowned. "Is something troubling you, Ezekial?"

Tamerlane held the hand out to the general. "Don't you see?"

But of course there was no fire now. Nothing. The skin wasn't charred or even marked at all. It was fine.

Tamerlane's mouth opened and closed. Slowly he shook his head.

"Are you feeling well?"

"I—yes, sir," he replied to the general. He brought the hand down, more puzzled than ever. "Yes. It was—I must have imagined it."

Nakamura nodded and was about to say something when the intercom crackled, followed by word from the bridge of the *Lagos* that the fighter escorts had punched a hole through the naval blockade. A window of opportunity to send troops down to the surface had opened, and Nakamura intended to take advantage of it.

"Brace yourselves," the general ordered the troops that filled the compartment.

The bay doors opened on the bottoms of the Anatolian ships and rows of troop transports blasted out. At the head of the formation flew First Legion's command shuttle, angling quickly down and plunging into the atmosphere. In the passenger section, Tamerlane simply closed his eyes and waited.

The ride down was increasingly bumpy but ultimately successful. The *Lagos* descended through the Adrianople sky as a dark gray lump, blunt and ugly, steam jetting from its exhaust ports in a roar of sound that was momentarily deafening to those below. It settled to the ground in a broad field of low, yellowed grass that was already mostly covered by troop transports and freight-carriers, and Tamerlane had the hatch unlocked and swinging open before the engines had even cycled down.

"Glad you could join us," boomed a voice in greeting as Nakamura and his honor guard climbed out. Tamerlane followed them and looked up at the sound; the sunshine was almost blinding to him at first, but he quickly made out the massive form of Colonel Agrippa standing just ahead, hands on hips, waiting to greet them. Tamerlane shot a salute back at him and couldn't help but add a smile to it; the man was remarkably likeable.

They had set down just to one side of the bulk of Legion III's transports, he realized then. Soldiers with green piping on their shoulders moved about here and there, loading boxes of ammunition and other supplies onto transport sleds and gathering in small clumps for quick combat briefings.

"Your troops are massed mostly to the east of here," Agrippa stated, pointing that way. "They have missed you," he added. "They're not the same without your leadership, General. And, much as I hate to admit it, we could actually use the help."

Nakamura nodded acknowledgement to Agrippa while Tamerlane half-smiled.

"What's the strategic situation?" Nakamura asked.

Agrippa led them around to a display board that stood on a tripod next to the landing foot of one of his ships. He motioned toward it while accessing it via the Aether, and it came to life with color-coded representations of troop formations and positions.

"The Chung are a resilient and persistent foe," the blond man began. "They had landed here before we arrived, and had dug themselves in pretty solidly. Over the past forty-eight standard hours, my Golden Phalanx company has led a series of probing actions—" He traced a line with his finger along the map, leaving behind a white streak. "—here, and here, and here. I must reluctantly admit that all were repulsed with little to show for it." Next he pointed to a section of the display, and it lit up bright red. "We are therefore shifting our emphasis to a single, larger action, and are preparing to assault this position. We of the Third Legion believe it to be the key; if we can smash the Chung here, they will lose their hold on the entire continent, and should have no choice but to fall back to their own landing grounds—and, if they do not evacuate immediately at that point, we can move in and annihilate them."

Nakamura nodded. "Well, if Beyzit is convinced of it, that's good enough for me. The Thunderbolt is rarely wrong about such things."

Agrippa regarded him, tight-lipped. "That is a fact, sir."

5

The assault began precisely according to plan. Very quickly, though, everything went off the rails.

Tamerlane was dispatched to round up the elements of First Legion that were already planet-side, while Nakamura met with General Beyzit in Third Legion headquarters for a quick strategy session. Once plans were agreed upon and in place, Nakamura returned to his army and ordered them into positions.

"Beyzit was not happy to see me, I can tell you, Ezekial," the general reported in confidence as they waited in their temporary headquarters tent for the time for the attack to arrive. "I got the impression he quite liked being the ranking officer on Adrianople."

"I'm sure," Tamerlane replied. "Of course, I've never heard of him being in a *good* mood—about anything." Then, "It does seem rather odd, though, General."

"What's that?"

"Having both of you here, on-planet, at once."

"The Thunderbolt expressed a similar view," Nakamura replied. "That's why he is currently on his way up to his base ship in orbit."

Tamerlane reacted to this little announcement with surprise. "Cutting and running?"

Nakamura gave him a sidelong glance. "You should say that a little louder, Ezekial. I'm sure there are some few loyal Third Legion troops around us right now that *didn't* hear you."

Chagrined, Tamerlane pursed his lips and looked away.

"But it doesn't seem that strange to me for us both to be here," Nakamura went on. "It is, after all, the main theater of the current war."

Tamerlane noted that the general, while trying to convince him, didn't seem terribly convinced himself.

"What?" Nakamura asked, seeing that Tamerlane was visibly conflicted.

"It's like Kampong all over again," the colonel groused. "We keep being sent to locations where we're most likely to get killed."

"Or locations where the best soldiers in the empire are needed," the general said. Again, he didn't sound entirely convinced.

Minutes later, the signal arrived: all forces were ready.

Nakamura stepped out of the tent, Tamerlane just behind him. The darkness was almost overwhelming; it was nearly midnight, local time. He inhaled the chilled air, then nodded to a signal officer. "Give the word."

The word was given. The assault to break the siege of Adrianople had begun.

7

The lynchpin of the hastily-constructed Chung fortifications on Adrianople was a bowl-shaped valley only a few kilometers west of the major city on the major continent. Since the bulk of First and Third Armies was deployed within a hundred kilometers of there, and since even their ground transportation—hovertanks, levitating troop carriers, and the like—could travel very quickly when necessary, only a few minutes passed between the order to attack and the arrival at the valley of the vanguard.

The first strike came from above, from the *Lagos*, still high in Adrianople orbit. The debris of the enemy ships it and its cohorts had defeated upon their arrival had been cleared away, and now *Lagos* targeted the center of the enemy's valley stronghold. Cloud cover was dense, and accuracy could not be guaranteed. If successful, however, this first gambit in the battle could swing both momentum and the odds in the Empire's favor from the very start.

It all happened in less than a second: the huge warship fired a high-powered energy beam from its snout that streaked down like a lightning bolt and struck the center of the Chung defensive fortifications. Before the air could cool along that line—indeed, before the vacuum it created could be re-filled by the surrounding air—the ship launched a tiny missile that streaked down through the cylinder emptiness it had left behind. Moving in a vacuum, the missile thus achieved incredible speed and carried with it devastating kinetic power. It struck, and when it did, it vaporized everything within a quarter-mile radius of impact, leaving behind a crater never more than a hundred meters deep at its center point.

The blast wave washed over First and Third Armies, and Nakamura immediately signaled the attack. The hovertanks were unleashed first, their heavy metal shapes zooming over the smoking landscape, picking out important targets and blasting them with their massive particle-beam cannons mounted atop low swivel turrets. Then the troop carriers rushed forward, swinging into positions of cover and erupting with soldiers who instantly fanned out, blast-pistols and heavy quad rifles at the ready.

The entire action played out in less than an hour. Nakamura announced he was going in to personally inspect the results and nobody objected. The Chung lines had collapsed; their positions had all crumbled and the fight was going out of them in record time. The first strike on the center of their formation had decapitated their command structure even more effectively than anyone on the other side of the fight could have hoped. Now, leaderless, any chance for an orderly retreat had devolved into a rout as far less able and less experienced junior officers issued conflicting and contradictory orders. Legion I overran the western lines and kept going, while Third Legion blasted away at the Chung in the east. Nakamura watched it all play out on the displays in his camp and prophesied that the two forces would link up just north of the valley, beyond the new crater. That, he declared, was where he would meet them.

The heavily-armored command hovercar zipped over the blasted battlefield, a phalanx of escort vehicles that included three hovertanks in close formation around it. Nakamura stood on the front deck, an odd and antique-looking device held to his eyes. The local Aether had been horrendously disrupted if not intentionally jammed during the main part of the attack, and he didn't trust it yet to offer him a true enough image via his ocular implants. So he did it the old-fashioned way—with a pair of binoculars.

The vanguard of each army had signaled moments earlier that the Chung had surrendered—or been eradicated—across the entire line. There should be little danger now. Even so, Tamerlane stood just behind his general, seeking any potential dangers, his eyes as keen as a hawk's. Behind them, Agrippa towered like some lost oak, in constant contact with his Golden Phalanx company and occasionally dispatching messages to his immediate superior, General of Third Legion Abdul-Rashid Beyzit, aboard his flagship in orbit. The Thunderbolt, for his part, had made his preferences clear: He was not coming down to the surface of the planet under any circumstances short of a direct order from the Emperor or Nakamura. No one had the courage to ask him why that should be.

After circling about the massive crater and reaching the north side of the valley, Nakamura signaled a halt. His big vehicle slowed and stopped, the support units continuing to curve around.

Nakamura climbed down, his black boots crunching on the ashy, barren ground. Nervous as always when his commanding officer insisted on visiting a still-"hot" battlefield, Tamerlane hurried after him.

"The Golden Phalanx, serving as vanguard of the Third Legion, will arrive in approximately thirty minutes, General," Agrippa called down from the observation platform. "First Legion is about five minutes beyond that."

"Thank you, Colonel. I look forward to seeing your 'Kings of Oblivion' once again."

Agrippa grinned at the general's use of the entirely unofficial but cherished old nickname for the Phalanx.

Nakamura strode across the wasteland, the soil crunching as he stepped. Clouds of dark smoke and dust rose up as he moved, dirtying his camouflage uniform—it was mostly a tan and green pattern, but with a tiny bit of red along the cuffs and collar to indicate Legion I.

Tamerlane caught up with him and started to speak when the first of the explosions struck, heralding the ambush.

The hovertank off to the west exploded in a blinding flash of explosives and fuel. An instant later, the one to the east did likewise. The third and final one, to the south and moving along the rim of the crater, survived for one more second before it joined its brethren.

With the third one, Tamerlane managed to actually see the beam that struck it. He pointed and cried out, "High-powered energy cannon—there!"

"Back aboard, General!" shouted Agrippa, even as the big man issued orders to his subordinates to fire up the engines and prepare to move out with all possible haste.

Nakamura recovered from the shock quickly and hurried back toward the vehicle. Tamerlane tried to help him, only to be rebuffed: "I'm fine, Ezekial. See to yourself!"

Tamerlane noticed then that the air cover was gone. The first thing the Anatolians had done after the lightning strike from orbit was to blanket the area with atmospheric fighter planes, in order to maintain air superiority over the battlefield—but not a single aircraft could be seen now. *What exactly is going on?*

He turned to point this out to the general—and all hell broke loose around them.

Explosions, a hail of bullets and a barrage of blinding energy beams rocked the air.

Tamerlane leapt forward into Nakamura's back, driving the general down into the dirt just before the deadly hail could strike them both.

They rolled over and Nakamura was staring, wide-eyed, at nothing. "A trap," he managed at last, focusing on Tamerlane's face, coughing from the cloud of ash they'd stirred up. "It was a trap!"

More gunfire, this from much closer. Tamerlane rolled to his feet and, crouching, gazed across the gray landscape. Soldiers were advancing—and they were moving very, very quickly. Too quickly, he realized. *Inhumanly* quickly.

Tall and lanky, they loped across the barren field like antelope. They wore body armor seemingly composed of glass, colors flashing and swimming across the surface. They carried what looked like long, skinny rifles in one hand and blades of similar shape in the other. Their voices were high-pitched, their language incomprehensible.

"Dyonari!" Tamerlane called out.

From above them on the vehicle's deck, Agrippa cursed. "There have been rumors in this sector that the Chung had actually made alliance—or at least entered into some sort of non-aggression pact—with alien powers."

"Astonishing," Tamerlane replied. "Our fights are *our* fights—*human* fights. How could they get involved with *xeno-forms*?"

"I don't much care," Agrippa replied with a shrug. "Enemies are enemies. Once you've killed them, they're pretty much dead. It never seems to matter then what they *used* to be."

Nakamura spat ash, then growled. "I should've known there was more going on here than met the eye," he muttered. "They want to capture us alive. They want hostages."

"We'll see about that," Tamerlane responded. His blast pistol was in his hand as he helped Nakamura into cover behind the big slabs of broken concrete. "Get ready!"

And then the aliens were upon them.

The first Dyonari warrior to reach them, nimble as a gazelle, leapt over the concrete blocks and over their heads as well and confronted them from behind. It brandished its deadly-looking sword—a gleaming, transparent curved blade that looked as much like glass as did the armor it wore—and screeched something at them in its own language. Tamerlane brought up his blast pistol to fire, when suddenly with a bellow Agrippa leapt from the top of the transport and crashed down on the alien with savage fury. He punched it in the face once, twice, then drew his pistol and, as it staggered back, disoriented, he fired point-blank into that same rage-contorted face. The alien dropped, lifeless.

"You have to shoot them where they're vulnerable," the big man explained. "Most energy-blast shots to their armor will just deflect away."

"I was fighting the Dyonari before you were born, son," Nakamura replied. "If you—"

Whatever else the general was going to say was lost as a second and third Dyonari arrived, blades swinging.

The transport hatch had opened in the interim and the dozen First Legion soldiers inside boiled out. They rushed around to take up defensive positions in front of their officers, and the now half-dozen-strong crowd of alien attackers crashed into them. The humans never had a chance; the Dyonari were taller, stronger, and far more agile, and they danced in and out of the formation, not even bothering to fire their guns but relying entirely on their blades. Within half a minute, the soldiers had been carved to pieces.

Tamerlane looked on, aghast, firing his own pistol whenever a target presented itself but rarely managing to connect with the incredibly fast-moving enemy—and, of course, when he did, the blast usually deflected away. He realized full-well that, had the Dyonari not been there to take them captive but instead merely to kill them, they all would have been dead by now. Even Agrippa wouldn't have lasted terribly long, though he was certainly giving a good accounting of himself; the big blond soldier was about as powerful and nearly as fast as the aliens, and on two occasions he managed to grasp a Dyonari by the arm and sling it down to the ground, where a shot or a series of punches put it out of commission.

A wave of coldness passed over them then, and Tamerlane heard a voice that at first seemed to be coming from all around, but which he quickly realized was inside his head: *Humans. Officers,* it said. *Surrender now. We have no wish to slaughter you as we have your soldiers.*

"Get out of my head, aliens," Agrippa cried, rushing to attack the nearest Dyonari and smashing it in the glass-armored gut with his fist.

You are surrounded. You cannot defeat us all. Cease your resistance.

Tamerlane looked to Nakamura; the general scowled.

"I would say we're in an untenable position," the colonel stated angrily.

"They've blanketed the Aether," Nakamura told him. Of course, Tamerlane had already figured that out for himself, since he'd been trying to call for reinforcements from the moment the aliens had appeared, only seconds earlier, and to no avail.

Agrippa was about to be overwhelmed as three Dyonari advanced on him; quickly he beat a strategic retreat to where the other two officers had taken defensive positions behind the concrete slabs.

"The thought of surrender—and particularly surrender to aliens—galls me," the big man barked, "but we can't just allow the general to fall into their hands this way—" He trailed off, unsure of what to say or do next.

The Dyonari had regrouped a short distance away, behind a bit of cover, and were holding off on pressing the attack.

Possibly they sensed via their telepathic powers that the humans were discussing the concept of surrender, and were allowing them time reach that decision.

"Surrender, hell," Nakamura spat. "I'll go down fighting, sooner than that." He drew his blast pistol and held it up, checking its power charge.

"General, I don't think—" Tamerlane began.

Nakamura ignored him. Before either of the other two soldiers could stop him, the general charged out into the open, aiming his pistol at the nearest alien warrior, firing shot after shot. Caught completely by surprise, the Dyonari warrior failed to move for a mere heartbeat—and a blast of super-heated plasma from the gun took it between the eyes.

Nakamura was already running past it, seeking the next target, as it fell to the ground.

Tamerlane gawked. He'd known the general most of his life, and knew how fiercely determined the man could be— and how reluctant to concede anything on the battlefield. But *this*—this was *suicide*. Cursing, he rushed out into the open, hot on Nakamura's heels.

The Dyonari realized what was happening now. Three of their warriors emerged from their own patch of cover and raised their swords. The others behind them leveled their long, glass guns at Nakamura.

Tamerlane cried out—there was absolutely nothing he could do. He reached out for the general, seeking to grasp him, to pull him down, out of the way. His fingers stretched out—out, in the direction of the general—in the direction of the enemy—

Heat. He distinctly felt a wave of heat passing through his body. Had he been shot? What was happening?

His fingers tingled. There was a burst of light directly in front of him. Ignoring it, his eyes focused beyond Nakamura on the enemy figures that were about to fire. He willed destruction on them.

There was a larger flash, this time across the gulf of open ground that separated Nakamura and him from the enemy. The flash was followed by screams—psychic screams, reverberating through his head.

An instant later, the three Dyonari warriors directly ahead burst into flames.

The telepathic backlash from the aliens' surprise, followed by their pain—their *agony*—drove the three humans to their knees.

"What happened?" Nakamura managed to gasp, his eyes squeezed tightly shut as the fading echoes of the screams reverberated within their heads. "Did our... reinforcements... arrive?"

Tamerlane stood on wobbly legs as the psychic wave receded. His brain felt as if it were vibrating within his skull from the force of it. He looked around, seeing the hulking shape of Agrippa moving up next to them, shaking his head violently from side to side like a huge dog that has heard an uncomfortably high-pitched sound. Across the field, he saw the remains of the three Dyonari he and the general had attacked, now in the form of sizzling mush inside their half-melted glassite armor. Beyond them, the other dozen or so aliens were backing away slowly, warily, seemingly as uncertain of what had just happened as the humans were.

"Ezekial," came Nakamura's voice as he struggled to his feet. "Look."

The colonel looked where the older man was pointing—at Tamerlane's own right hand.

Flames flickered and danced along its surface.

Tamerlane cried out and jerked it back, waving it about. The flames fluttered but didn't die.

He staggered back, clutching his hand to his middle and wrapping his other arm over it, desperate to snuff out the flame. He stood there a moment that way, the others looking on in puzzlement, then drew his hand out again. The flames were gone. The hand itself appeared perfectly normal, as if nothing had happened. No burn marks, no blackening, no damage whatsoever.

And what was more, it didn't hurt. Not a bit.

"By the gods," Agrippa gasped as it slowly became apparent what had happened. He pointed to the dead aliens. "You—you did that."

Tamerlane looked from the bodies to Agrippa and back down at his hand. He shook his head slowly. "No. How—how *could* I have—?"

You employ some new weapon against us, came the voice of the aliens, once more resounding within their heads, *but it will not save you. Surrender now.*

The Dyonari halted their retreat, regrouped, and began to advance once more.

"Try it again," Nakamura ordered.

"What?" Tamerlane was taken aback by this. "But—I don't know how I did it the first time, sir," he protested.

"From a functional standpoint, there is little to understand," Agrippa pointed out. "You pointed at them, and they burned."

Tamerlane glanced over at him and saw that the big man's expression revealed his extreme discomfort with all of this—but, for the moment, a weapon was a weapon, and they were desperately in need of one. He shrugged and nodded.

"Get behind me," he said in a quiet but tense voice.

He raised his hand up before him and flames sprang again from it, flickering along the length of his fingers. He stared at it with widening eyes but resisted the panic that threatened to overtake him. It was a most disconcerting feeling to see one's hand actually on fire—and to do nothing about it!

Still uncertain of exactly what he was doing, he raised the arm and directed it, gun-like, at the line of alien troops. The other two men stood a bit behind him and watched very closely.

The air around the charging Dyonari shimmered and then grew blood red. Suddenly flames erupted all around them, from the ground, from the air, and from their own bodies. It engulfed them in an instant, swallowing them up. The screams this time were almost overwhelming.

Tamerlane looked back at the other two men, his mouth hanging open and his eyes like saucers.

Nakamura's mind was racing ahead of the others. "The expedition," he said. "Our journey into the Above and the Below. That *has* to be it. *Has* to be. Something happened to you there." He paused, then, "But… you didn't go alone. That would mean—"

The general leaned past Tamerlane and reached out with his left hand, directing it at the remaining Dyonari. They had started to pull back a second earlier but were now hesitating, seemingly contemplating one last charge. Apparently reaching that decision, they brandished their long, glasslike swords and rushed across the battlefield.

Flames sprang to life on Nakamura's fingertips, then flashed outward.

A sheet of flame filled the air in a circle around the aliens and closed in from all directions. They cried out both verbally and psychically, seeking a way of escape from the constricting doom, finding none. The circle of fire contracted smaller and smaller, tighter and tighter, until it washed over them, somehow taking root in their armor, boiling them inside it. Their psychic screams were muted somehow, this time. Or perhaps that mental sound was simply expected this time, and the humans were more prepared for it.

For the next few minutes, the three human soldiers searched the area for any other Dyonari troops, but found none. The battle was over, and they had won it—or at least survived it—but nothing was the same as it had been before.

Once they had gathered together again near the transport ship, Agrippa stood there in the open, hands on his hips, staring at the other two men—the only two other survivors of this portion of the battle. He regarded Nakamura and Tamerlane with pursed lips and a furrowed brow, seemingly uncertain of exactly what to think. There was appreciation visible in his features, and respect—but a degree of concern, as well, if not outright fear.

"Speak your mind, Colonel," Nakamura ordered after several seconds of silence on everyone's part.

Agrippa nodded. "I withhold all judgment on my part until I hear your story, General," he said. "And," he added, a second later, "it is increasingly apparent to me that you two gentlemen have quite a story to tell."

The tide of the larger battle turned very quickly once Nakamura and Tamerlane discovered their newfound abilities.

Leading the First and Third Legion advance, flames blazing out ahead of them and burning the enemy where they stood, they routed the Chung forces with relative ease. The waves of interlinked and antigrav-supported hovertank units that descended from orbital transport ships like floating islands of steel were scarcely needed; the enemy had been for the most part driven off planet before the first one reached the ground.

Of the Dyonari, there was not a trace; none were seen again on Adrianople after the encounter in the valley. Presumably the "sound" of the psychic screams they had unleashed there had been more than sufficient to scare any others away forthwith.

Practical men above all else, Nakamura and Tamerlane made certain the battle was won and Adrianople liberated before they turned their attention to what seemed to them at the time the less important subjects: How had they come by this strange power—and what did it mean for the future?

"You must be right, General," Tamerlane stated. "It was something we were exposed to in the Above. It has to be."

"Or in the Below," Nakamura pointed out.

"You were in the *Below*?" Agrippa asked, startled. He sat at the far end of the table, hunched forward, studying the two men. Till that moment he had worn a mostly neutral expression.

"We got the grand tour on that trip," Tamerlane replied. "It's...complicated."

"I do not doubt it." Agrippa reached out and lifted the glass that had been set before him, containing the finest of Adrianople's vineyards, but he didn't drink. "I knew, of course, about your rescue mission to save the Emperor," he added, "but I had only heard he was lost in the Above." He stared down at the tabletop for a moment, clearly shaken by the revelation. "You mean the Emperor was trapped *in the Below?* Down with the demons and the darkness and...?"

"That's precisely what I mean," Nakamura snapped.

Agrippa shook his head slowly in wonder and consternation. Distractedly he set the glass back down, untasted. "I had no idea."

Unsurprised, Tamerlane chuckled at this. Nakamura did not.

"I had not thought to check the *official* reports of our actions there," the general noted, sipping from his own glass.

"He means the propaganda version," Tamerlane explained needlessly. "The version where the most interesting details were omitted."

Agrippa's bright blue eyes flashed from the general to the colonel and back. He nodded sharply. "I understand what he means. Please—continue, sir."

Nakamura gave a very abbreviated account of the rescue mission to save the Emperor and the Ecclesiarch. He concluded with, "The gods alone know what sorts of radiation we were exposed to while we were there."

"Radiation," Agrippa agreed, "and who knows what else."

Nakamura hesitated, then nodded. His eyes narrowed; he was watching the big man carefully.

"Science and scientific concepts seem to sort of... *bend*...in the Above," Tamerlane said, feigning obliviousness to the developing subtext. "They beyond any recognition. Same in the Below." He shrugged. "I guess there's no telling what we got into."

"Or what got into you," Agrippa added somberly.

Both of the others now looked at him, regarding him uneasily.

"There's no reason to believe this—this power—poses a danger," Nakamura said, glancing at Tamerlane. The colonel nodded his agreement.

"As yet," Agrippa stated.

They sat in silence for a long, uncomfortable moment, the only sounds coming from outside the tent, as the First and Third Legion units continued breaking down their equipment and loading it on the transport ships.

At last, Nakamura set his glass down and stood. "Colonel, we thank you for your assistance today. And we thank Legion III too, of course. Exemplary performances, as always."

Agrippa nodded once. He did not rise.

"Ezekial, if you would accompany me to the shuttle, I'd like to get—"

"Please, General," Agrippa said with a smile that was suddenly cold, "stay a bit longer."

"I'm afraid we can't. Much work to be done—reports to file on the action today, unit evaluations to look over—"

"I will have more food brought in," Agrippa suggested, slowly rising and moving around the table. His bulk seemed to nearly fill whatever corner of the tent he occupied. "We must celebrate this victory properly."

"Most gracious of you," Nakamura said, moving quickly toward the exit, "but I would prefer to—"

Agrippa looked away for an instant, receiving a private message via the Aether. Then he looked back at the two First Legion officers. "I'm afraid you can't depart just yet—sir. They've arrived."

Nakamura reddened. "Can't depart? Have you taken leave of your senses, Colonel?" He glanced at Tamerlane, who shook his head very slightly, as if to say, *I have no idea.* He turned back to Agrippa. "Who has arrived?"

Before the blond man could respond, the broad flap of the tent opened and a man clad all in white strode in. He was dark-skinned—making for a sharp contrast with his uniform—with a blunt nose and broad cheeks. His immaculate uniform—seemingly part military, part religious in its stylings—sported slender gold braiding along the hemlines and across the chest. He looked more the part of a brawler than an officer—though in what army, Tamerlane at first had no idea.

Nakamura got the idea more quickly. "The Ecclesiarchy." He looked from the man in white to Agrippa, who stood off to one side. "You called them."

"I did. Sir."

"You don't trust us."

"I followed protocol, sir," Agrippa responded. "I trusted you would understand."

Tamerlane got it. "You called the Ecclesiarchy—*on us?*" He started toward the blond colonel, anger flaring in his eyes. "You're accusing us of—"

"Colonel Tamerlane!"

At Nakamura's sharp exclamation, Tamerlane froze in his tracks. Agrippa, meanwhile, had not moved, not reacted in any manner whatsoever. That actually aggravated Tamerlane as much as anything else had.

"Colonel Agrippa witnessed the two of us engaging in the use of rather...*unorthodox*...abilities today," the general stated. "And we have told him we recently visited the underverse—the *Below*—home to demons and other creatures of malevolent origins and intentions. By notifying the Holy Church, he merely did what he believed was right, as a soldier in the Imperial military."

Tamerlane, scowling at the other man, reluctantly nodded and returned to Nakamura's side.

The general turned to the man in white.

"Interesting new uniforms. Very...*militant*," Nakamura noted, before addressing the man directly. "So—you're here on behalf of the Ecclesiarchy, to debrief Colonel Tamerlane and myself, I take it?"

"I am Father Octavion," the man said, "and I have been sent here to arrest you both. *General*," he added almost contemptuously.

Nakamura started at this bit of information.

"You're *what?*" Tamerlane exclaimed, moving toward the man in white. "On whose authority could you—"

"On the authority of the Ecclesiarch," the priest snapped.

"If we are accused of a *violation* of a religious nature by His Majesty's government, it is the role of the *Inquisition* to arrest us and to bring charges. *Not* the Ecclesiarchy."

"The Ecclesiarch possesses all the authority he needs to detain you, General," the priest replied sharply. "Please come with me."

"That's not happening," Tamerlane snapped.

The man in white regarded him with open contempt.

"I'm happy to talk with the Church to explore exactly what has happened," Tamerlane continued. "But I won't be treated like a criminal over it." He leaned in on the priest. "Particularly when whatever-it-is that's happened to us happened *while we were rescuing the Emperor himself!*"

Nakamura stepped between them, raising a hand to restrain Tamerlane. "Octavion," he began, clearly trying to sound warm and kind, "I have known Wallin Zoric—the Ecclesiarch—for many years. If I might speak with him, I'm certain we can resolve any—"

"Wallin Zoric has not been Ecclesiarch for nearly two months," the priest said, cutting him off. "The old fool finally passed away—gods preserve his soul."

Nakamura staggered back a step, shocked. "Zoric—*dead?* Then—who is—?"

"You will meet the new Ecclesiarch in due time, General. Now—again—I must insist that you come with me."

The space outside the tent was suddenly filled with soldiers—soldiers in *white* uniforms. Of the First and Third troops, there was no sight.

Nakamura looked them over and exhaled slowly. He appeared to have conceded the situation. "Come on, Ezekial," he said. "We can't turn down an invitation from the Ecclesiarchy—particularly when it's offered in such a *friendly* and *collegial manner.*"

Tamerlane scoffed at this but reluctantly he followed his general out of the tent. White-clad soldiers moved into position on either side of them. He looked back one last time and his eyes met those of Agrippa, now back in his seat on the far side of the table and brooding. The look he saw was not one of leering or gloating but of grim resolve, perhaps tinged with a bit of regret.

He really thinks he's doing the right thing by turning us in, Tamerlane concluded. *The fool.*

The tent flap swung closed.

BOOK THREE
THE COUNCIL OF ASCANIUS

1

Nakamura and Tamerlane tumbled out of the airlock and into the deadly void of space. Considering they both wore only their regular crimson smartcloth uniforms, this represented a serious problem.

Tamerlane thrashed about, spinning head over heels, desperately seeking and failing to find any handhold on which to grab. As the last of the air fled his lungs, he couldn't help but reflect that he never would have dreamed he'd be murdered by a priest.

It had begun a short while earlier, as the Ecclesiarchy transport craft shot up out of Adrianople's atmosphere and closed in on the Church's massive cruiser where it orbited in its own flight path, a few thousand miles beyond the military fleet. The two ships docked smoothly, the smaller shuttle pulling alongside and locking onto a slender metal connecting tube that extended from the larger vessel.

The High Priest, Father Octavion, stood and moved to the hatch. He waited as the two First Legion officers he had arrested were helped up by Ecclesiarchy subordinates. The chains connecting the manacles at their wrists and ankles jangled noisily.

"Is this truly necessary, Eminence?" General Nakamura asked, his simmering anger scarcely restrained as he held the manacles and chains up where Father Octavion had no choice but to see them.

"I'm afraid that's one of our regulations," the warrior-priest replied.

"A regulation for handling accused heretics and convicted criminals," the general snapped back. "Not high-ranking officers!" He breathed deeply, attempting to calm himself. "I can understand the Ecclesiarchy's...shall we say, *interest*, in what the Colonel and I have been doing on Adrianople. In the course of winning the war there," he added with no small sense of satisfaction. "But we have not yet been accused of anything, have we? Nor faced an Inquisitor or a military tribunal. Much less been convicted of anything. And, as I am the ranking officer of the Emperor's forces in this theater, I do have some say as to how anyone—prisoner or not—is treated here. Do you disagree? Or have you some charge against us to level—*now*, at this very moment?"

The priest's eyes narrowed as he returned Nakamura's gaze. Then, with a smirk, he shrugged and stepped forward, unlocking and removing the manacles and chains from each of them. "Very well. It matters not," he muttered—and neither of the two soldiers bothered to ask him what he meant by that utterance. "Now," he went on, "if the two of you will come this way, I will see you aboard the *Karilyne's Sword*, the flagship of our local presence."

"The *flagship*?" Nakamura repeated, surprised, as he rubbed at his wrists. "You mean you have multiple ships in this sector? The Church has never been permitted to do that—to operate more than one ship in a particular planetary region. Where did you—"

"That's a question better left for the Ecclesiarch himself," Octavion interrupted, "though I believe it is within the bounds of protocol for me to state that, well, things have *changed.*" He flashed a very-white smile at the general. "Now—this way, if you will, gentlemen," he said again, nodding toward the hatch.

Tamerlane could practically feel the rage and frustration building within Nakamura and rising to the surface. But the general managed to keep it in check. He looked back at Tamerlane and angled his head toward the exit. "Fine. I have quite a few questions for him, actually," he said.

"I thought you might," Tamerlane agreed. "I have a couple more."

Nakamura chuckled, though there was little humor in it. "Alright," he said. "Let's go."

They moved through the seating area and to the exit, sliding past the High Priest, who offered them a "you first" gesture with one hand, and out into the connector tube that led to the larger ship. Octavion in his immaculate white uniform entered the tube behind them.

The two soldiers reached the far end of the connector tube, where the hatch leading into the larger ship stood closed and locked. The lights in long panels along the sides of the tube were almost blinding as they reflected off the gleaming metal and white plastic surfaces. Tamerlane turned back, waiting for Octavion to join them and open the hatch.

To his surprise, he saw that the High Priest had actually backed out of the tube, back onto the shuttle.

Nakamura looked back and saw this now, as well. "What are you doing?" he called after the priest.

But Octavion was gone, back inside now, and the hatch on that end closed as well, sealing them in with a resounding clang.

Tamerlane and Nakamura exchanged extremely nervous glances, realizing exactly how vulnerable they were, trapped in the docking tube. The colonel reached for the panel off to the right that opened the hatch, but all the lights on it were red. He moved to the manual wheel at its center, attempting to turn it, but it wouldn't budge. He banged his fists on the hatch, while Nakamura started back down the other way, toward the shuttle.

Another clang echoed through the tube. Nakamura reached the other end, tried and failed to open the hatch there. He turned back, his eyes widening as he looked at Tamerlane.

"They cannot seriously mean to—"

The docking tube separated from the shuttle as the smaller ship pulled smoothly away. The air inside the tube evacuated instantly, carrying the two soldiers with it. They fell into the void.

2

What exactly is this shindig we're being sent off to," Major Niobe Arani wondered aloud, "and could it actually, *possibly* be so important that they need Imperial Special Forces to serve as part of the security?"

She stood at a table in the passenger section of the Imperial transport liner *Endymia,* patiently reassembling her sniper rifle. After two weeks on **Trezibond**, where her unit had been essentially locked down, unable to leave the base and under strict orders not to speak to anyone outside of their little group, she was happy to at least be on the move again. Unfortunately, they were still for the most part locked down—but on a ship, now, instead of a planet—and on their way to some new and far-flung destination. All she really wanted was a break; a vacation; a chance to kick back for a few days and recharge her metaphorical batteries. Clearly that wasn't in the cards anytime soon.

"I've heard it's a religious conclave," the soldier to her right—Captain Durin— said in a quiet voice as he worked on his own weapons. "Maybe even naming the new Ecclesiarch—or introducing him, at least."

Arani considered this. "A new Ecclesiarch? Hmm." The thought was somewhat comforting to her. The Empire had gone nearly two months without a head of the Church, ever since the elderly but still seemingly healthy Wallin Zoric had suddenly and inexplicably dropped dead. "That might explain it," she mused, "but the security still seems excessive just for him. The Church has their own army—what do they need with us?"

The soldier to her right—Major Senjanik—leaned in close, his eyes flickering around as if he were afraid of being overheard. "I've heard a rumor or two, myself," he whispered.

Arani laughed. "We've *all* heard rumors, Den. Durin's here is the first one that's made the slightest bit of sense to me."

Senjanik's expression remained grave. "No," he whispered, speaking even more quietly. "Not about our destination. About the situation with us—the reason for the lockdown."

Now it was Arani's turn to frown. "Oh, really?" she responded—but now she'd lowered her voice, too. "So—what have you heard? And why should we believe it?"

Senjanik snapped the last component of his own rifle into place and held it up, sighting along the barrel. "I have a friend—*no names!*—inside the Church," he said in a now-barely-audible voice. "The word *they're* hearing is that somebody in our unit—in Special Forces—saw something they weren't supposed to see. And we're all on lockdown until it's sorted out, so that it doesn't get out to the press or the public."

Arani started to bark a laugh at that—and then her laughter caught in her throat.

Surely, she thought to herself, *surely it couldn't be what I saw...*

Her thoughts flashed back to that night on **Trezibond** when the soldiers under—what had his name been?—

Sergeant *Garner* had helped her disrupt a Vorthan cult and expose their high priest as none other than Colonel Nikolai Barmakid, former adjutant of First Legion.

It couldn't be that. Why would anyone in the Church—or the Empire in general—care if I knew that—?

She frowned. That *was* one of the things she had not been allowed to discuss with anyone—not even her fellow soldiers in her unit—since it had happened. And it hadn't subsequently turned up in any media coverage she'd seen, though admittedly she never got to see much of that, or cared to. So it *was* being kept secret, but...

The others had been talking while she was lost in thought. She looked back up at them and quickly surmised that they'd been throwing out other rumors that had been making the rounds, none of which had sounded remotely plausible to Arani the first fifteen times she'd heard them.

This, though—the thought that someone was keeping Barmakid's crime a secret... That somehow seemed much more plausible... and much more disturbing to her personally. After all, *she* was one of the few that even knew about it...

"I've heard we're headed for Ascanius," Captain Durin was saying. "That would fit with some kind of big religious ceremony."

Arani nodded absently. There was no doubt Ascanius was the planet one would choose for a religious ceremony, what with the massive Church of the Relique located there. With its kilometer-high dome and massive sanctuaries for numerous members of Those Who Remain, as well as the colossal main hall, it had been home to many of the greatest ceremonies and religious events of the past two millennia, including most recently the coronation of Emperor Janus IV.

"Any other rumors worth chewing on?" Durin asked.

Major Senjanik scowled and turned away, clearly taking all this much more seriously than many of his teammates.

Arani started to respond, then hesitated. Something was nagging at her. She mentally ran down the list of who else likely knew about Barmakid. There was the fire team that had helped her on Trezibond... and the officers above her, headed by General Nakamura.

She couldn't very well call up Nakamura to ask him about it, but...

She excused herself and left the compartment, moving out into the corridor beyond. The hatch slid closed behind her. Cool air blew from various vents along the walls, and the occasional crewmember hurried past. She stood there a second, breathing the fresher air, then oriented herself and walked briskly toward the communications center.

The lockdown they were under included very limited use of the Aether network, and it was being closely monitored. So she resolved to use the ship's main comm array to openly make her call. If the higher-ups didn't like it, at least they couldn't accuse her of trying to sneak around and do something surreptitiously.

As she rounded the first corner, she thought she heard something behind her. She started to turn, then dismissed such concerns, figuring that with as many people around as the big transport was carrying, there were bound to be people in every nook and cranny of every deck. She continued on, pausing at the next intersection to reorient herself and remember which way led to the comm center.

It was the faintest click that sounded behind her, but it was just enough—and just *familiar* enough—to send her diving out of the way the instant before the energy blast sizzled by. She hit the floor of the corridor and rolled, instinctively reaching for her pistol—only to realize as her hand met only her hip that her weapons were back in the passenger cabin.

Continuing her roll until it took her back up into a tight crouch, she stared down the hall in search of her attacker.

No one was there.

Frowning, puzzled, she considered what to do. Part of her demanded that she rush down the hallway and find her attacker. Another, probably much wiser part of her, screamed that she was unarmed and exposed out here, and should seek immediate cover before whoever-it-was came at her again.

Torn by indecision, she remained in that crouch for another two seconds, then sprang to her feet and ran back down the corridor in the direction from which she'd come— and the attack had come. Along the way, she accessed the Aether network. The rules said no normal use of the link, but this hardly qualified as "normal." She needed to report the incident as quickly as possible, and that was the fastest way.

Even as the link came up in her virtual vision, however, she hesitated. If what she was beginning to suspect was even partly true, it had been someone in her own unit that had tried to kill her. If that was true, it was unquestionably at the orders of someone higher up—in her unit, or in First Legion, or...

She stood outside the door to her team's cabin, her eyes flashing this way and that, her mind racing. Was someone trying to silence her—permanently? If so, who? And— what about the others who knew what she knew?

That might go a long way toward shedding some light on the situation, she realized. If any members of the fire team that had helped her on Trezibond had experienced any threats or violence, then the situation would rapidly move from the realm of wild speculation to that of serious possibility.

Her heart still beating rapidly, she riffed through the listings of other units in Legion I in her virtual vision, until she found the one she was looking for. "Ah ha. Sergeant Garner. There you are." She placed the call, sending a request into the *Endymia's* Aether link and from there out to the vastly larger network.

The call took only a few seconds to process, since most of the Aether's signals traveled via hyperwave through the boundaries of the Above, reducing transit time to the functional equivalent of much, much faster than light.

Unfortunately, there was no answer—at least, at first. Then, after a couple of relay clicks, the call was picked up by a woman with a husky voice. "This is Major Shae. Can I help you?"

Arani was taken aback. "I'm sorry," she said, "but I was attempting to reach a Sergeant Garner."

A pause, apparently as Major Shae checked to see who she was on the line with. The pause then went on even longer—just long enough to begin to unnerve Arani. "Ah— Major Arani. I'm afraid the sergeant is unavailable."

Arani frowned at this. "Unavailable?"

"Yes."

Arani shook her head slowly, groping for what to say.

"So—if that's all, I wish you a good day—"

"Wait," Arani replied quickly. "Please."

"Yes?"

"When you say the sergeant is unavailable, what do you mean by that? If I may ask."

Another pause. "Actually, Major," Shae said finally, "I am not at all certain that you *may* ask that."

"What?" Arani was now completely taken aback.

"Our unit is under communications lockdown," Shae explained, "as I believe yours is. You should not be making this call at all."

"It's an emergency," Arani said quickly. "In that case— may I ask why Sergeant Garner has a major serving as his answering service?"

Nothing.

"Can you connect me with any of the other members of his fire team, then, Major Shae? Anyone who was with him on Trezibond?"

Yet another moment of silence. Then, "I have to let you go, Major. Good day."

Before Arani could say another word, the connection severed at the other end, leaving her with nothing but the hollow tunnel sound in her virtual ears. Frustrated, angry, and a tiny bit afraid, she shut it off on her end and looked around.

What to do now? She didn't know.

Is there any doubt something big is going on—and someone very high up doesn't want me talking to anyone? Doesn't want me alive, now, apparently?

She turned to enter her unit's passenger cabin when the Aether came to life once again, this time with an announcement from the bridge: "Ladies and gentlemen, we have arrived at our destination. If you will all strap in, we will be landing momentarily." She opened the cabin door and hurried in, slipping into her crash couch just as Senjanik was buckling his own restraint belts in place.

"Where have you been?" he asked, his voice low.

She shook her head. "I'll tell you later," she replied. Then, "Maybe," she added. "Not sure I really want to tell anybody anything right now."

Senjanik gave her a quizzical look before returning his attention to his buckles.

I have to get off this ship, she told herself silently as the vessel began to shudder with entry into the atmosphere of the planet. *I have to get off as soon as we're down, and find someone—anyone—I can talk to. Someone I can trust.*

"Welcome," the ship's captain was announcing over the local Aether link. "Welcome to the holy world of Ascanius."

Someone I can trust, she repeated to herself, *but—is there anyone in the entire Empire at this moment that fits that description?*

She was terrified that the answer to that question was a resounding *no*.

3

Tamerlane, standing as he was at the opposite end of the tube when it separated from the shuttle, saw what was happening and understood that Nakamura would be flung out into space first. As the air rushed out, he leapt up and pistoned his legs against the hatch of the bigger ship behind him, driving himself forward at great speed just as the vacuum grasped him. He shot down the length of the tube and exited it into open space only an instant behind the general. He reached out, knowing he would get only one opportunity to do this, and grasped for the other man as he went by. His right hand slipped off the smooth smartcloth of the general's sleeve but his left hand managed to snag his collar and he held on for dear life—for both their lives.

The dark red smartcloth that comprised most of the two men's uniforms was already doing what little it could in such an environment; it was hardening into an armored shell to protect their bodies from the cold and the vacuum, while exuding a transparent helmet cover up from their collars that automatically extended over their heads to hold in what little atmosphere remained. It possessed no on-board oxygen supply, however—whatever remaining air they had with them now would be all they would have; Tamerlane understood that this amounted to a few seconds of breathing at best. When that was gone, they were finished.

Tamerlane pulled Nakamura tightly to him. They continued to spin, but now they moved together as one unit. The colonel could see the two ships flashing by repeatedly, with the glowing blue-white sphere of Adrianople far beyond, the tiny lights of the First and Third Legion fleets twinkling around it. Those other ships were much too far away—there was no way they could ever reach them before their air ran out. Their only chance lay in getting back aboard one of the two vessels that lay near them; then they'd have to take their chances with the Ecclesiarchy troops within. But that was a problem that lay literally a lifetime in the future; for now, the only priority was to get back inside a pressurized, oxygenated environment. The shuttle seemed like a bad option; that was the crowd that had engineered this little "accident." In any case, that small craft was already pulling away and zooming back down toward the planet surface.

Our new abilities, Tamerlane thought then, even as he grew dizzy and nauseous from the head-over heels spinning. *The fire. Is there any way we could use it to—*

His thoughts were interrupted as he realized that Nakamura was already very clearly thinking along those same lines, and was doing something about it. The general was directing his hands outward, creating bright bursts of flame before them in space, at regular intervals. This puzzled Tamerlane at first. A couple of seconds later, it became apparent that Nakamura was using the fire to stop their spin, pulsing the flames like a rocket engine to steady them.

Once they were motionless, a few seconds later, he called to Tamerlane over a private Aether connection and gave him instructions. Tamerlane acknowledged and together they channeled their powers to create a sort of propulsion effect, driving them back toward the ship.

It had all happened very quickly, but had still taken too long; their air was almost gone now. But they were moving, and moving with impressive speed, closing rapidly on the hull of the Ecclesiarchy cruiser. *But*, Tamerlane wondered—*now what?*

Nakamura was reaching out with his hands again, this time toward the cruiser. Flames sprang up across the gleaming metal of its silver hull—flames apparently feeding purely on other-dimensional fuel sources, as there was nothing but vacuum here for them to draw from. Tamerlane joined in and together they hit the side of the cruiser with a concentrated blaze that burned like a blowtorch. This had the added benefit of slowing their velocity toward that metal bulkhead. In the instant before their momentum carried them into the side of the ship, the circular patch of hull they had been focusing their flames upon gave way, melting into vapor. Air rushed out past them as they passed through into the ship and were immediately pulled down onto the deck by the artificial gravity.

Surrounded by air again, albeit rapidly outward-gushing air, they could hear—and what they heard was the wailing of alarms: *Hull breach, hull breach!*

Automated systems unleashed robotic arms that sprayed quick-drying foam across the hole, sealing the breach. Atmosphere gushed back into the space where they stood and their smartcloth uniforms responded by softening into cloth and quickly folding back into normal configuration, the helmets disappearing into the collars.

The two men stood, leaning forward, hands on hips, gasping for breath, as the sound of booted feet on metal deck drew nearer and nearer. When they finally straightened and looked up, they saw that they occupied a sort of dead end corridor, with a cadre of white-garbed and blast pistol-armed Ecclesiarchy soldiers arrayed across from them, blocking the only way out.

"General! Colonel!" cried the ranking officer—or rather, priest—of the company. He moved forward, concern etched across his dour features, and executed a quick sign of blessing in the air with his right hand. "By all of Those Who Remain! Thank the Above that you're both alright!" He shook his head in seeming astonishment. "There must have been a malfunction in the docking systems—!"

"Yes," Nakamura managed to croak. "I'm certain that's what it was."

Tamerlane attempted to discern if the priest was being sincere or merely playing a part, pretending—if he was part of this conspiracy or not. Meanwhile he simply glared at the men in white, his mouth firmly shut.

The priest ordered his underlings forward, to help the two men along. "To the infirmary with them," he commanded. "They must see the doctor at once!"

4

ou still think my so-called 'conspiracy theory' is crazy, General?" Tamerlane sent across their private Aether link. "You honestly don't believe that someone higher-up has been trying to put us in positions to get ourselves killed?"

"I didn't think there were many people in the entire Empire 'higher up' than me, to be honest," Nakamura replied across the link, as he sat back in the chair next to the exam table. The doctor had looked both of them over and, to his astonishment, had found no serious or permanent damage. "But I'm starting to believe the Ecclesiarchy at least *thinks* it's higher up than me—than *anybody*. Though why they should think that, or when such a thing came to be, I have no idea."

Tamerlane sat up on the exam table. He swung his legs out and hopped down, feeling none the worse for the wear. He started to reply when the door slid open at the far side of the medical facility and in glided three figures—three very familiar figures—clad in jet black robes.

"My dear General! And the Colonel! So—we meet again," came the voice of the tall, gaunt man in front. "I must confess that I have been hoping for this opportunity—though I never dreamed it would come along so soon." He turned to the two white-clad Ecclesiarchy soldiers who stood just inside the doorway, and waved them away. "Go, go. I would interrogate these men in private."

The two dark-haired Ecclesiarchy warrior-priests exchanged uncertain glances.

"Fear not," he added. "If there are any messes—as often occur in my work, I find—my two acolytes here are fully capable of cleaning them up. Though," he added, leaning toward them conspiratorially, "you might want to stand by outside with wet towels, and perhaps a vacuum. And a plastic bag or two."

The two white-clad soldiers blanched. They looked at the two young and athletic figures in black who flanked the Inquisitor, looked at one another, then seemed simultaneously to reach a decision. They nodded and hurried out of the room. The door slid closed behind them.

"So. General," the tall man stated, smiling slightly, when they had departed. "How have we come to such a pass?"

"Grand Inquisitor Stanishur," Nakamura stated by way of greeting. "Well. I'm pleased to see you and yours survived our little adventure."

"Indeed," the Inquisitor said. Then he added, "Though, fortunately, *we* were not possessed."

Tamerlane and Nakamura exchanged puzzled looks.

"Possessed?" the General sputtered. "You think we were *possessed?*"

The Inquisitor shrugged noncommittally. "That *is* the word going around the Ecclesiarchy. Much of the Inquisition believes it, too. Which, I would imagine, is why the two of you are here, now."

Nakamura darkened. "That is ridiculous!"

This time the Inquisitor merely smiled innocuously. "Well. You did exhibit some rather...*unusual*... abilities during your actions on Adrianople over the past few hours," he noted. "But you were already being...shall we say, *monitored*... after your long period of recovery following the expedition. There was some concern even before the events of today that something might be... Oh, what is the word I'm looking for here?" He chewed his leathery lip for a few seconds, then brightened. "Ah, yes. *Incubating*."

"*Incubating*?" Tamerlane blurted, shocked.

"Preposterous," the general barked. "There is no evidence to suggest—"

As Tamerlane listened to Nakamura angrily defending the two of them from the Inquisitor's veiled accusations, he realized with a start that a black rectangle had appeared in the corner of his virtual-reality vision—the view from which he operated his link to the Aether network. It looked somewhat like a stylized letter "I," and he recognized it at once. Quickly he authorized it to connect to the private link he had set up with the general, and the unspoken voice of the Grand Inquisitor boomed over it, in their heads.

"Gentlemen! Calm yourselves. I am not here to accuse you of anything—I merely repeat the whispers of the upper levels of the Church, for the benefit of those who are listening in. I do not necessarily subscribe to their views."

Nakamura's verbal rant came to an abrupt end. "Then why are you here?" he sent back silently.

Inquisitor Stanishur pursed his lips, then looked about the room. "They will grow suspicious if we suddenly go from loud argument to deathly silence," he stated over the link. He motioned sharply to his disciples. One of them—the female, Delain—raised a black-gloved hand. She held a small box, and touched a stud on one side. There came a flash that caused everyone present to blink.

"Their cameras and listening devices have been knocked offline," the Inquisitor said aloud. "We can speak in privacy now, and for another couple of minutes. Then, of course, their soldiers will descend upon us, to find out what has happened—and what we are up to."

"What *are* we up to?" Tamerlane asked, intrigued.

Stanishur moved around to face them more directly, his black robes fluttering behind him. The two acolytes stood to either side, hands folded in front, heads bowed.

"I must speak candidly with you," he began. "And I must rely on you to keep my words in confidence."

"These people just put us out an airlock," Nakamura grumbled. "By contrast, Inquisitor, you look like my best friend."

Stanishur actually chuckled at that. "Very well." He moved in closer to them, speaking softly. "I have *heard* things...*seen* things...in the Imperial court... that have caused me great concern. And I fear that, like the two of you, very soon I will no longer be in a position to do anything about it."

"You think they're going to oust you from your position as Grand Inquisitor?" Nakamura asked. "Why?"

"It has already happened once," the gaunt man said, "with the Ecclesiarch. They forced poor old Zoric out almost immediately after we returned from the Above."

"I thought he died," Tamerlane said, frowning.

"Oh, he *did* die," Stanishur replied. "Eventually. But his power, his office, had already been stripped away by then. Whether that alone killed him, though, or someone helped the process..." He shrugged. "But there is a definite sense that someone—someone very high up in the Empire, and very behind-the-scenes—is, shall we say, *encouraging* a changing of the guard at all the key positions. A new Ecclesiarch—though no one has officially been named yet... a new Grand Inquisitor, if they get their way with me—and only a quirk of the rules of the Church has prevented my ouster thus far—and, from what we've just seen, a new supreme military commander."

Nakamura reluctantly nodded. He motioned toward Tamerlane. "The Colonel here has previously suggested that something along these lines was happening, but I had no idea it was this...*pervasive*," he said. "No idea so many people and institutions were involved, one way or the other." He brought a hand to his chin and rubbed it absently, clearly very concerned.

"Have you noticed," the Inquisitor asked, "that you and General Beyzit of Third Legion have repeatedly been placed in harm's way?"

"I have noticed that, yes, definitely," Tamerlane responded with a scowl.

"And during those actions, General Attila and Second Legion were nowhere to be found. And meanwhile his attack dog, Iapetus, has been given free reign."

Tamerlane frowned. He hadn't actually extended his thinking that far yet. "So—Attila is involved somehow? You believe he's part of it?"

"He is involved," Stanishur said, "or at least favored by those who are pulling the strings. If all had gone as they clearly planned—had their intrigues come to fruition—the two of you and General Beyzit would now be dead— Agrippa too, though he likely won some temporary favor by turning the two of you in—and General Attila would be the sole military commander of the Empire."

Neither soldier replied to that. They didn't like to consider that one of their own could be actively involved, or even complicit, in such a thing.

"And Attila would be serving—who?" Stanishur added. "The Emperor?" He shrugged. "Perhaps. Perhaps not. I do not know."

"Who else?" Nakamura asked. "Who else *is* there, that could be directing all of this?"

"That is something," Stanishur replied, "that we need to find out. Very, very quickly."

"How can we do that?" Nakamura asked. "What are you suggesting?"

"We must move while I still hold my office and my authority," the Grand Inquisitor stated, "and while the efforts against the two of you—and the attempts on your lives—remain cloaked in the appearance of 'accidents,' and with no official arrest orders issued."

One of the acolytes leaned in and whispered something to Stanishur. He frowned and nodded once. "We have been supplying the watchers of this room with false data from the time we entered," he told the soldiers. "But now they are growing suspicious. We must hurry."

"You said we must move," Nakamura said. "Move how? Where?"

"There is a conference convening even now—a grand council, the likes of which the Empire has rarely seen since the days of its founding. We must go there. We must gain an audience with the Emperor. And we must observe those around him—those seeking to guide him in making *and changing* governmental and religious policy. Only then will we know how to strike—and *whom* to strike."

Nakamura considered this, then nodded. "The Colonel and I should be expected to attend something of that nature. I'm surprised I haven't been informed of it already."

"You were not to be invited," Stanishur stated. "You were to be *dead* by then." He snorted a laugh. "*I* wasn't invited, either. *Me!* The Grand Inquisitor! Not invited to a grand council! Need you any further evidence of this conspiracy?"

Nakamura shook his head. He appeared sad—very sad—and almost deflated, Tamerlane thought. It upset him to see it, perhaps even more than the conspiracy itself.

"Where is this council to be held?" the general asked.

"On Ascanius."

"Why there? It's pretty far out along the Fringe."

Stanishur shook his head. "I do not know. There is a vague religious significance to it, I am told, but no one has yet indicated a specific reason."

Tamerlane looked up. "If old Zoric has been ousted, just who is the new Ecclesiarch?" he asked. "You haven't told us that yet. Is it anyone we'd know?"

"No word as of yet," the Inquisitor replied, looking away. "But...there are persistent rumors that the Emperor will be moving someone over from the military."

"The military?" Nakamura reacted with surprise. "A soldier—head of the *Church*?"

"Someone who has spent a lifetime obeying the Emperor's orders without question," Tamerlane noted, "rather than someone who has spent a lifetime defending the faith and the Church."

"That—that would be an outrage," Nakamura stated, shocked.

"On many levels," Tamerlane added.

"Yes," Stanishur agreed. "The Church and the Inquisition—reduced to mere tools in the hands of the Emperor and the political leadership." He could only shake his head. "You begin to see now the full depths of this problem we face, I take it."

The two men nodded.

"We have to get to this council, Stanishur," Nakamura snapped. "Immediately."

"If it can be done, I will see it done," the Inquisitor replied. He turned to his acolytes and whispered something. Each replied in turn.

"Wait," Tamerlane said, standing and moving forward. "There's one more thing I need to know, before we jump in with both feet."

Stanishur turned back to him. "Yes, Colonel?"

"I gather that we're accused of being possessed by demons. I assume that supposedly happened during our expedition to rescue the Emperor. And certainly our newfound...abilities...might seem to lend a bit of credence to that charge." He leaned in toward Stanishur. "Yet you, Inquisitor, seem perfectly willing to believe in us, without question, and to bring us into your confidence. I'd like to know *why* that is."

The Grand Inquisitor gazed back at him impassively for a long moment. Then the corners of his wrinkled mouth turned upward in a rictus-like smile. "A perfectly reasonable question, Colonel," he said. He spread his hands wide. "I do not believe this newfound ability you two have manifested marks demonic possession," he said in a quiet voice. "To the contrary, I believe it represents a *gift* from the gods, to the most holy of all within our empire."

Tamerlane smiled flatly at him. "I'm pleased to hear you say that, Inquisitor—and I appreciate the compliment—but, if I might ask, what exactly makes *you* feel that way, in contradiction to most of the rest of your order and the Ecclesiarchy?"

The Grand Inquisitor considered this for a second. "Perhaps it would be better if I simply showed you," he said. He extended his pale, cadaverous hand in their direction. He held it out, palm facing upward.

"I'm afraid I don't understand—" Nakamura began.

But Tamerlane got it. "Oh. Of course." Laughing, he waited patiently.

Puzzled, Nakamura looked from the wrinkled hand to the colonel. "Wha—?"

Tamerlane nodded back toward the Inquisitor. "Look, sir."

Nakamura turned back, and there he beheld a flame—bright and strong—dancing on the Grand Inquisitor's palm.

5

Arnem Agrippa tossed aside the sword and shield with which he had been practicing and strode to the far side of the room. His noble face was creased with anger and frustration

"So we're done?" called the dark-haired man who had been mock-fighting him for the past half-hour. "Had enough, have you? Ready to declare me the better man?" Major Selim Iksander chortled as he hung his own weapons carefully on their pegs along the wall.

Agrippa ignored him at first, instead staring out the viewport at the wash of stars beyond.

Iksander approached the massively-built blond man and leaned in so that he, too, could see out the port to where Agrippa was looking. He studied the starfield for a few seconds but saw nothing amiss. "Mm. Stars." He turned to his commander. "They're all still there, then, Colonel? None have gone missing?"

Agrippa made a sour face, then snorted a laugh.

"I haven't bothered to count," he grunted. "At least, not today. But I think it's safe to assume so."

Iksander moved away, taking a towel from a nearby bench and wiping his face and neck with it. "I expected you to be in a better mood now that we're done camping out on Adrianople." He shook his head in disgust. "What a mess that was. But you got to hand the whole thing over to Vostok and simply fly away. So—what's got you so distracted? If you don't mind my asking," he added. "Sir."

Agrippa shook his head. "I don't know." He continued to stare out at the long night. "Yes, I do." He turned to face Iksander. "It's the general. Nakamura. And Tamerlane."

"You're unnerved by their blasphemous behavior and freakish mutant powers, are you, sir?" Iksander asked, all innocence and sincerity on the surface but with his tongue obviously well-in-cheek to those who knew him.

Agrippa knew him. They'd served together on a dozen campaigns over the years, coming up together in Third Legion, favorites of "The Thunderbolt," General Beyzit. Beyzit had even given Agrippa his nickname—"The Golden"—and his company its official designation, in his honor: "The Golden Phalanx."

"No," the blond man replied, very serious now. He met Iksander's level gaze. "I'm unnerved—if that's the term you wish to use—by the fact that I turned those two brave and accomplished soldiers in to the Ecclesiarchy."

"As you had to," Iksander stated in a neutral tone.

Agrippa merely looked at him, and eventually Iksander relented. "Yes, okay," he said. "You turned two good soldiers in to the Holy Church—an organization neither you nor I nor anyone in The Thunderbolt's army has ever thought much of."

Agrippa nodded.

"And now you feel guilty."

"Obviously."

"So—what is to be done, then?"

Agrippa pursed his lips and turned back to the starfield. "I don't know," he admitted at length. "I don't know that

225

there's anything we *can* do—at least, not in the immediate future. We have this new assignment."

"As security," Iksander practically spat. "*Security*! *Us*! The Golden Phalanx! The Kings of bloody Oblivion—sent to stand guard at a fancy committee meeting, when we should be out smashing the Riyahadi, or the Chung, or—"

Agrippa motioned for him to settle down, and he did.

"Let's not get ourselves arrested for treason," the colonel cautioned. "We will of course discharge the duties we are assigned. But—" he appended, trailing off.

"*But* you won't be passing up any opportunities to make up for what you now believe was an error in judgment," Iksander finished for him.

"Well said."

Agrippa reached down and lifted a heavy practice sword, swung it back and forth a few times, and sighted down its length.

"So," the big colonel concluded after a few moments, "let the Golden Phalanx—the 'Kings of bloody Oblivion,' as you so colorfully called us—do our jobs as security guards for whatever group is having this little meeting on Ascanius, and then—" He strode back out onto the practice mat, motioning for Iksander to join him. "—and then, when we are done, we shall see what we shall see, as concerning the general and the colonel."

"Works for me," Iksander said with a shrug.

"That was easy," Agrippa rumbled, his blue eyes meeting those of his old friend and comrade.

Iksander shrugged again. "You're the brains of the operation, sir. I just wait for you to point at targets, and then I shoot them. Or chop them down. Or punch them. Or whatever works."

"Even if that target lies...shall we say... somewhat close to home?"

"I've never heard a syllable of treason from you or anyone else in Third Legion—not even just now," Iksander stated by way of reply. "I simply do as I'm told. I find it works better that way." He snorted again. "Better for everyone involved. I've never had any desire to be any smarter than I already am."

"You're smarter than you let on," Agrippa told him. "You're proving it now."

"No idea what you're talking about, sir," the dark-haired soldier said, shaking his head. "Now—can we get on with this?"

"By all means."

Iksander screamed bloody murder and lunged with his sword at the colonel. Agrippa blocked his blow—it was a new attack from Iksander, or at least one Agrippa hadn't encountered before, and very creative—and spun about. In one very quick and continuous move he shoved his old friend to the side, smacked him on the ribs with the flat of his blade, and took up another defensive position—one he had honed to perfection in uncountable sparring sessions with his best troops.

"Ascanius first," Agrippa whispered to himself as a sort of solemn pledge, as Iksander charged again, "and then, yes—then we shall see what we shall see."

ou will stand aside. *Now.*"

Grand Inquisitor Stanishur, resplendent in his black robes, loomed squarely in the doorway that led out of the medical facility. To either side stood his two acolytes, Brother Chopra and Sister Delain, hoods up over their heads and hands crossed at their waists. Behind them waited General Nakamura and Colonel Tamerlane, noticeably ill-at-ease to be in a situation where they had absolutely no control over what was happening, and had to depend on someone else to determine their fate. Facing them on the other side of the threshold was a veritable battalion of Ecclesiarchy soldier-priests in stainless white uniforms and body armor.

"With apologies, Inquisitor," the white-clad man in the front of the crowd said, "I cannot allow those men to leave." He wasn't holding a weapon—none of them were, yet—but from his stance and the tone of his voice it was very apparent that violence was well within the realm of possibility. He was tall, though not quite as tall as Tamerlane and not nearly as tall as Stanishur, and in his mid-twenties, with very short, brown hair and pale skin. The eight-pointed golden star on his lapel, one of the primary insignia of the Church, was echoed by a tattoo onto his left cheek. His blue eyes blazed as he glared at the Inquisitor.

"Your name?" Stanishur asked him.

"Father Reichenbach, disciple of Malachek," the young man replied instantly and formally.

"Reichenbach," the Inquisitor repeated, nodding. He smiled at the man. "Well. I had not been informed that the Emperor had chosen yet another new Ecclesiarch."

The man was taken aback. "I—excuse me?"

"Or that he had selected *you* for that role."

Now the man was utterly flummoxed. "I—Inquisitor, I'm afraid I don't understand what you are saying. Why would you think that *I*—"

Stanishur spread his hands. "Well, my dear fellow—as you are attempting to tell me what to do, I can only assume you are the new Ecclesiarch." His mouth parted into a chilling smile. "Because no one of lesser rank would dare do such a thing."

The man swallowed with some difficulty.

"Or—am I mistaken, somehow?"

The man started to speak, but Stanishur interrupted him. "As a disciple of Malachek, I would further assume you possessed the common sense—let alone the *wisdom* of that very god—not to bar my way."

The man, Reichenbach, faltered, momentarily wrong-footed. He moved backwards a half step.

That was all Stanishur needed. He swept through the doorway, brushing past Reichenbach, closing the space between himself and the rest of the arrayed troops in an instant. The others hurried after him.

"No—*wait*," Reichenbach cried, recovering his wits and scrambling to catch up. "Don't let them pass," he shouted to the troops.

The nearest Ecclesiarch soldier-priest stepped out of formation and grasped the Inquisitor by the upper arm.

Quickly—so quickly the eye could barely follow it—the acolyte on that side, Brother Chopra, struck the man with a series of martial arts blows that left him a crumpled mass on the floor.

Wide-eyed, Tamerlane caught Nakamura's attention and gave him a look that carried a clear message: *Impressive!*

Nakamura's expression in return was one Tamerlane had seen before, and he instantly understood it: *Now what?*

He had no answer, at least for the moment. These people in white were Imperial troops, the same as Nakamura and himself; they simply served the Church instead of the First Legion. He had no desire to fight them—to *hurt* them. Better to *talk* their way out.

In short, this was Stanishur's play, at least for now.

The Grand Inquisitor was helping the soldier up that Chopra had beaten down. "I apologize for my aide's…*over-enthusiastic* reaction," he told the man with a tight smile. "But, you see, he has been trained from childhood to protect me. No one is permitted to lay hands upon an Inquisitor—and certainly not upon the *Grand* Inquisitor."

The leader moved back into Stanishur's path. He now held a blast pistol in his right hand. "That's enough," he said, still shaken but now embarrassed and angry.

"Oh, my dear Reichenbach," the Inquisitor said, *tsk-tsk*ing. "The only thing worse than laying a hand on my person is brandishing a firearm in my presence."

Brother Chopra started forward again, but this time Stanishur held up a hand, restraining him.

"Wait. Before events escalate beyond our abilities to control them," the dour Inquisitor said directly to Reichenbach, "I suggest you simply let me and my party pass. We intend to return to our ship and depart this system immediately."

"You and your servants are free to go, of course, Inquisitor," the Ecclesiarch soldier stated with a slight bow.

"But, as I said before, I cannot permit you to take these two men with you."

Stanishur's face creased into a look of utter incomprehension. "Again, father, you seem to labor under the extremely false impression that *you* can issue orders and directives to *me*." He leaned down over the man, eclipsing him in shadow. "I have urgent business with the Emperor himself. And I am indeed taking these two men with me."

Reichenbach glared back at him, fists involuntarily bunching.

"If you have a problem with *that*, father," Stanishur went on, "you have a problem with *me*. And with the Holy Inquisition itself." He regarded the man with seemingly genuine curiosity. "Is that the case?"

The violence that erupted mere seconds later seemed to indicate that the answer lay in the affirmative.

Reichenbach raised one hand and dropped it sharply, signaling his orders. The white-clad soldier-priests immediately responded, surging to the attack. Pistols came out of their holsters, and the color and intensity of the energy discharge indicated they were set to "stun"—but to the more powerful, vicious, debilitating "stun" setting that generally left targets hospitalized at least briefly.

The Inquisitors gave them no opportunity to target them. The two acolytes became twin swirls of dark, blurred motion, slicing through the white-suited soldier-priests like small tornadoes, their hands deadly weapons. Stanishur, meanwhile, drew matching, antique-looking pistols from his robes and opened up on the crowd in white, blasting away rapid-fire.

Behind them, Nakamura and Tamerlane looked on in surprise for a split-second, once again taken aback by the resourcefulness—and the resources—of the Inquisitor. Then they joined in, punching and kicking their way into the crowd.

For nearly two full minutes the battle raged, with several of the Ecclesiarchy troopers falling but none of the opposing five injured. Such a situation could not last forever, though—particularly within the narrow confines of the spacecraft corridor. Sister Delain was the first on that side to be struck by an energy pulse, and she fell at Stanishur's feet, half-paralyzed. As the remaining four were momentarily distracted by her plight, a soldier in white managed to get a clear shot at General Nakamura and clipped him in the arm. He spun about, shocked, his arm growing numb.

Seeing this, understanding how the battle inevitably was going, given the numbers and the constricted nature of the arena where they fought, the Inquisitor held up a hand. "Cease your fire," he called out, his voice loud and commanding. "Everyone."

Tamerlane wasn't sure what the old man had in mind. Surrender? Some clever stratagem he'd inexplicably waited this long to enact? And indeed he would never find out for sure. For at that moment, General Nakamura stepped forward, pushing past the Inquisitor, his functioning hand—the one that hadn't been stunned—outstretched and raised before him.

"You know what the Colonel and I are capable of," he called to the Ecclesiarchy soldiers. "You've all seen what happened on the planet's surface by now, I'm sure." He raised the hand higher and flames danced all along his fingers and up his wrist. "Move aside—clear the corridors and allow us to pass—or I will burn you all where you stand."

For a moment, no one reacted at all—though individuals on both sides of the confrontation frowned and looked to others for some kind of guidance.

Tamerlane moved up alongside the general and raised both of his powerful arms up over his head, where all could see. Flames flickered over his limbs as well.

"This man is General Nakamura, the supreme Imperial military commander," Tamerlane barked, his eyes flickering from one white-clad soldier-priest to the next.

"And he carries with him the holy fires of the Above," Stanishur added in reverent tones. "He has been touched by Those Who Remain, and now embarks upon a holy mission in their name!"

The soldier-priests exchanged nervous looks, growing uncertain.

"He means to depart this ship," Tamerlane continued. "You will *not* hinder him. Am I understood?"

Slowly, very reluctantly, the Ecclesiarchy troops pulled back, clearing an open path down the corridor.

"What are you doing?" Reichenbach squawked. "We have our orders! They are to remain in our custody until further notice!"

Again the white-clad soldier-priests hesitated, torn in two directions, yet for another instant the avenue of escape remained open.

The three Inquisitors and the two Legion I officers wasted no time moving quickly along it. Stanishur led them, calling back to the others, "My ship is docked this way. Come along!"

Just like that, they were past the troops and jogging along an empty corridor toward the docking area.

"We will shoot you out of the sky if you attempt to disengage your vessel," Father Reichenbach shouted at them, as defiant as ever.

"No, you will not," Stanishur replied.

"You are violating the direct orders of the Ecclesiarch," Reichenbach retorted, hurrying along behind them. "I will have every right to do so!"

"I'm not arguing that you won't *try*," Stanishur countered. "I'm simply pointing out that you will not—that you *cannot—succeed*." He paused before rounding the last corner that led to the docking port for his ship. "My acolytes were not idle while I spoke with your prisoners here," he went on. "Particularly Sister Delain, who enjoys a close working relationship with starship computer systems—especially those using the coding language of Ecclesiarchy machines."

Reichenbach's eyes widened. He hurried along after them. "What—what do you mean by *that*?" he demanded.

Sister Delain worked her magic on the airlock controls and Brother Chopra tugged the hatch open. As the others quickly filed through and onto the ship that lay beyond, Stanishur looked back at the chief soldier-priest one last time. He chuckled.

"I mean that, were I you, I would be extremely careful about believing anything my ship's computer systems told me for the next, oh, thirty hours or so. And especially careful about firing any weapons—no matter what direction you might *believe* them to be pointed in."

Cursing, infuriated, Reichenbach whirled to face his own people and began screaming orders, including the command to inform the Ecclesiarchy of what was happening here and where the prisoners were headed. He'd scarcely begun when reports came at him from every direction of the local network. "What do you mean, the long-range Aether connection is down?" he asked, incredulous. "And the hyperdrive, as well? How can that *be*?"

The Inquisitor clambered aboard his small vessel and the hatch clanged shut behind him. He nodded to his acolytes and they hurried to the forward area of the ship, climbing into the pilot's and navigator's seats. They manipulated a few controls and the ship broke loose and streaked rapidly away from the Ecclesiarchy cruiser.

Nakamura and Tamerlane settled into the surprisingly comfortable seats in the passenger compartment; the upholstery was black with gray trim and silver metal fixtures. In reply to their question, Stanishur grinned his skeleton smile. "Never fear, gentlemen," he said. "Sister

Delain assures me that, due to the virus she introduced into their computer systems, Father Reichenbach and his ship and crew will remain trapped here, unable to talk to anyone or go anywhere, for at least the next twenty-four hours. That should be more than sufficient to see us safely to Ascanius, without any sort of alarm being raised." He paused as the young woman in black leaned in, whispering something further to him. Then he laughed. "She adds that, should Reichenbach or his friends prove so foolish as to actually attempt to *fire* on us…"

At that moment, a bright flash filled the rear viewscreen. A second later, a shockwave briefly rocked their ship.

Stanishur shook his head mournfully. "I told them. I *warned* them not to trust their instruments—not to fire." Then he looked up at the two First Legion men. "Allow me to revise my previous statement, gentlemen," he said. "We are now safe from the ship we just departed… for an *indefinite* period of time."

Tamerlane gazed up at the image on the screen of the rapidly expanding fireball that seconds earlier had been the Ecclesiarchy cruiser. He didn't find it as humorous as the Grand Inquisitor seemed to—that much was certain. But he did feel a very definite sense of relief, mixed with a sickening depression. To have spent his entire adult life— and a fair amount of his childhood—serving with the Imperial military, the very thought of any of the Imperial institutions being arrayed against him, and actively trying to capture or kill him, left him almost physically ill.

"We will rendezvous with the Inquisition mothership in precisely twenty-seven minutes," Stanishur reported a few seconds later. "From there, it's straight on to Ascanius— and the Emperor."

7

Major Arani disembarked from the transport *Endymia* alongside the rest of her company, but new orders arrived via the Aether the moment her booted foot touched the surface of Ascanius.

She strode out onto the broad, flat, concrete plain and gazed out at the sea of spacecraft parked almost nose-to-tail for as far as the eye could see. Waves of heat rippled and distorted the horizon as she turned, taking it all in. Yet the immense array of starships was only the second-most amazing sight to see on Ascanius—as she herself realized only a moment later. When she had rotated halfway around, she gasped and slowly moved her eyes upward, readjusting her mind to comprehend what she was seeing.

The great Church of the Reliquae towered over her—over the ships, over the entire plain. Its dome, topped with a tall spike of a steeple and gleaming white in the sunlight, loomed a kilometer up into the blue, cloud-flecked sky. It was one of the two or three most visually-impressive structures in the entire Empire, and seeing it in photos or even in holo scarcely did it justice. It was immense and imposing and powerful.

She came back to reality as the rumble of other descending spacecraft and the roar of atmospheric fighters washed over her, physically moving her with their backwash like waves in the ocean. One in particular was nearly blotting out the sun for the moment, as it dropped toward a reserved space very close to the front of the church complex.

"Wow," exclaimed one of the troopers coming down the ramp behind her as he stared up at the dome. "Never saw it in person before."

The sound of another person's voice served to bring Arani back to reality. Ignoring the man behind her, she replayed the orders that had arrived via her link and nodded to herself, not surprised in the slightest. She was being dispatched to sniper cover duty in the upper levels of the church complex—a job that meant she would be all alone. A perfect place for some accident to befall her.

She hurried across the concrete plain to the nearest hover-tram, climbing aboard with others from her unit to be ferried across the kilometers of landing field to the complex itself. A few minutes later she was back on her feet and passing through the broad double-door entrance on the east side of the church; security forces obviously were not making use of the ceremonial main entrance, an arched doorway that looked to have been constructed for the use of giants.

Into the grand old edifice she went, moving alone, making her way up flights of stairs and along narrow corridors. The Aether presented her with a map of the complex in her virtual vision, her assigned position highlighted clearly.

Eventually she emerged onto the balcony that was to be her domain for this mission. It was small—only four elegant chairs occupied most of it— and as she moved out onto it and peered over the railing, she saw that she had climbed higher than she'd realized. Her head swam and she actually had to grip the railing to keep from losing her balance; she was perched something like a quarter of a kilometer above the marble floor of the gargantuan main hall.

She studied the space beneath her carefully, comparing it to images she'd called up via her link. The altar and other religious artifacts normally present in the center of the main hall had been moved aside, and now a long, broad table of rich, dark wood and inlaid stone filled the center space. Thirteen very fancy chairs sat behind the table, the center one tallest and inlaid with gold and jewels.

All that, just for the new Ecclesiarch? she wondered. *I mean, I know it's an important office, but still—that looks like a set-up the Emperor himself would—*

She frowned. There still had been no official word from higher up as to exactly *whom* this service—whatever it was to be—was for. She had been assuming it was to announce or swear in the new head of the Church, but...

Surely not, she thought. *Surely not him. Wouldn't they have* told *us?*

The main doors opened. They were huge, metal and wood affairs inlaid with gleaming gemstones and golden filigree. They moved slowly, and it took a remarkably long time for them to open all the way in. When they finished moving, a blast of horns echoed out, and everyone who had been milling about far below in the sanctuary or main hall moved quickly to attention and bowed.

By Those Who Remain, Arani thought, shocked. *It* is *him.*

Janus IV, the Emperor himself, strode through the entrance, surrounded by his vast retinue of aides, assistants, bodyguards, and assorted other hangers-on. Along with him came the Empress herself, Lisbeth Salome Rahkmanov, and both of the royal children—the teenaged heir apparent and the little princess. The huge Emperor's Guard troopers, impressive as ever in their brightly-colored synthetic crystal armor, stomped along in the wake of the party.

What is he doing here? Arani wondered. *What could possibly be happening that would merit his traveling out here, to the heart of the Ecclesiarchy's domain?*

The Imperial party moved at a slow but steady pace along the broad red carpet that led from the entrance to the huge table in the center of the sanctuary. Light streamed in from the arches spaced around the lower section of the dome high above, giving the entire affair an ethereal quality— doubtlessly the intent of the original architects, some two thousand years earlier.

Hypnotized by the sight of such royal splendor, Arani jumped when a voice suddenly called to her over the Aether: "Arani, are you in position? Are you at your assigned spot?"

"I am," she replied reflexively. Then, puzzled by the informality of the contact, she asked, "Who is this?"

The doors to the balcony behind her burst open. A silent hail of deadly dart flechettes sprayed out at her.

Tamerlane leaned over to Nakamura, speaking in a whisper. "General, I know you didn't wish to harm any of our people—and I consider even the Ecclesiarchy to be 'our people,' as I know you do, too. I didn't want that Reichenbach guy dead—though I'll admit I did want to beat the stuffing out of him. But, I have to ask..." He raised his hand and flames flickered across his fingertips. "Would you actually have done it? Were you bluffing, or would you have unleashed the *fire* on them?"

Nakamura met the colonel's eyes, then looked down at his own hand, flexing it slowly as the feeling returned to it. "I don't know, Ezekial," he said. He looked up and met his adjutant's eyes again. "Would you?"

Tamerlane considered this for a second, frowning.

"I would have, yes," he said. "I would've hated it—and I hate that those people were killed anyway—by their own stupidity!—but, *yes*. The overall survival of the Empire *must* come first. And I honestly do believe we are on a holy mission now, sir."

"You believe Stanishur's propaganda, then? That we've been touched by the gods—gifted with their holy fire, for some special purpose?"

"Maybe so. There is without question a vast conspiracy unfolding around us. The Emperor may be in the process of making himself an absolutist dictator, or else someone near him is exerting a tremendous amount of control over him, forcing him to do these things—and placing him in grave danger in the process. We have to expose this—this person, this conspiracy, whatever it is—and bring it out into the open, where it can be dealt with." He offered a slight shrug. "If someone—the gods, whatever—have given us an extra advantage in order to fulfill that purpose, I say we use it."

Nakamura took this in, chewed on it, and nodded.

"We have to believe that, Ezekial," he replied at length. "We have to. Every bit of it. After all, the alternative is that we—all of us here on this ship—are *possessed*..." He squeezed his eyes closed and brought his hands up to his face, then shook his head firmly. "You have to be right— we must be acting in the direct service of the *gods* now. The alternative is simply too horrible to contemplate."

Major Niobe Arani leapt out over a quarter-kilometer drop of empty space. She leapt for dear life.

She had been ready for an attack, having made up her mind before landing on Ascanius that it wasn't paranoia if they really were out to get you—and that someone really was out to get her. She had been poised to respond to an attack from behind, and had done just that. However, she hadn't expected a projectile attack, assuming that anyone who wanted to kill her would also not wish to draw the attention of the people down below—the very important people, now entering for some sort of religious ceremony.

A silent projectile weapon, though—that's what got her. Or rather, *almost* got her.

As soon as it fired, she understood what it was: A flechette sprayer. Not much good over any distances but utterly devastating up close. Most importantly, it was almost silent as it fired its barrage of high-velocity razor blades.

She leapt, in the only direction that seemed safe. Ironic that "safe" should mean "out over a balcony's edge and down toward a marble floor very, very far below."

She didn't fall that far, of course. She scarcely fell far at all. Her short, ninjato-style sword was already unsheathed and in her hand as she moved, and she jabbed its virtually frictionless blade into the ancient woodwork of the balcony, swinging down and around by its handle and thus allowing the hail of blades to pass just overhead. Her momentum carried her back around in a gymnastic arc that brought her back onto the balcony a few feet to the left of where she'd been a second earlier.

The attacker—a figure clad all in white, with a hood and mask covering most of his face—was startled by this move and stood motionless as she landed before him. Belatedly he brought his gun up to fire again, only to have it knocked from his hand by Arani's sword. Blood splattered across the elegantly-carved wall of the balcony, and the man in white, eyes wide now, whirled and fled.

Arani tried to access the Aether, to report what was happening and to call for assistance—but she was not at all surprised to find she could not link in. At first she thought the signal itself was being jammed, but then she realized it was still there—she had simply been locked out of it.

Cursing, she crouched down and then sprang through the doorway from the balcony back out into the corridor, keeping low to avoid another possible attack. None came. She looked up and saw the figure in white racing away down the dimly lit hall.

No one else was going to help her, she knew. No one would possibly even believe her. They might even accuse her of planning to shoot someone from her assigned perch—the Emperor, even. The gods only knew what punishment the Inquisition would create for that crime.

No—she needed to catch this guy. She needed to ask him a series of questions, and she needed to present him to the highest possible authority she could find, as proof of her innocence.

She just had to hope that, whoever that higher-up was, he or she wasn't part of the conspiracy, as well.

10

The Inquisition ship *Confessor* cleared the last line of Imperial picket ships and angled down toward the surface of the planet below. Aboard it anxiously waited five individuals—individuals who might be seen as patriots or as renegades, depending upon one's point of view.

Whether those five could successfully make their way past layer upon layer of Imperial security and actually set foot on Ascanius had depended entirely upon two things: One, that the conspiracy against them was confined to a few individuals near the top of the power structure, who had been issuing very specific and secret orders against them to only a small number of operatives such as Reichenbach, and two, that the combination of Nakamura's fame, Stanishur's cunning, and Tamerlane's hands-on knowledge of Imperial security could allow them to talk their way past or otherwise overcome any resistance they did encounter. The odds for the one had seemed good; they had monitored the Aether net from the time they had left Adrianople and there had been no alerts, no declarations making them outlaws in the eyes of any imperial personnel. The conspiracy, it seemed, was indeed limited. As to the second, they had breezed past security with remarkable ease simply by claiming that Nakamura and Stanishur were aboard, that the attendance of both had been requested by His Majesty—a most logical assumption, if in reality a lie—and that they were running late for the start of the Council and had no time to waste. Once their identities were confirmed, they were allowed to proceed with no delays.

Thus at no point in its journey to Ascanius was the *Confessor* boarded by naval warships or blown out of space, and eventually it settled to the ground on a broad, flat landing field that stretched on for miles in every direction.

The field had been blasted out of former farmland and forest and paved over just for this occasion, and it was already nearly covered in carefully-parked rows and columns of ships of all shapes and sizes; ships that had flown in from all parts of the Empire.

The occasion was the Council of Ascanius, the greatest convocation of Imperial religious, political, and military leaders in living memory. And it convened inside the only structure in the Empire glorious enough to merit so momentous a gathering: The Chuch of the Reliquae.

That church was in actuality a massive cathedral constructed in ancient Byzantine style, with a huge interior space topped by a towering dome that loomed almost a kilometer above the plain. The entire building was encased in a gleaming shell of pink-veined marble and inlaid with gold and precious stones. No expense had been spared in creating this, the finest cathedral to the gods in all the Empire.

No sooner had the Grand Inquisitor's shuttle landed in its hidden space to the rear of the great complex than he was up and moving toward the exit hatch, urging the others along quickly as well. The five hurried out of the ship and across a narrow metal bridge to a wooden door that was almost entirely hidden from view. Stanishur produced an ancient-looking metal key from somewhere in his robes and unlocked it, and with the help of his acolytes got it to swing open with a resounding creak.

"I like having ways in to places that cannot be overridden by some technician at a console a thousand light years away," he informed them as they passed through and into the church. He shoved the door closed and its manual lock clicked shut again.

When the door closed, they were plunged into darkness. A moment later, flames sprang to life in braziers set at regular intervals against the wall along the length of the corridor.

"I also like lights that cannot be turned off by anyone but me," he added.

Tamerlane gave Nakamura a quick smile. "I'm beginning to wonder how we ever got anything done without the Inquisitor on our side," he said.

"I'm wondering how he hasn't already taken over the Empire," Nakamura responded, only half in jest.

Stanishur turned back to them as he led them along the hallway. "Gentlemen, please. I have no desire to do anything but serve the Holy Inquisition. My ambitions have always begun and ended there."

"Thank goodness," Tamerlane said.

This time even the Inquisitor chuckled.

They continued on through a winding labyrinth of cross-cutting corridors for some time. Tamerlane and Nakamura had no idea where they were now, but Stanishur never faltered.

"I know every inch of this facility, gentlemen," he stated when Nakamura finally dared to bring that point up. "I've been coming here since I was a small child, raised by my predecessor in this office."

Tamerlane started at that and glanced over at the general; he realized that to some degree it gave the Inquisitor and him something in common. He'd never expected to be able to say such a thing.

Nakamura finally called a halt to their movements and the five of them gathered in a loose circle at an open intersection of brick-lined corridors. The flames on either side of them danced and sent shadows cavorting across their features.

"This is a delicate situation," the general stated to the others. "It's worth a few moments to consider what we face, and what we know."

Tamerlane nodded. He and the general wore their dress uniforms of red and gold while, across from them, the Inquisitor and his two acolytes remained in their usual black.

"On the one hand, we are some of the highest-ranking officials in this empire," he went on. "On the other, none of us was invited to this event. I have no idea how we will be treated when we encounter anyone else present. Will they obey our orders? Will they report us to whomever is behind this..."

"Conspiracy?" Tamerlane supplied.

Nakamura shrugged. "As good a word as any. Or—will they simply try to capture or kill us? We don't know."

"That is why I am presently attempting to get all of us to the central chamber unobserved, via my secret ways," Stanishur interjected impatiently. He motioned toward the hallway ahead. "So, if we might—?"

"I understand and appreciate that, Inquisitor," Nakamura said. "Nonetheless, I don't like the idea of skulking about down here in the shadows. It makes us look guilty, I fear. Guilty of… *something*, at any rate."

Tamerlane considered this; it was a thought that had crossed his mind, as well.

"I believe we should make our presence known sooner rather than later," the general concluded. "Known to the *Emperor*."

Stanishur laughed. "Yes, I take your meaning. Start at the top—because if *he* is involved in this, as well, then we truly have no hope at all."

No one could argue that.

"Very well," the Inquisitor said at length. "I will lead the way to the main sanctuary. We can emerge through the doors of the eastern nave. No one should see us before then, but we will not suddenly come upon His Majesty like hidden assassins that way, either."

"There will be snipers in the main hall, positioned high up," Tamerlane noted. "If even one of them is part of the conspiracy, they will shoot us down before we can get halfway to the Emperor."

"I believe I can address that concern," the Inquisitor stated.

"Oh?" Nakamura considered this, glanced quickly at Tamerlane and received a shrug and a nod, and turned back to Stanishur. "Very well," he said. "I don't know how you could do it, but I've seen no reason so far not to take you at your word."

Stanishur merely laughed.

"We will look awfully much like assassins, no matter how we approach the Emperor," Tamerlane said after a second. "If I was there, as part of the security detail, and I saw a group like us emerge from out of nowhere and try to get close to the Emperor, I'd give the order to open fire. I wouldn't think twice. I doubt they will, either."

Nakamura closed his mouth in a tight line, then nodded. "Yes. That's so."

"Here's another thought," the colonel added. "Let's just come out and say it. No point in being coy at this stage of the game. Let's hypothesize for a moment that our worst and darkest secret fear is true—that we *were* all possessed by demons while we were in the Below."

"Ezekial," Nakamura began, agitated.

"Let him finish, please, General," the Inquisitor said quickly. "I'd like to hear this."

Tamerlane shrugged. "Just say that it's true. If we were—and if our goal was to kill the Emperor, or possess him somehow, or whatever—wouldn't we be behaving exactly, *precisely* the way we all are right now?"

No one said a word for several seconds. They all exchanged glances.

"Yes," Stanishur said finally. "Yes, Colonel. We would."

Tamerlane looked up at him, his normally smooth face lined with concern.

"But," the Inquisitor went on, "we are not. We have not been possessed. And the actions we are taking are in the best interests of the Empire and of the Emperor himself."

"You're sure about that," Tamerlane stated flatly, though he meant it as a question.

"I am," the Inquisitor replied, his eyes steely and cold.

Nakamura inhaled deeply and exhaled slowly. "Very well, gentlemen," he said, and, "lady," nodding to Sister Delain. She favored him with a very tiny half smile. "Let's go. Let's get this done. The gods will decide our fate—and that of the Empire we all serve."

Their resolve once more in place, the five started off down the brick-lined passageway again.

A second later, the wild-eyed soldier appeared in their path, bloody sword swinging back to strike.

11

Tamerlane's pistol was aimed directly at the woman's head, his finger ready to squeeze the trigger.

She looked a fright; only a bit over five feet tall, her long mane of black hair was tousled and standing out, and blood streaked her right cheek. She held a short sword of some sort with both hands, ready to swing. Her expression was a frightening mixture of frantic and furious.

"Who are you people?" she finally blurted, after a very long couple of seconds in which no one moved or spoke, waiting to see what would happen next—and what needed to be done.

Nakamura studied her uniform—jet black, with matte gray insignia designed not to gleam in darkness and give her position away. "Major," he said. "Special Forces. Of *my* army, it would seem," he added.

Tamerlane recognized the insignia then and nodded his agreement. In fact, her name was embroidered on a patch over her left breast: ARANI.

"*Your* army?" the woman asked, blinking. "What do you mean, *your*—" Then she gathered her senses enough to take in the names and ranks displayed on the two officers in front of her. Her jaw worked soundlessly for a second, before she blurted, "General! General Nakamura!"

The older man smiled flatly. "Yes," he said, still keeping at least one eye on the sword at all times. "And this is Colonel Tamerlane, my adjutant," he said, "as well as the Grand Inquisitor and his acolytes." He frowned. "And now that we have made the proper introductions, Major— perhaps you would be so kind as to *lower your sword. Now.*"

There was steel in the general's voice and Arani felt it. Nervously, carefully, she lowered the weapon, and Tamerlane in turn did likewise—though he kept the pistol in his hand, ready, in case this woman turned out to be the homicidal maniac she appeared to be.

"What are you doing down here, sir?" Arani asked, still wild-eyed.

"If you don't mind, Major, I believe I will ask the questions first." Nakamura took four quick steps past her to the next intersection while Tamerlane kept the gun at the ready. He looked down each of the perpendicular passages and saw nothing. Then he turned back to the woman.

"What are you doing down here? It looks as if you've been hunting someone."

Stanishur pointed to the blooded blade and added, "It looks to me as if she already *found* someone."

"Someone tried to kill me, General," she answered, slowly recovering her composure. "I was assigned sniper cover duty on one of the balconies above the main hall. Someone broke in and tried to shoot me with a flachette gun."

"And you're still alive?" Tamerlane's eyes widened. "That's impressive."

"I'm Special Forces, Colonel," she snapped. "We are expected to be able to perform at a maximum level of effectiveness. That includes defeating attempts to kill us— no matter how clumsy or how sophisticated."

Tamerlane nodded approvingly.

"Anyway—I chased the man a long way. Cornered him at one point, got in a lick—" She nodded to the bloody sword she held loosely now in her right hand. "—but he got away again. I tracked him this far."

"We have not seen anyone since we entered, I'm afraid, Major," the General said. "This person must have gone a different way."

"Who was it?" Tamerlane asked. "Was there anything to indicate where they came from, who they work for—?"

"He wore white," Arani replied.

The general and the colonel exchanged knowing glances.

"We've had a run-in or two with some very... how shall I put it... *aggressive* soldiers in white of late," Nakamura told her.

"The Ecclesiarchy," Tamerlane growled. "Still up to no good."

Major Arani frowned at this exchange. "You mean— *you're* involved in this, too?"

"What do you mean by '*this*,' Major?" the Inquisitor asked, leaning into the conversation.

Arani shook her head, clearly groping for words, for thoughts, struggling to grasp all that was happening.

"People have been trying to kill me," she told the others at length. "I believe it's because of something I was involved in, back on Trezibond." She hesitated. "But—no!" She backed up, the sword twitching upward in her grasp. "You were there. You knew about it, too!" She looked on the verge of losing her somewhat tenuous control again.

Nakamura raised his hand slowly. "Hold on, Major," he said, his voice calm and warm. "Tell us what you mean."

"Barmakid," she spat. "I was part of the team that took down Barmakid—that exposed him for what he is. A cultist."

Nakamura nodded. "I remember now, yes. Go on."

"Afterward, I was ordered not to speak to anyone about it. Any of it. Especially about Barmakid himself. And in the time since, someone has tried to kill me—*twice*."

"I was asked to keep that quiet, as well," Nakamura interjected, "by someone within the royal family. I had assumed it was to protect his family's name. Now, I'm starting to wonder—" He turned to Arani. "—seeing as how essentially the same thing has happened to us as happened to you."

Arani took this in with no small degree of shock.

"Continue with your story, please, Major," Tamerlane prompted.

Arani nodded. "When I tried to talk to the others involved in the operation," she said, "none of them answered my call. I was routed to some major who cut me off." She ended the statement with a disgusted grunt, and the sword bobbed in her grasp.

Nakamura looked to Tamerlane. "So," he said. "It involves Barmakid. I'm not surprised, somehow."

"You truly think this is connected to what we've been dealing with?" Tamerlane asked.

"It must be," the general replied. "It all seems to be about keeping his dealings with the dark powers secret."

"But, why would anyone be interested in keeping that quiet?" Tamerlane shook his head. "I mean, I can understand his family wanting it hushed up, but this—this has to be from higher up—from the royal family itself, or someone even closer to it than you, or the Inquisitor here."

Stanishur nodded. "Someone very close to the Emperor himself. Gentlemen, if I believed in our mission before, I most certainly do now."

"Then let's get on with it," Nakamura said. He nodded toward the Inquisitor. "Lead on."

"What is the mission, sir?" Arani asked as she fell into step with the other five, headed back down the winding passage.

"We're here to talk to the Emperor," Tamerlane stated.

"So—he really is here, then? We were never told specifically, but I suspected..." Arani was quiet for a moment as they hustled along. Then, "You may have trouble getting to him," she said. "There's all kinds of extra security. They're preparing a really big ceremony in the main hall, it looks like."

"We may have to interrupt it," Tamerlane replied.

12

Horns blared from either side of the cyclopean hall as Emperor Janus IV Rahkmanov seated himself in the largest chair—though the word "chair" was hardly adequate; it was more a throne than anything else—positioned at the middle of the massive table. On his left hand sat his wife, the Empress Lisbeth Salome, her dress exquisite in shimmering blue and green, her hair perfectly styled. Their four children, two boys and two girls ranged from ages seven to seventeen, sat at attention like little soldiers at a little table a short distance behind them, dressed in finery of their own. At the Emperor's right hand sat a tall, slender, dark-haired man with very tan skin, clad in a tight-fitting uniform of military appearance—save that it was white as snow. He held a long, spear-like scepter of silver in his left hand, its end resting on the marble floor beside him, and his dark eyes sparkled as he gazed out. Various men and women of the Ecclesiarchy, clad in exquisite robes of white inlaid with gold filigree and diamonds, were seated further along that side, while on the other, beyond the Empress, sat the heavy-set form of General Esteban Attila of Second Legion—"the Bold"— and his second, Colonel Ioan Iapetus—called "the

Unyielding." The hall before them was filled with hundreds of immaculately-dressed dignitaries—from Imperial bureaucrats to planetary governors—seated in rows of chairs that stretched to the rear of the sanctuary.

At the signal of the second blast of horns, the crowd quickly settled down to silence, and then the Emperor stood regally. His purple and gold robes hung in almost toga-fashion from his shoulders and arms, and golden jewelry sparkled on his fingers and arms. He gazed out over the crowd of well-dressed individuals from across the Imperium assembled in the hall and smiled benevolently.

"Before we begin," he said, "I have a bit of news that I insisted on announcing myself." His smile turned impish as he bent down and reached under the table, then straightened. In his right hand he held a shining golden object and, upon seeing it and realizing what it was, the crowd issued a collective gasp.

"The Sword of Baranak has been recovered," he told the audience. "Our greatest treasure belongs to the Empire once more!" He held it up, waved it about momentarily, and bowed slightly as the crowd greeted this news with a hearty round of applause.

When the crowd died down a bit, the Emperor seated himself and laid the sword across the marbled surface of the table before him. Then he turned formally to the man to his right. That man in turn looked to the man to *his* right, who stood and addressed the assembly.

"You have all of our thanks for that wonderful piece of news, sire," he said. Then he got to the gist of his own remarks. "I am High Priest Salid Donnan," he said, and while his speaking voice was soft, it boomed out via amplification across the vast chamber. "It is my honor to welcome all of you to the Church of the Reliquae, and to this great convocation, which shall henceforth be known as the Council of Ascanius."

There was a murmur of appreciation from the crowd.

"We are gathered here for two important reasons..." He hesitated, smiling faintly. "...And for a third that will become apparent once we are underway." A slight murmuring from the crowd as whispered speculation rippled throughout the hall. "First," he continued, "it is my duty and my honor, in the name of our great Emperor who has graced us all with his presence today, to introduce the new Ecclesiarch who he has chosen to step into the shoes of the late Wallin Zoric and lead this Holy Church, guiding us with reverence and faith into the future." He stretched a hand out toward the man in the military-style white uniform, seated between himself and the Emperor. "That man is Nikolai Barmakid."

The reaction was muted at first. Barmakid was not a priest and never had been; he had no connection to the Ecclesiarchy. He was a soldier. All that was known of him by the general public—and by the noble families gathered there—was that he had recently stepped down from his post as adjutant to General Nakamura of Legion I. Clearly, they reasoned now, it was so that he could accept this new assignment. And if the Emperor wanted him for that position, he must be the right choice. The applause picked up, echoing throughout the massive sanctuary.

Donnan seated himself and Barmakid stood, raising his right hand to the crowd in acknowledgement. The silver scepter was still clutched in his left. He bowed his head.

"Thank you, Father Donnan," he said as the applause died down, "and all of you." His dark eyes peered out at the crowd. "It is my very great honor to accept the appointment by our Emperor as your new Ecclesiarch."

A figure in black appeared beside the Emperor then, leaning in to whisper something in his ear. Janus IV nodded and stood, addressing the audience.

"The former colonel's scholarship and published works in religious philosophy are of course well-known across the realm," the Emperor said, much to the surprise of those in the audience who knew anything about religious philosophy and writings about it. Of course, the Emperor's staff had been hard at work for days, producing volumes of such scholarship to disseminate to libraries and media outlets across a thousand worlds, all bearing Barmakid's signature, and his degrees in theology and divine studies had all been successfully implanted—and back-dated—into the appropriate registries. Where two weeks ago his official accomplishments were confined to his service to First Legion, he now had a pedigree in theology second to no one in the Empire. "We are very fortunate that he has agreed to serve us in this new capacity, and the Empire will only be the richer, spiritually, for it.

Barmakid bowed low to the Emperor, who seated himself and motioned for the new Ecclesiarch to continue.

"Mine is not the only high office to have a new occupant," the man in white stated. He turned to the heavy-set soldier in the dark blue dress uniform seated to the left of the Empress. "General Attila is well known to everyone in this hall. His exploits and accomplishments on behalf of the Imperium throughout his illustrious career have rightfully earned him the nickname, "The Bold." Today I officially announce his accession to the position of Supreme Commander of the Empire's armed forces, succeeding the late General Hideo Nakamura—may his spirit be preserved forever by Those Who Remain."

As the new Ecclesiarch, Barmakid led the assembly in a quick word of prayer, while the other priests along the table traced various signs in the air before them. Then the Emperor rose and reached out, clasping hands with Attila, who nodded his head brusquely at his ruler.

"Our next order of business," Barmakid said when they were done, "concerns the wars we are currently fighting along three fronts. While primarily a military and political matter, the Holy Church has a role in those conflicts and therefore our position on them must be made known."

Barmakid strode out from behind the table and stood before it, addressing the massive crowd. "These wars were launched by the rival states that surround us, by selfish and small-minded leaders who look upon our realm with jealousy and envy. But it turns out that their militaries are as feeble as their governments are short-sighted. Their advances have been or are being repulsed on every frontier. We advance in every direction."

The crowd cheered, and Barmakid smiled broadly. He glanced back at the Emperor, who was nodding his approval.

"Furthermore," the man in white went on, "we anticipate that our own Empire will shortly be much increased in size, both in terms of territory and population, as well as resources, as those hostile powers fall by the wayside. It is not inconceivable that, before this standard year is done, the Anatolian Empire of the Emperor Janus IV Rahkmanov will stand as the only power of any significance in the human sector of this galaxy!"

They cheered louder.

"So let any who question the actions of our Emperor and his military staff in this precarious moment of our current campaign consider those facts before they speak out," he concluded. "Such voices of surrender and defeatism will not be tolerated—and it shall fall to the Church, and to the Holy Inquisition, to root out all opposition and expose it."

The cheers were mixed this time; some applauded louder, others not at all. Expressions ranged from enthusiasm to astonished disapproval.

Barmakid pressed on. "And that brings me to the final issue before us—and the one upon which the balance of this Council will focus, as we call upon the knowledge and guidance of our brothers and sisters in the Holy Church and the Inquisition."

The crowd refocused on Barmakid, listening intently to what he was saying now, as a wave of fear ran across the hall.

"All current laws in the Imperium will be rendered null and void at the conclusion of this Council," he announced. "The old constitution, treacherously forced upon the Emperor's great grandfather more than a century ago, will be abrogated at that point. A new set of laws—drawn up by the Emperor and the Holy Church, and ratified by this august body here today, will set this Empire upon a new course—a course of power and glory and honor."

The crowd was not at all happy about what they were hearing now.

"So—we are here to debate these changes, then?" asked a voice from the first row of the audience—a space reserved for the most powerful individuals in the Empire, aside from those at the table itself.

Barmakid gazed down and recognized Governor Rameses of Ahknaton. He smiled. "Oh, no, Governor—we are here to *inform* you of the changes. They have already been decided upon and are essentially in effect now."

Rameses gasped, turning to look back at the crowd arrayed behind him. From that crowd, murmurs were quickly growing into outright cries against what the new Ecclesiarch was saying.

Frowning, Barmakid motioned with his right hand and hundreds of soldiers in the white livery of the Church stepped out of the shadows, guns at the ready. If anything, this stirred the crowd up even more. Things were about to spiral beyond all control when a new voice called out across the chamber:

"Your Majesty—I have known you all your life," the voice said, carrying easily throughout the hall without amplification, "and I can only conclude that this man Barmakid has somehow beguiled you."

Everyone in the sanctuary looked from the Ecclesiarch to this new figure striding boldly in from a side entrance, a small group hurrying along with him. Collective gasps sounded as at least one of the other four was recognized: General Nakamura.

The Emperor stared at him, wide-eyed, but said nothing. The Ecclesiarch had no such problems speaking his mind. "Inquisitor," he called, "I do not believe you were invited to this event."

"It matters not," Stanishur replied, halting at the edge of the perimeter formed by the first row of seats. "The constitution guarantees the Inquisition a number of seats at any official convocation, and as ranking member of that institution, I certainly qualify for a seat. And I claim it."

"The constitution is void," Barmakid said. "Did you not hear me a moment ago? Or were you still busy sneaking in through the service entrance?"

"The constitution is not void, by your own admission, until the end of this Council," Stanishur fired back. "Until that time, I remain your humble Grand Inquisitor—with a seat at the table and a voice in any decisions." He glared at the four black-clad Inquisitors already seated at the table, and vaguely recognized them. "Certainly a more important voice than any of these wretched creatures you've unjustly promoted through the ranks, doubtlessly to rubber-stamp your decisions. For shame!"

The four clearly balked at this characterization but none could truly dispute it and none possessed the wherewithal to stand and challenge Grand Inquisitor Stanishur.

"You would no longer *be* Grand Inquisitor but for a technicality in the rules," Barmakid grumbled.

"Yet that technicality does exist, and thus I am still Grand Inquisitor."

Barmakid started to argue again when the Emperor seemed to suddenly wake and cried out, "For the sake of the gods, Stanishur—come up here, then."

The Inquisitor approached the table and bowed to the Emperor, then flashed the new Eccelsiarch a look of utter contempt.

"Who are these people who accompany you?" the Emperor asked, noticing the rest of the group for the first time.

Nakamura stepped into clearer view.

General Attila rose to his feet almost involuntarily. "You!" cried the man known as "the Bold"—hardly bold at all at this moment.

The Emperor gasped. "Nakamura? Hideo? But—I was told you were *dead*!"

The general smiled back at his ruler. "Perhaps, sire," he said. "Politically, if not physically." Flames danced across his fingertips. "But I'm feeling much better now."

13

Tamerlane followed the Inquisitor and the general out of the tunnel and through one last doorway. The next thing he knew, they were emerging into the grand hall itself, the main sanctuary of the Church of the Relique. A broad arc of seated dignitaries blocked off much of his view but, far ahead near the center of the chamber, he could see the Emperor and a host of other Church and political and military figures seated behind a table on a raised dais.

Tamerlane turned to Arani and reminded her of her first part of their plan. She nodded and accessed the local Aether network, connecting directly to every Special Forces sniper in the building. Most of them, she knew, would be safely hidden in balconies like the one she'd originally been assigned to. A few others would be scattered out, here and there, in whatever spots seemed particularly advantageous.

"Major Arani to cover squad," she called. "I am entering the sanctuary alongside General Nakamura, Colonel Tamerlane, the Grand Inquisitor and two of his assistants. Do not fire. Repeat—*do not fire.*"

At first no one argued. Then one of the men from a different unit called back, "Major—I don't see any of their names on the approved list. Are you certain—"

"Think about who they are, soldier," Arani sent back angrily. "Do you want to be the man who goes down in history for assassinating our top general or the Grand Inquisitor? Do you suppose the Inquisition would take it kindly if any one of us pulled the trigger on their leader?"

After that, no one bothered to argue. The Ecclesiarchy troops, overhearing, reacted about the same way—they had started in toward the interlopers but now they moved back, nervous and unsure of what to do or how to react.

The party moved out into the crowd along one radial aisle, drawing closer and closer to the dais and the Emperor. For a few moments no one took notice of them. Then Stanishur approached near enough to see who the new Ecclesiarch was, and to hear his words. His head nearly exploded in fury. Hurrying forward, he shouted up at Barmakid and that man in turn shouted at him.

Arani looked at the others, forlorn. "There went the element of surprise," she lamented.

"It wasn't going to last long, anyway," Tamerlane replied.

"Barmakid!" Nakamura cursed. "A heretic! A cultist! As head of our Church! It defies logic—defies reason!"

"Something very, very strange is most definitely going on," Tamerlane said by way of agreement. "There's no other way to go from accused cultist, stripped of your titles and position, to leader of the Holy Church, in only a few weeks."

The Emperor was speaking to Nakamura now, and in response the general followed the Inquisitor up onto the dais. For his part, Barmakid looked ready to chew metal and spit nails.

"Majesty," the Ecclesiarch said with a bow, "I must object to these two—*trespassers*—being allowed onto this panel."

"Trespassers?" The Emperor scoffed. "These men are two of my oldest and most trusted advisors."

Barmakid reddened but didn't reply.

Instead of taking a seat, Stanishur stood before the table and bowed again to the Emperor. "Majesty," he began, "I can only imagine that you are not fully aware of the changes this...*man*...and his cronies in the Church have proposed."

"You know nothing," Barmakid shouted. "You cannot comprehend what we are accomplishing here today."

"Colonel Barmakid," Stanishur snapped, evoking the man's ire by using his old military title rather than his new Church one, "I was not aware you were such a religious and legal scholar." He nodded toward the other members of the Inquisition—all much younger—seated along the far side of the table. "Perhaps my colleagues in the Holy Inquisition have read some things I have not had the opportunity to see yet."

"Well, I—"

"But," he went on, "I *did* know *this* about you. I did know you were captured recently by the military on Trezibond, leading a cult that worshipped Vorthan."

The Emperor looked from Stanishur to Barmakid, his face reflecting surprise and confusion.

Barmakid was already on his feet; now he nearly came over the table at the Inquisitor. "*Lies!*" he cried. "How *dare* you?"

"We have a witness present," Stanishur stated, his dark eyes flashing from the Ecclesiarch to the Emperor.

Barmakid recoiled slightly, then seemed to recover. "If you mean the general here, I know for a fact that he witnessed no such thing. He was merely told about it—told *lies* about it, by my enemies. Or perhaps one of his over-zealous underlings saw someone who *resembled* me, or who wore a similar uniform, and reported this to the general erroneously."

Stanishur scoffed at this. Then he motioned toward the audience. "Major—if you would come forward?"

Major Niobe Arani emerged from the crowd and tentatively approached the dais.

Barmakid stared down at her. There was curiosity in his eyes at first, then confusion, then something like fear. He opened his mouth, seemed to think better of it, and closed it again. He gestured.

Tamerlane, standing a few feet behind Arani, noticed the slight hand movement Barmakid made. He leapt forward, tackling her and driving her down. A heartbeat later, a blast of energy seared down from one of the balconies and passed through the space Arani had been filling.

Reacting to this, the Inquisitor leapt to his feet and gestured with both hands. A cloud began to form rapidly a few meters over their heads, dark and almost entirely opaque, across most of the center of the hall. Another blast came sizzling down but this one missed by a wider margin.

"What is this?" the Emperor demanded, on his feet and furious. "By all the gods! *Stop shooting!*"

"Hold your fire," Nakamura shouted to the Special Forces troopers hidden in various spots around the walls of the old facility, while sending the same message over the Aether. "That's enough!"

Another shot blasted down, and another. Whoever was shooting now, they clearly felt no compunction to obey orders—or, at least, not Nakamura's.

Tamerlane, busy trying to get Arani to safety, looked up as a clanking sound echoed from the direction of the Emperor. There, emerging from behind the dais, came seven huge figures, gleaming in crystal armor of various colors. Their boots shook the ground as they moved, and they quickly took up protective positions around the Emperor, each gazing upward, searching for the source of the shots, attempting to see past or through Stanishur's conjured cloud.

"Get these people out of here—in an orderly fashion," Tamerlane commanded to the Ecclesiarchy soldiers all around. The white-clad warrior-priests looked from him to each other, uncertain whether or not to obey him. Meanwhile, the crowd was disintegrating on its own, most of the dignitaries in terror at the shooting. They were surging toward the exits, threatening to trample one another. "*Now*!" Tamerlane shouted. "There's no time for you to consult the gods about it first! *Get them out!*"

Another shot blasted down, this one striking the first row of seats—now empty—and vaporizing several chairs.

Tamerlane quickly ran through the Aether links of each of the snipers in his virtual vision and couldn't find any that hadn't acknowledged the order and backed off. He shook his head when the general looked to him for that information.

"It's not anyone under our control, Majesty," Nakamura in turn reported to the Emperor. "It's a renegade—an assassin—off the net. Working with Barmakid, I'd imagine."

The Emperor looked at Barmakid. "Ecclesiarch," he called, "what is happening here? Is what these people say about you true?"

Barmakid staggered back a step, astonishment etched on his face. "Majesty," he stammered, "I have only done what you wished—what you *ordered!*"

The Emperor stared back at him for a long moment, silent. The figure in black that had whispered to him before reemerged from behind the throne and again spoke in entirely inaudible tones to him. A short distance away, still protecting Arani, Tamerlane looked on and frowned; he could see someone conversing with the Emperor but his vision was somehow blurry at that spot; he couldn't quite make out who it was.

The Emperor nodded then and straightened. "Lies about your Emperor represent the most vile form of blasphemy!"

he shouted, looking directly at Barmakid. "I have been deceived! Guards!"

Two of the elite, crystal-clad Emperor's Guards—Tamerlane recognized them instantly as Rashid in garnet and Abdul in sapphire—surged forward, reaching out to attempt to seize Barmakid. The Ecclesiarch moved quickly, though, leaping down from the dais and avoiding the grasping armored hands.

"Majesty—wait," he called to the Emperor as the sapphire Guard jumped from the dais after him with a remarkable agility and grace. "It's not too late—this situation can still be salvaged!"

Osman, the Emperor's Guardsman in emerald, suddenly rocketed off the ground and into the air, the antigrav flight pack that was incorporated into his armor sprouting a pair of broad repulsor wings that carried him up through Stanishur's smoke cover and beyond it. He had a lock on the source of the fire and he shot like a missile towards it, soaring in seconds up above one of the lower balconies and then dropping heavily onto its ledge. The soldier in black who had until a moment earlier held that position scrambled backward, his sniper rifle clattering to the floor. Osman leaned forward, grasped the man by the collar, and flung him over his shoulder, over the balcony rail, and out over the main hall. He tumbled like a rag doll for two long seconds before impacting the marble floor with a thud.

Nakamura saw the sniper hit the floor and cursed. "So much for interrogating him."

Barmakid took heart at this. He stood before the Emperor's table, Stanishur lurking just to his right like some cobra about to strike. "Terrorists!" he called to the Emperor. "Our Council was disrupted by terrorists! But the heroic Guard defeated them!" He turned to Stanishur, leering. "A shame the High Inquisitor and General Nakamura, among others, were killed before the terrorists could be stopped."

The Emperor only stood there, seemingly deep in thought—or else having gone utterly blank. "I—I—don't—" he stammered, his eyes moving from Nakamura to Barmakid to Stanishur. "I don't know—"

The figure in black leaned in again, whispering.

Nakamura meanwhile was shocked by what he was seeing and hearing. "Sire—you don't mean you're in league with this foolishness? You cannot mean Barmakid was operating under your orders?" He looked to Tamerlane, faltering; the thought of the Emperor he had served for years—served since that man was a child—being somehow responsible for this insanity... It was almost more than he could bear.

"Colonel Tamerlane!" came a cry from the rear of the chamber, and Tamerlane turned back at the booming bass voice. Pushing their way through the crowd was Colonel Arnem Agrippa and his Golden Phalanx, all suited up in their fine metal plate armor and brandishing heavy blast rifles. They carried their helmets under their arms.

Tamerlane met them a short distance from the dais and saluted. "Glad to have you here, Colonel," he said. "Things are getting rather tense."

"We were on our way to assist you," the big, blond man reported. "I felt guilty about my role in turning you in to the Church—particularly after a few back-channel reports of a...shall we say, *peculiar* nature... reached me along the way." He nodded toward the dais, where the Emperor, Nakamura, and Barmakid were shouting at one another. "What I've seen and heard since our arrival—it's all being transmitted over the Aether, you know—has only reaffirmed my decision." He moved in closer. "I'm sorry I doubted you, Ezekial. I should have known better." He extended a massive hand.

"I appreciate that," Tamerlane replied, clasping the hand. "Now—stand by, because I have no idea how this will develop next."

On the dais, the Emperor turned away from the argument with the general and the Ecclesiarch to speak again with the man in black—the man no one present could quite look upon, or mentally acknowledge was even there. That strange figure issued more instructions to the Emperor, now in a hissed tone that was almost audible to the others nearby. This time Janus turned to face the man and actually said something back. The conversation grew heated, and at last the Emperor shouted, "I am in command here. Me! I will decide what happens—no one else!"

The figure in black hesitated, seeming to grow larger—to expand somehow, beyond mortal bounds—but then it shrank back, bowed its head, and faded into the background again. The Emperor turned toward the others and shouted for his Guard. He started to issue a new order but before he could say anything intelligible he choked and leaned against the table, coughing violently. Nakamura hurried to his side, instinctively coming to his assistance. Tamerlane left Agrippa and his men where they stood and hurried up to join Nakamura at the dais, now that the crowd was being ushered out of the sanctuary in an orderly manner. Stanishur and his two trusted acolytes, as well as Major Arani, all drew nearer as well. The eleven other individuals, men and women of the Ecclesiarchy, Inquisition and Imperial bureaucracy, were on their feet, sticking close to the Emperor but clearly wishing they could be somewhere—*anywhere*—else.

The Emperor coughed again, even more violently, then raised his head and glared out. He screamed in wordless rage and fury, a sound no one had ever heard him make before. It scarcely sounded human.

The Empress rushed to him, the others moving aside for her as they realized who she was. The four children crowded close by, the younger ones crying. Nakamura saw them and ordered, "Get the royal family to safety," but no one responded to his order. Everyone was staring in shock at the Emperor. Nakamura turned back and looked.

The Emperor's eyes were burning bright red, glowing like hot coals, with rivulets of crimson energy trailing from them like streams of blood.

Before anyone could react further, Janus shouted to the nearest of his Guard, the one in the ruby armor, "Zeyid! Kill them!" His voice was hoarse and raw but it carried a more commanding force than anyone had ever heard from him before.

Zeyid stood there, his massive quad-rifle held at the ready, his armor sparkling crimson; he had been conditioned from birth to obey the Emperor without question or hesitation, but of course he required specific orders first. Being told simply to "Kill them"—that was an order he could not carry out, for his logical mind demanded to know the specific target being selected among this crowd of officers, soldiers and dignitaries.

And so Zeyid of the Emperor's Guard did something his kind rarely, if ever, did: He spoke. And in doing so, he did something no Guardsman had ever done: He questioned his Emperor.

"Kill who, sire?"

"All of them," Emperor Janus IV shouted, his voice now warped almost beyond recognition. He reached down and grasped the golden sword that lay before him, raised it overhead, and screeched. "Everyone! *Kill them all!*"

The Guardsman hesitated, processing this, considering it carefully. Then he nodded his gleaming helmet once and raised his gun.

14

The Guardsman was raising his quad-rifle—though, to do what, none would ever know— when Agrippa and his Golden Phalanx came charging up the aisle.

"Belay that order," General Nakamura shouted. "Stand down, Guardsman. That's an order!"

Zeyid hesitated again, looking from the general to the Emperor.

"Your master is not well—surely you can see that," Tamerlane added forcefully. "Stand down!"

The Guardsman in emerald tromped over, the sapphire one just behind him. None of them spoke—at least, not in a way that anyone else could overhear—but clearly a conversation was happening, likely over a private Aether link.

Zeyid in his red addressed Nakamura then, or at least started to. "General," he said, "I concur that the Emperor is—"

"I gave you an order!" Janus screamed, and blood flew from his mouth as he did so. His next words were unintelligible as his voice dissolved into a horrific gurgling sound. Blood spilled out of his mouth onto the marble-faced table.

Looking on in horror, the Empress screamed.

No one was looking at the Guardsmen now, and so no one saw their own transformations begin. They, too, screamed and gurgled, but their helmets blocked off the sight and much of the sound of what was happening to them for the moment. Tamerlane did, however, see them raising their guns and leveling them at the last of the retreating crowd and at the individuals on the dais. He shouted a desperate warning and grabbed Nakamura, who was standing beside him, flinging him down.

The guns blazed to life, energy bolts slicing into the crowd.

Agrippa and his men saw what was happening and, though it violated every principle they held dear, they in turn opened fire with their heavy blast rifles on the Emperor's Guard.

The result wasn't quite what Agrippa had hoped for: The impact of the Phalanx's superheated-plasma shots didn't penetrate the hyper-dense crystal armor of the Guardsmen but it did at least deflect their aim, substantially reducing the number of casualties caused by the first barrage.

Furious, almost mindless, bellowing their inhuman rage, the seven Guardsmen rushed toward the Phalanx troops. Their first shots took down two of Agrippa's warriors in a combined hail of particle-beam and depleted-uranium slug fire before the crystal-clad men seemed to lose interest in their guns, dropped them or flung them aside, and simply charged. They smashed their massive bodies into the metal-armored Phalanx soldiers and drove the nearest ones down to the hard marble floor. Red and green and blue crystal fists rose and fell, crumpling metal plate and metal helmets. The Guardsmen—or whatever they had become now—howled like banshees as they fought, all military training gone, now mindlessly seeking nothing but blood and death.

274

From atop the dais, Nakamura looked on in horror. "Sire," he cried, "call them off! Something is wrong—they are out of control!" He moved around to where he could see the Emperor, and started once more to implore his master to listen to reason—at which point he actually saw Janus's face, and abandoned any hope of success.

The Emperor's face was splitting down the middle, blood fountaining out. Hands that were no longer human but clawed monstrosities reached up and tore away the remaining flesh.

From that moment, events played out very rapidly. The Emperor's body rose up, inflating, seemingly growing exponentially in mass even as it metamorphosized into a hideous, inhuman shape. The head warped and distended until it was more snake than man, with rows of jagged fangs dripping venom. The body now grew luminous scales and twisted into a long, narrow form that towered over the table and the dais.

"By all of Those That Remain," Stanishur gasped. "The Emperor is possessed!" He held up his hands and traced signs of protection against demonic forces in the air.

General Attila had leapt up from the table when the transformation began. Now, his face twisted with horror, he drew his pistol and charged at the thing that had been the Emperor. The massive creature spun about, raking him with razor-sharp claws before flinging his body into the air. Attila landed with a crash on the top of the table.

The Emperor-demon cast its terrifying gaze about, then seemed to notice the golden sword it still clutched tightly in one of its own gnarled fists. It stared down at the weapon, snarling, as if the sword were burning it. Casually it flung the golden weapon away, to land with a clatter some distance across the hall.

"Demons!" cried someone from behind Tamerlane, pointing. "The Guard—they are demons!"

Tamerlane followed the sound and saw. Horror washed over him.

In the midst of their battle with the Golden Phalanx, the members of the Emperor's Guard were also growing, their crystal armor cracking and falling away as the bodies inside them morphed and expanded. Clawed talons raked at Agrippa's men as demonic fire blasted out from monstrously deformed mouths, scorching the soldiers inside their suits.

"Help them!" Tamerlane shouted to the white-clad Ecclesiarchy soldiers, most of whom were simply standing about, transfixed by what they were seeing. He pointed to the Phalanx, which was being pummeled nearly to death; Agrippa himself had his ceremonial sword out, slashing to little avail at the talons that clawed at him. "Go!"

The warrior-priests ignored him. They appeared determined not to live up to the first half of that description. Furious, Tamerlane grabbed the nearest one by the collar and pointed him at the demonic creature that had been the Emperor. "*This* is what you've been following!" he shouted into the man's face. "Do you understand that now? You have to act! You have to help!"

The man Tamerlane was holding tore himself free and ran. This broke the dam and numerous of his brothers and sisters did likewise, some of them actually trampling dignitaries in their haste to escape. From there, anarchy broke out. Others of the Ecclesiarchy—the few still left—chanted some few feeble words of prayer for a few seconds before, staring aghast up at the Emperor, they, too, lost their nerve and fled.

Cursing the priests as they ran away, Tamerlane snatched up a dropped blast-rifle. He opened fire on the Emperor's Guardsmen, if they could even be called by that name any longer, but his best efforts seemed hardly noticed by the monsters that now existed where moments earlier had stood the finest warriors in the Empire. Only one returned fire, unleashing a deafening, blood-curdling shriek as it did so. Had the blasts been fired by a Guardsman in full possession of his faculties, Tamerlane would have been a dead man that instant. Instead, fired by a demonic entity whose brain was filled only with the most basic, brutal urges, the shots mostly missed; one struck Tamerlane's hip and deflected away harmlessly, thanks to the smartcloth of his uniform, while another struck his boot and sent him stumbling down.

By the time he had struggled back to his feet amidst the growing pile of rubble that covered much of the marble floor, the demon that had shot at him had lost interest and had returned to battling Agrippa's Phalanx. Frustrated, unable to help, he realized then that he'd forgotten the general. He whirled about to look for him.

What he saw instead was the gigantic demon looming over everything.

The Emperor's transformation must now have been complete, for the human form was gone entirely, replaced by a gigantic snake-demon that lashed out with incongruous, almost comically stubby arms to slash those around it to shreds. Three of the Inquisition men lay in pools of blood, along with two of the Ecclesiarchy officials. Hanging motionless on his back, draped over the table, was the broken body of General Attila. Nakamura was staggering back, having been struck a glancing blow by one of the claws. Of Barmakid and Colonel Iapetus, there was now no sign whatsoever.

The Empress had vanished from sight during the demon's first onslaught, but now her head appeared over the table— apparently she'd been trapped under some rubble momentarily. Tamerlane saw her and raced in her direction, leaping onto the dais, even as she looked about frantically and called for her children.

The eldest child—the Archduke—got to her first. A strapping young man of seventeen standard years, Augustin Rahkmanov was heir to the throne of the Empire. He had been trained from birth in all forms of martial arts and the effective use of modern and ancient weapons.

All of that training availed him naught.

He moved past his mother and drew his ceremonial energy-sword, brandishing it at the demon, tears streaking his cheeks. The demon swiped at him with a razor-clawed arm and practically eviscerated him. Screaming, the Empress bent over him—and the demon lashed out with its spiked tail, impaling her where she stood.

Tamerlane arrived an instant too late to help either of them. He barely dodged in time to avoid the tail's backswing.

Cursing, he snatched up the Archduke's energy sword and leapt off the rear of the dais, searching for the other Imperial child—the daughter, Marens. Tamerlane was determined to save her, at least—to get her out of this slaughterhouse before it was too late. She was, after all, the only member of the royal family left now.

There was no sign of her. Tamerlane ran from one end of the dais to the other, avoiding the thrashing tail of the massive demon while calling the girl's name, to no avail.

"Ezekial!"

It was Nakamura's voice. Tamerlane remembered then that the general had been injured. He leapt back onto the dais and spotted Nakamura lying to one side; hurrying over, he helped him up.

"I'm alright," the general reassured him, quickly inspecting the three bloody gouges in his side. The smartcloth uniform he wore had already acted to seal up the wounds and stop the bleeding. They moved around the end of the table farthest from the demon and crouched down, out of range—for the moment—of the thrashing, bellowing demon.

"I couldn't find the little girl," Tamerlane spat. "She's gone. The rest of them are dead, but—"

"We will *all* be dead if we don't end this quickly," Nakamura said, the strength coming back into his voice. "You know what we have to do."

The colonel hesitated. "Sir— do we dare? It's still the Emperor—"

Nakamura shook his head sadly. "I don't believe it has been the Emperor for some time. Not since we brought it back from the Below."

Tamerlane's expression revealed his shock and disgust. "We brought it out," he breathed. "Yes."

"And now we send it back."

Tamerlane met Nakamura's eyes and he nodded.

Together they stood. The demon that had once been the Emperor of Mankind saw them and surged forward, jaws opening and talons reaching.

Nakamura and Tamerlane raised their arms, palms open, toward it. Flames began to flicker across their fingertips.

Something smashed heavily into their backs, knocking them forward. The sword flew from Tamerlane's hand.

Tamerlane tumbled to a halt and sat up, his vision a blur. Nearby, the general was on his hands and knees, head down, clearly disoriented.

A blood-curdling roar hit them then with what felt like actual, physical force. The colonel looked up—directly into the sharklike face of a demon. Shards of sapphire armor were still falling away from his expanding, glistening, blood-covered body.

"Abdul," Tamerlane whispered, knowing this creature was no longer the Guardsman known as Abdul in any conceivable fashion.

The creature roared again. Tamerlane shouted for the general to snap out of it—to move! The older man didn't respond. He was still hunched forward, insensate.

Another creature appeared next to the first one. Parts of its body were still covered in the emerald armor of Osman.

It opened its jagged maw and that horrific, deadly orifice hovered over Tamerlane.

There was nowhere to run, no chance of escape. Frantically, he reached for his gun. It was gone; he saw it where it lay on the floor a distance away. The sword he'd picked up a few moments earlier was long gone, lost in the confusion.

"General!" he called again.

The fang-filled maw descended.

15

Barmakid raced through the carnage, heading for a hidden tunnel that he knew would get him out of the church. He cursed violently as he ran; everything had been going so well, and then in an instant everything had fallen apart.

He had been shocked when representatives of the Imperial government had come to him in his cell, after his capture by the Arani woman, and released him, bringing him not to humiliating trial—or rather, torture—before the Inquisition but instead to a private audience with the Emperor himself, along with General Attila and...someone else. He could never recall precisely who the third person had been.

At any rate, they had offered him the position of Ecclesiarch, head of the Holy Church of Those Who Remain. When he had protested that he had no experience in religious affairs, the Emperor had pointed out two things: Barmakid was a high priest of the cult of Vorthan, and being Ecclesiarch was probably preferable to being a prisoner of the Inquisition. Barmakid could not refute either of these statements. He accepted the offer on the spot.

He did, however, manage to ask why His Majesty would want an admitted Vorthan cultist as Ecclesiarch. The

Emperor's response had been enigmatic: "Change is coming, Nikolai," he had said, "and an intimate knowledge of the teachings of the god of toil and fire would not be out of place in the realm to come."

And so Nikloai Barmakid had been transformed from disgraced former soldier to honored religious leader. He had called for the Council at Ascanius at the Emperor's command, and had begun to supervise the rewriting of the Empire's laws.

And then Nakamura and Tamerlane had shown up, after everything Barmakid had done to ensure their deaths. And then all Hell had broken loose—quite literally.

Demons? Monsters of the Below? That was something Barmakid had known *nothing* about. He was as shocked as anyone else by that little development.

In any case, the jig was up, the Empire was surely doomed, and it was now, in Barmakid's view, every man for himself.

He rounded a corner and came up short, nearly plowing into a figure in black that loomed just ahead, blocking the entrance to the escape tunnel. His first thought was that it must be the strange figure he'd seen lurking in the Emperor's presence. At closer inspection, though, he realized he knew exactly who it was.

"Colonel Iapetus! Well. Very glad to encounter you here." He smoothed out his blood-splattered white uniform and drew himself up to full height. "I need an escort to see me safely out of the church."

Iapetus simply gazed at him, almost clinically—or the way someone might study a bug.

"Colonel?" Barmakid repeated.

Iapetus frowned. Then he stepped forward. He moved very quickly, with great precision. His hands grasped Barmakid by the neck and, in a compact but powerful move, took the man off his feet. Then he leaned in close.

"So," he hissed. "You're a *cultist*. A stinking *Vorthan* cultist."

Barmakid's eyes widened. He was choking, but he managed to gasp, "No—*no!* They made those things up... to discredit me..."

"A *lying*, stinking cultist." Iapetus snorted his derision. "Nakamura, on the other hand, couldn't lie if his life depended on it. Certainly not to the Emperor. Tamerlane either." He shook his head. "I don't like either of them. Not at all. But I respect them."

"No," Barmakid gasped. "No—"

"You, on the other hand..."

Iapetus removed his right hand from the man's throat, then reached up and gouged out first one eye, then the other. Barmakid wailed in agony and thrashed wildly. Iapetus released his grip and Barmakid collapsed to the floor, his head making a sickening thud as it hit the cold marble.

Iapetus stood over him and surveyed his handiwork thus far. He nodded to himself. And then he got down to business.

16

I t was an absolute madhouse. An insane asylum.

As Planetary Governor Amon Rameses of Ahknaton came to his senses again, his ears were assaulted by a cacophony of sound from all around: energy weapons discharge, crashes and collisions, explosions, and screams. Above all else, screams.

He lay in darkness, and at first felt a shock of fear as he thought he'd gone blind. Then he reached up and felt a slab of wood that lay over him, blocking out the light. His eyes slowly adjusted and he could see the bulk of it resting on a massive chunk of masonry to his right, preventing it from crushing him.

Using all his strength, he was able to shove enough of the wood panel aside—splinters jabbing his fingers—to make an open space through which he could crawl. He pulled himself up and out, climbed to his feet—and saw that he was right. It was a madhouse. It was hell itself—complete with demons.

Fortunately for him, those demons all seemed occupied battling a small battalion of metal-armored soldiers that he quickly recognized as Agrippa's Golden Phalanx. "Well," he muttered to himself as he brushed off his elaborate

COLOR COLOR suit, "that's as much as could be hoped for. If the Kings of Oblivion can't beat these creatures, surely no one can, and we're all dead."

And that made for the perfect justification in Rameses' mind for him to flee.

Picking his way over and around the wreckage, even as new pieces smashed down around him, he headed for the nearest exit—not the main one, part of which was now blocked by debris and the rest of which was still jammed with people trying to get out, but a side tunnel he spotted as he frantically searched for just such an alternate route.

As he moved toward it, he saw a man in black entering it far ahead. His first thought was of the strange figure who had lurked behind the Emperor at the start of the Council. But, no; that man—if man he was—had been odd, almost ephemeral, as though he were only partly there and partly somewhere else. The figure who had jogged into the tunnel was a soldier, wearing a type of black uniform he recognized now and remembered all too well.

The fanatics of Legion II. The soldiers of Colonel Ioan Iapetus—the man known throughout the Empire as "The Unyielding." The man who had humiliated Rameses in his own palace.

Rameses scowled in distaste as, negotiating a particularly hazardous set of obstacles that filled his path, he thought back to the incident on Ahknaton.

And now here was one of those soldiers—perhaps even Iapetus himself—fleeing the scene of battle.

The chance to embarrass Iapetus filled Rameses with a renewed enthusiasm and energy. He practically leapt the last few piles of debris along with the injured and the dead—he scarcely took notice of them at all, in his sudden determination to confront his quarry—and rounded the corner into the tunnel.

The man in black nearly ran into him coming back the other way.

Rameses stopped short and stared into the face of the hated Iapetus himself. Flustered, he couldn't speak for a moment.

Iapetus sized him up. "Going somewhere, Governor?" he asked, contempt obvious on his face.

Rameses felt anger and resentment—along with disappointment—flooding through him. Normally he would have refrained from doing anything to antagonize this notoriously ruthless killer. But these were hardly normal times, and he couldn't help himself.

"I was following you," he blurted. "I saw you leaving."

"Ah," Iapetus replied, a slight smile forming at one corner of his mouth. "No. I wasn't leaving. I simply had an errand to see to."

"What?" Rameses felt wrong-footed. "An errand?"

Then the governor spotted something lying on the floor of the tunnel a short distance ahead. It looked like a body, and—was that *blood* pooling under it?

Rameses started forward, seeking to go past the man in black and investigate further.

Iapetus held up a hand and stopped him. "Don't believe you want to go that way, Governor," he said. "Nothing you need to see there. Or get involved in."

Rameses glared at the man, and at the hand that held him back. "How dare you?"

"Let me call some men over to see you to safety," Iapetus continued, ignoring the hostility that practically radiated from Rameses.

"I—I'm not seeking safety," the governor asserted, his voice growing louder and more strident. "I was simply wondering what you were doing." He attempted to push past the colonel. "If you've hurt someone—"

"Oh, I've definitely done that," Iapetus replied. He lowered his arm and shrugged. "Fine. If you're determined to get into it, then go ahead. I have work to do—" He nodded back toward the great hall. "—out there."

WIth that, Iapetus strode away, never looking back. Rameses watched him go, wishing he had a gun and the nerve to shoot the man down. Then he turned and made his way slowly into the tunnel, his eyes locked on the crumpled shape of the body that lay there on the tiles. Reaching it, he knelt down and rolled it over.

There was just enough of the face left to identify it. Barmakid. The Ecclesiarch. The *cultist*, if Nakamura and his friends were to be believed. The traitor to mankind.

Rameses took all this in and cursed. Iapetus had killed the one person no one would blame him for killing. In fact, he'd probably be hailed as a hero, if all was as it now appeared.

But the way he'd killed Barmakid...

Rameses shuddered.

Iapetus was an animal. A thug. A barbarian.

And, he swore to himself as he made his way down the remainder of the tunnel and toward safety, a day of reckoning between them was coming. Surely it was. And *soon*.

17

grippa stood on legs grown somewhat shaky from only a few minutes' combat with the demonic Guardsmen. Blood trailed down his face and his right arm from numerous cuts and gouges. His blast pistol wasn't working, either because he'd already depleted the battery or because he'd fired it so many times in quick succession that it was overheated. Angrily he reholstered it and cast his gaze about for another weapon.

And he saw one.

He started toward the gleaming shape that lay on the floor nearby, and only as he moved to reach for it did his mind fully register exactly what he was seeing. It lay where the mindless creature that had been the Emperor had flung it in its rage.

A demon leapt before him, interposing itself between him and the weapon. He ducked and rolled, the razor-like claws just missing over his head. He continued his roll between the creature's legs, coming out behind it. Like a coiled spring released, he dove for the weapon and his fingers closed on its grip just as the demon whirled around to attack again. He sprang to his feet and raised it up before him, brandishing it at the hideous demon. A bright, pure light shone from its gleaming surfaces.

He held the Sword of Baranak.

The demon fell back, hissing and growling, raising a clawed hand to block the light. Agrippa wasted no time; he attacked, swinging the blade mercilessly. It sliced into the demon and sickly-smelling green ichor sprayed out. Agrippa looked down at the sword in his hand and smiled. *This isn't so bad a weapon at all,* he realized. *If only it could be mine on a permanent basis..!*

The demon charged him again, crouching, springing, coming in low. Agrippa met it with a roundhouse swing that lopped its head clean off its shoulders. The grotesque, larger-than-human snake-head bounced and rolled across the fine marble floor, leaving a trail of blood in its wake—blood that sizzled like acid. The body, meanwhile, collapsed and began to spontaneously combust.

Agrippa stared down at the burning demon's body and a sense of accomplishment swept over him. *So,* he thought. *We can kill them. Or, at least,* he amended, raising the golden sword in his right hand and inspecting it, *we can if we have something like* this.

He started to dive back into the scrum of combat that was happening behind him. It consisted of the rest of the Emperor's Guard—now in their demonic forms—battling the surviving members of his Phalanx. Before he could move, however, he noticed out of the corner of his eye the predicament General Nakamura and Colonel Tamerlane had found themselves in: they were injured or at least dazed, and two of the demons were closing in on them, about to kill them. The one closest to the general was bending over him even now, grotesque mouth open wide, about to devour him or at the very least bite off his head.

With a cry, Agrippa crossed the space between them in a series of powerful bounds, the golden sword drawn back. As he reached the general and the demon, he brought the blade around with all his might. A weapon that had once belonged to the mightiest of the gods— Baranak, god of battle and lord of the Golden City—it still possessed unearthly power. It sliced into the demon and cleaved the creature in half.

Nakamura and Tamerlane had recovered sufficiently by then that they both made it to their feet again, and both fired their blast pistols at the other demon attacking them. The barrage caused the beast to recoil momentarily, but when they paused, it surged forward again—directly onto the blade Agrippa held out, point-first. Wailing, screaming in a tongue rarely heard on our plane of reality, the demon burst into flames and collapsed into a blazing heap.

Tamerlane grinned at Agrippa and Nakamura gripped him by the shoulder, nodding. The tide seemed to be turning.

Then came a bellow that shook the very foundations of the Church of the Reliquae.

All three men looked up and saw that the demon that had been the Emperor had now grown so vast and bloated that its head actually reached up inside the dome itself, while its arms had extended to many meters long and were now flinging about, smashing into the walls and sending chunks of masonry raining down to impact the floor with deafening force. Again it bellowed, the sound like a heavy freighter ship lifting off from a spaceport. In response, the surviving Emperor's Guard demons bounded across the wreckage of the sanctuary to gather at the gargantuan monster's feet. They turned and faced outward, howling their wordless rage.

"What are they doing?" Tamerlane croaked, his mouth filled with dust and smoke.

"Nothing good," Nakamura replied, as Agrippa looked on in silent astonishment.

The demonic creature thrashed hard to its left, its bulk smashing into the walls of the cathedral. The ground shook and more chunks of masonry fell, exploding like bombs as they hit all around the humans. The dome high above cracked . The demon reared back and struck the walls again, even harder, and this time the dome collapsed.

The three officers dove for cover, scrambling beneath the table as bricks and marble plates smashed to the floor all about.

"It wants out, I think," Tamerlane said.

"I don't know if this sword will stop it," said Agrippa, holding the golden blade up before him. "It's grown so vast…"

"We have another weapon," Nakamura stated. He motioned to Tamerlane, who nodded. Together the two men clambered back out from under the table as the deadly hail abated momentarily. Agrippa, curious, followed them.

"Colonel," Nakamura called, facing Agrippa, "if you would be so kind as to attract its attention…?"

"Sir." Agrippa saluted crisply, then bounded toward the thing's leg. A Guardsman demon bellowed madly and charged out to meet him, but the blond man hacked it down where it stood. Then he drew back the blade and plunged it into the Emperor-demon's leg.

The mighty beast unleashed a deafening roar. It spun around, wrenching the sword from Agrippa's grasp. It bent down, one savage claw reaching for him.

"Now!" cried Nakamura.

Tamerlane stepped up beside his general and together they raised their arms, hands open and palms facing outward. The Power of the Above filled them, transforming as it passed through their bodies, becoming the antithesis of the demonic flame.

The holy fire flooded out, engulfing everything.

BOOK FOUR
THE TAIKO

1

The golden Sword of Baranak lay on the long marble table where Agrippa had set it when the battle was done, amid chunks of stone and plaster and splatters of blood—all reminders of the nightmare they had just passed through, and out the other side. Some of them, at least.

The holy fire unleashed by Nakamura and Tamerlane had washed over the monstrous demon and dissolved it like a sand castle struck by a tidal wave. Its bones—if bones ever supported its gelatinous bulk—had dissolved within seconds, leaving only bubbling, stinking, putrid gobs of jelly that sizzled for an hour or more after the battle was over. Flames danced here and there, the thing's mass continuously reducing as it burned, melting away—or perhaps returning from whence it had come.

Within minutes, all that had remained of the behemoth was a black smear across seemingly an acre of the marble tile.

Now Tamerlane stood near that awful stain, leaning over the sword and the table that supported it. He gazed down at it in wonder. It seemed to radiate power from every inch of its gleaming form. With the battle over and it's immediate expediency done, no one dared pick it up; it was a sword of kings, of emperors, of the gods themselves. And now all of those who might claim such titles were dead—dead or gone beyond the reach of Man.

The acrid smell of smoke and blood and other, more unspeakable things, still hung in the air. Tamerlane wrinkled his nose at it and scowled as he stood near the spot where, only a short time earlier, the Emperor had held court. Now that man—the unquestioned ruler of the Anatolian Empire—was dead, along with his wife and children. The thought of it all nearly staggered the colonel, and he could merely shake his head slowly as he gazed across the chamber at the destruction that had been wrought by the battle with the demons.

Possessed, Tamerlane thought, astonished. *The entire party that we rescued from the Below—the Emperor and the Guard—all of them possessed by demons.*

It's partly our fault, then, he concluded. *If we hadn't gone in after them... if we hadn't brought them back out from the depths of subspace, where we already knew evil entities dwelt...*

But such thoughts were meaningless. Of course they had gone into the Below in search of the Emperor. Of course they had brought him back out. They could scarcely have done otherwise.

And it was done. The only question they faced now was, *What next?* What was to become of the Anatolian Empire that Janus IV had until today ruled?

"This Empire is dead."

Tamerlane looked up, startled from his thoughts by so unfathomable a statement. "What?"

Planetary Governor Rameses had approached while Tamerlane was deep in thought and now stood before the broad table, hands on hips, face a mask of disapproval and disgust. The colonel straightened instinctively, while simultaneously taking the man's measure. At some point in the last few minutes he had traded his ceremonial Egyptian-style robes for an officer's uniform of the Empire. Tamerlane noticed, however, that the usual various Imperial insignia were missing from the lapels. An aide stood behind him, holding his crooked, red-and-gold-striped staff.

"It's all done," the ruler of Ahknaton said, turning from the table to glance at Tamerlane for a moment, then looking away again. "Finished."

This rankled Tamerlane more than he could have imagined it would have before it had been said aloud.

"No—with respect, Governor," he said, the anger within him welling up nearly into outrage. "It's not dead."

"Ridiculous," Rameses snapped, this time not bothering to look Tamerlane's way. Instead he turned toward the sound of boots crunching their way through the rubble, and nodded to the approaching form of Governor Tokugawa, the ruler of Edo. "It is time for the planetary governors to assert direct control over their territories—would you not agree, Iyesu?"

Before Tokugawa could answer, Tamerlane stepped forward and cut him off. "That would lead to chaos. Our enemies would descend upon us—pick off our worlds, one by one." He glared at Rameses intensely, until the governor had no choice but to look back at him. "The Empire is not dead," Tamerlane repeated. "It merely needs a ruler."

"You forget yourself, Colonel," Tokugawa snapped, appalled at Tamerlane's manners. Rameses meanwhile regarded Tamerlane with an expression of scorn and contempt.

"The entire royal family is *dead*," Rameses almost shouted. "There is no one *left* to lead it!"

The others in the chamber were taking note of the conversation—and its elevating tone—and turned to watch. At the far end of the room, General Nakamura frowned and started toward them.

Tamerlane saw him coming and knew the general intended to shut Tamerlane up. But that couldn't be allowed. Tamerlane understood very well that all of history turned on but a few moments—moments of vast consequence and import. This, he knew in his bones, was one of those moments. The very Empire itself hung in the balance. If things were going to be said and done—things Tamerlane had long believed in, quietly—they needed to be said and done *now*. Now, or not at all. There was no more room for manners, for niceties, at this crossroads of history. No time for that at all. This was it. There would surely be no second chance.

"When I desire the counsel of a mere *colonel*," Rameses was saying, his tone reflecting the impatience of a man whose plans are being disrupted, "I will be sure to—"

"One moment, Amon," said a short, stocky man in flowing robes of purple and gold, who had just slipped up behind them. He reached out and placed a hand on Rameses's shoulder—something that caused the ruler of Ahknaton to jerk around, before he realized it was the ruler of Bursa, bloodied and bandaged from the recent events but still alive, who addressed him.

"Suleyman," Rameses almost gasped, restraining himself. He frowned. "You wish to encourage the radical politics of this—this *soldier*?"

Governor Suleyman Mehemet allowed himself to smile. "We were all soldiers once—and so much younger than we are now. Less set in our ways. More open to new ideas." He winked at Rameses. "And the young must have their say—no?" He turned his gaze slowly to Tamerlane. "Please—go on, Colonel. I for one am not entirely convinced as to who here is the *radical*—and I am most interested in where you are going with this."

Others were approaching now, as well. Colonels Iapetus and Agrippa moved in closer, listening intently. Majors Barbarossa and Vostok exchanged troubled glances.

Behind them all, Inquisitor Stanishur and his aides swept forward, black robes flowing. Within seconds a crowd of dozens of men and women of the military and the Imperial government had closed in around them, looking and listening.

"My position is simple," Tamerlane called to the assembly. "We cannot allow the Empire we have all fought and bled for, our entire lives, to evaporate because of this incident. On the contrary—this incident proves that all of mankind faces a much more formidable foe than we had ever suspected. We need unity now—more than ever—not division."

"We need the strength of our individual worlds, each at its most efficient," Rameses countered. "With the central government dissolved and power devolved to the planets themselves, we can more effectively fight whatever enemy we face."

"We can more effectively die, one planet at a time, each one of them alone," Tamerlane stated.

"I will not debate this matter with a common foot soldier," Rameses barked.

"Foot soldier?" Nakamura exclaimed. He moved forward. "Governor—while I am not pleased that my subordinate is making a spectacle of himself here, I do believe that he—a full colonel in His Majesty's military—deserves some measure of respect and—"

"His Majesty is dead," Rameses snapped, cutting the general off. "Just like his empire."

Governor Tokugawa moved between them, hands raised to settle them both down. "There are others to be heard from," he said, looking out at the crowd. "What is the Church's view of all this? We must have the opinion of the Ecclesiarch before we can go further."

"The Ecclesiarch probably won't be addressing that, or anything else, I'm afraid," Agrippa observed in his booming voice. "The pretender, Barmakid, is dead. My men just found his body in a side passage." He snorted. "Someone took out a great deal of hostility on him before he died."

"The priests are all dead," Major Barbarossa added, nodding to the carnage around the big table. "And as for their little army—" He snorted a laugh. "They ran away and still haven't come back."

"There is no one here to speak for the Church," Rameses concluded.

For a moment the impromptu assembly was silent. Then Inquisitor Stanishur moved forward and intoned, "I can speak for the Holy Church—and I will." He looked toward Tamerlane momentarily and a hint of a smile touched his lips. "Both Church and Inquisition have always supported the Empire, and we will continue to do so. The Empire must endure!"

Some of the others turned to one another and nodded, muttering words of renewed hope and confidence at Stanishur's proclamation. Rameses, however, shook his head. "No one here disputes the importance of the Inquisition, Stanishur," he stated. "But you do not speak for the Holy Church."

At that, the crowd dissolved into loud and increasingly angry argument.

The Grand Inquisitor raised one bony hand and held it aloft until they silenced themselves. "The Ecclesiarch has been revealed to all as a traitor and a heretic," he stated in solemn tones. "A cultist and worshiper of Vorthan. A servant of the dark forces. And the Emperor was taken entirely—may Those Who Remain accept and preserve his soul. We cannot know how deeply the taint reaches—how many others within the Church have also been swayed by the dark powers, or possessed outright. The Inquisition therefore relieves the Ecclesiarchy of its authority—for now, pending a full inquisition into its members and practices—and assumes for itself that authority within the Empire."

More shouting and confusion greeted this.

"There *is* no more Empire," Rameses asserted angrily, above the din.

Stanishur ignored him. Again he motioned for silence, and it was a testament to the esteem with which he was held—and the fear his organization perpetuated—that the throng quickly silenced itself. "It is as Colonel Tamerlane has stated it," he said. "The Empire endures—it merely requires a new ruler."

Rameses glared at the older man. "And it is as I have said: There *is* no one left to rule."

"Then we must *find* someone," Stanishur replied, his flinty eyes gazing out at the crowd of soldiers and politicians surrounding him. "Someone that *all* can accept, and respect, and obey."

Now everyone in the room was looking at everyone else in the room. Had the plots and machinations being mentally conceived at that moment made actual sounds, the hall would have been filled with a deafening cacophony from the sheer number of them.

Tamerlane shifted his gaze quickly from the Inquisitor, who had in effect legitimized his position and backed his play, to the man he most feared could still disrupt it: Rameses. Indeed, the Governor of Ahknaton did seem to be filling himself with a new resolve at that moment, and as his brows furrowed, he started to step forward, toward the marble table.

It was now or never.

History turned on its axis.

Tamerlane surged ahead, moving more quickly than Rameses. He reached out and down and his fingers closed upon the hilt of the Sword of Baranak. Those closest by gasped, startled, and then gasped again when they saw what he was doing. Rameses stumbled to the side as Tamerlane cut him off, and his face twisted with surprise and outrage. But it was too late.

"Ezekial," Nakamura began, reaching one hand out toward his old friend and subordinate, terrified of what might happen next. "You can't—"

Tamerlane raised the gleaming weapon over his head and cried, "This is the Sword of Baranak, most sacred object of the gods of the Above. It belongs to the rightful ruler of our empire—the true master of all Mankind."

Before any of the others could react—and indeed several were reaching for their sidearms to shoot Tamerlane down—he stepped forward, took a knee, and held the sword up to Hideo Nakamura.

"I believe this now belongs to you, General."

Nakamura's eyebrows arched. He opened and closed his mouth once, twice, but no sounds came out. All around him, no one dared move or look away. The fingers that had been brushing the handles of guns or tightening on triggers moved away. A soft murmur arose from the congregation, then quieted as Nakamura gathered himself and his emotions and looked up from the sword being proffered by Tamerlane to the faces of the men and women all around him—faces of soldiers with whom he had gone to war many times.

Silence reigned.

Then: "Take it," cried someone from the rear of the crowd.

"Yes! Nakamura is the one!" joined in another voice.

"He's the only choice!"

"The gods have favored him with their gifts—the holy flame that sent the demons back down to Hell," Inquisitor Stanishur added to the growing chorus. "They have delivered these Lords of Fire to us in our hour of need. The choice is therefore obvious."

Those closest by now—the top political and military leaders—began to smile at the idea. Nakamura was someone most of them respected—someone they could work with. Those closet by nodded and offered encouraging and supportive looks to the general. Rameses, however, turned away in frustration. Briefly he met Tokugawa's eyes and glowered. He, too, could feel history swaying in a dramatically different direction—a direction away from *him*.

The general meanwhile swallowed dryly and looked from the crowd back down to the sword. It gleamed and shimmered like a mirage in the desert and he found he couldn't quite focus his eyes upon it. He had been about to refuse, but now he felt somehow different about things. The longer he gazed at the sword, the more filled with energy he became, and the more confident—confident that he really was the right man for the job. He started to reach out, then hesitated and looked directly at Tamerlane. In a voice that was barely more than a croak, he muttered, "You may live to regret this, Ezekial."

Tamerlane smiled. "I would regret anything *other* than this."

Nakamura inhaled deeply, grasped the hilt of the sword, and raised it high over his head. Flames sprouted to life from along his arms and leapt up to wreath the sword in fire.

The crowd went wild.

2

The celebrations on Nakamura's behalf were extremely short-lived. The general made certain of that. This was a somber occasion, he stressed to everyone present, not one for merriment.

Very quickly Tamerlane moved the crowd of survivors to one of the adjacent, slightly smaller chambers, while an army of laborers was brought in to remove the bodies from the main hall and shore up the cracked and crumbling masonry. Major repair work to the Church of the Reliquae would be needed very soon, but there were more important issues to be tended to first. And there were decisions of great import to be made, as well. There was little desire on anyone's part to make merry so soon after such a horrendous disaster, but with the acceptance of Nakamura as the new leader of the Empire—and thus the survival of that empire beyond the end of the Rahkmanov Dynasty—there was much for which to be thankful.

Not everyone in the palace shared in the thankfulness, however. Governor Amon Rameses of Ahknaton kept to himself, brooding, lurking at a table near the exit, awaiting the first proper opportunity to leave without attracting any unnecessary animosity from the others—from Nakamura's loyal new devotees.

As he sat, drinking wine from a golden goblet, a man in black approached him and bowed.

Rameses looked up and regarded the man with cool appraisal. "You," he said. "I've seen you somewhere before." His eyes narrowed. "You were with the Emperor's entourage—though in what capacity, I have no idea."

The man in black nodded once.

"And you weren't killed by the demons, or by the soldiers, or by the ceiling collapsing. Congratulations," Rameses said with a smirk, before quaffing more wine.

"We should talk, you and I, Governor," the man said, ignoring the sarcasm. "In private. I believe we have things of great importance to discuss."

"Is that so?" Rameses asked, his expression reflecting extreme doubtfulness.

The man nodded again.

"What could there possibly be of such great importance to discuss with *me*?" Rameses grumbled, his fist tightening on the goblet to the point that it began to bend. "Didn't you hear? The governors—the worlds—won't be gaining any new autonomy, despite this catastrophe. We have a new ruler to hold it all together." Rameses snorted derisively. "And the worst of it all is—he's not *me*."

"There are certainly many things to regret at this juncture," the man in black replied, nodding slowly. "I, for example, am quite disappointed that things here went so wrong, so quickly. I worked very hard to place demons obedient to me and me alone within the Emperor and his bodyguards. I didn't anticipate that they would escape my control so soon, or that they would physically manifest into this universe at that particular moment. It was quite unfortunate."

It was obvious that Rameses had been paying the man scant attention before. Now, however, he blinked, frowned, and looked up directly at him. "What? What did you just say?"

The man continued on as if Rameses hadn't spoken. "But I shouldn't complain," he said with a shrug. "I was, after all, finally able to engineer an escape from my long imprisonment in the Below. And I have other plans in place, of course. Plans that might yet yield the results I seek."

"What in the name of the Above are you saying?" Rameses started to rise. "Are you a madman?" He looked ready to call for guards.

"Hardly. I am merely an individual with grand plans for the future. For this entire galaxy." The man in black gazed down at Rameses, and a light seemed to well up and flow from his eyes . Rameses saw it, felt it flowing toward him, into him, and felt a sense of peace and tranquility seeping through him.

"Which brings me to you, my dear Governor." The man patted Rameses on the shoulder as one might pat an upset infant to calm it. "I believe you and I can do great things together. Things that will shake this galaxy to the depths of its core." He smiled. "But, for now, you should simply forget my words of the past few moments—forget them entirely."

Rameses started to protest, but the anger had melted out of him. His expression softened as his mouth opened and closed soundlessly several times. He gazed off into the distance for a moment, blinked again, and looked at the man as if seeing him for the first time. "I—I'm sorry," he said. "Do I know you? What was it you were saying?"

The man in black allowed a thin smile to cross his lips. "I was saying that you should take heart, Governor, because this new regime of Nakamura's scarcely has its feet under it." His dark eyes sparkled. "And things are perhaps not set in stone just yet."

Rameses perked up at that a little. "Oh? And what would you have me do, then? And note," he added quickly, "that I'd prefer not to be executed for treason, the very first *victim* of this new regime."

"That is precisely what we need to talk about," the man replied. He gestured with one hand toward the exit. "If you would?"

Rameses frowned. "You're serious," he said. "You mean what you're saying."

"Indeed. I have great plans in mind. Plans for you, plans for our new *Taiko*—and plans for the *galaxy*."

Rameses stood quickly, already sobering. He gave the man one last appraising look and then strode for the doors. The man in black followed closely behind. As they passed through, the governor turned back to him and said, "We haven't been introduced. I don't know your name."

"My name," the man in black said with a slight bow, "is Goraddon."

3

There's still no sign of the little girl," Tamerlane reported, passing through the doorway into the general's new, temporary quarters in the Zatalyan Palace, the royal residence adjacent to the Church of the Reliquae. He approached the general with a team of four First Legion troopers behind him. They had searched high and low through the wreckage of the sanctuary and all around it, to no avail. "Even the DNA scanners reveal no traces of her."

"We have to assume the worst," Colonel Agrippa rumbled from where he sat in a heavily-cushioned chair nearby. "The Princess Marens must be dead."

Tamerlane sighed heavily. He wasn't ready to give up yet. But he didn't know what else to do.

"What of Rameses?" asked Nakamura as he lifted the Sword of Baranak carefully from the granite counter upon which it had lain these last few hours. "He disappeared from the church pretty quickly."

"I don't know," Tamerlane replied, shaking his head. "But I'm sure it doesn't bode well."

"My flagship observed his fleet pulling out of orbit about a half-hour ago," Colonel Agrippa stated. "I believe he and all of the Sand Kings have headed straight back to Ahknaton."

Nakamura frowned at this. "I knew he wasn't entirely happy with the way things turned out, earlier," he said, stroking his chin.

"That's putting it mildly," said Tamerlane.

"But to simply *leave*—to leave before anything else has been decided…?"

"If you're asking if it's as disrespectful as it sounds," Agrippa growled, "the answer is most certainly *yes*."

Nakamura sagged a little and shook his head. "Discord already." Then he straightened and regarded the assembly before him. "Never mind that. He'll come around. Let's get to it."

Agrippa grasped the ornate handles of the massive double-doors and pulled them open. The three men strode out into the broad meeting hall that lay beyond. Its center was taken up by a long, boardroom-style, dark wood table that had been brought in a short time earlier. Seated at either side of it were the true power-brokers of the Empire.

Nakamura set the sword down on the tabletop, like a symbol of office, and then took the seat at the near end; to his right sat his adjutant, Tamerlane, followed by Colonel Agrippa and his top aide, Major Iksander, along with Major Vostok, all representing Third Legion. To his left sat Colonel Iapetus and Major Barbarossa—all that remained of Legion II's leadership, following the killing of General Attila by the Emperor-demon.

At the far end of the table sat Inquisitor Stanishur, his two young and ever-present assistants standing behind either shoulder. Halfway down on either side were Governors Mehmet and Tokugawa; with Rameses having departed, they were the only planetary administrators left in attendance and thus now served as representatives for all the Imperial governors. Various other governmental bureaucrats and officials filled the remaining seats.

"Still no word from General Beyzit, sir," reported a lieutenant as Nakamura took his place at the table.

The general looked to Tamerlane. "I don't like the sound of that," he whispered.

"He seems to have dropped completely off the grid," the colonel replied quietly. "He hasn't answered any Aether contacts in days, either."

Nakamura shifted his gaze to Agrippa. "You have command of Third Legion until the Thunderbolt decides to check in, Colonel," he told the big man.

Agrippa bowed his head.

"Alright. Before we go any further," Nakamura began, addressing the entire room now, "I have to make one thing very clear: I am not claiming the title of Emperor."

The others looked at him in surprise and a moderate grumbling broke out among them. Quickly he raised a hand to restore the silence.

"I do not claim the title of Emperor—that title belongs to the royal family of Rahkmanov, not to a mere soldier who spent his entire life fighting in their service." He paused. "Instead, I take the title of *Taiko*."

The others frowned at this, uncertain. Tamerlane spoke up. "Yes, I know that title," he said. "An early Japanese governmental position. Senior official—regent—top administrator and commander-in-chief. But—not royal."

"Precisely," Nakamura agreed. "Leader, but with no claims to royalty."

The others exchanged looks with one another and no one objected. A few moments later, the title was ratified by acclamation.

"As *Taiko*," Nakamura said then, "I will have need of a council of advisors, loyal directly to me, whose opinions I can trust implicitly, and who I will always be certain will be looking out for the best interests of the Empire and all who live within it."

The others nodded at this.

"My *Hatamoto*," Nakamura continued, "borrowing from the same early tradition." He motioned toward the group seated before him. "I have made my selections. There will be three *Hatamoto*, and all three are present here."

The assembled officers and governors waited, obviously anxious and uncertain.

"They cannot be planetary governors," Nakamura added. He nodded toward Tokugawa and Mehmet. "Your responsibilities lie with your own worlds and your own populations. I would not divide your attention to such a degree. However," he added as they both frowned at the news, "I do intend to turn more power and authority over to the planetary rulers than you previously enjoyed under the late Emperor."

Their frowns softened somewhat. The glanced at one another and then both nodded, accepting this arrangement.

"Two of my choices would be obvious now," Nakamura went on, "except that, of the two other generals, one is dead and the other missing. I have no choice but to move down the ranks for my *Hatamoto*." He gestured toward Agrippa. "Colonel, as acting commander of Third Legion, and given your...*remarkable* contributions during the conflict we have just survived, I grant you promotion to general, and welcome you to my *Hatamoto*.

The big man smiled grimly and bowed his head in appreciation.

"With my accession to head of government," Nakamura went on, "First Legion needs a new general. The choice is clear. Ezekial," he said, looking to Tamerlane, "you have been my right hand for many years now." The *Taiko* favored Tamerlane with a smile. "You are given Legion I. Will you do me the honor of joining as the second member of my council?"

"The honor is mine, Gen—*Taiko*," Tamerlane quickly corrected himself. "And a greater honor than I ever expected to receive."

Nakamura nodded his head to the new general in appreciation, then regarded the rest of the gathering. "That leaves only Second Legion leaderless, and my council short one member." He appraised the expressions and postures of each man. Once he had done this, he looked straight at Iapetus.

"Colonel," he said, "I would have your thoughts on this matter."

"Mine?" Iapetus spread his hands before him. "I assume I will be passed over." He turned to the man seated to his left. "I was preparing to congratulate Major Barbarossa here on his meteoric rise over me." He looked back at Nakamura. "What use are my thoughts to you?"

"You assume much, Colonel," the *Taiko* said evenly. "And you *presume* much."

"I speak my mind, sir," he replied. "I prefer that people always know precisely where they stand with me. I am not fond of subterfuge."

Nakamura held Iapetus's gaze for several long, tense seconds. Then, "Very well. What do you make of my choices thus far?"

Iapetus extended his lower lip in thought for a moment, then shrugged ever-so-slightly. "Agrippa was a given. Tamerlane is a good man and a good soldier, and he's practically your son. Of course you would choose him—I would scarcely expect anything different. Who here would have?"

Nakamura nodded. "I appreciate your frankness, Colonel."

"I'm not done," Iapetus said.

All at the table reacted with restrained but obvious surprise at this. Eyes widening, Nakamura gestured for him to continue.

"As I said, I can understand why you chose them. They are logical. *Predictable.*" Iapetus paused for a moment. "*But.*" He shrugged again—an almost microscopic movement, but noticeable nonetheless. "Ezekial is too careful, too deliberate. Not decisive enough. Not strong enough—*ruthless* enough." He spared Tamerlane a quick glance. "No offense intended, Colonel," he added. "Or rather, *General*," he corrected. "I merely offer my honest evaluation."

"None taken," Tamerlane stated, eyes narrowing.

"And Agrippa is a fine soldier, a fine warrior—none could dispute that. But—a top-level advisor on all Imperial policy?" He chuckled. "No."

No one spoke. All eyes flickered to the big blond man. Agrippa did exhibit any reaction at all.

"If you want this new regime to survive," Iapetus concluded matter-of-factly, "I would be the best choice to for your council, and to lead Second Legion. But you won't choose me—and now everyone here understands why."

Nakamura couldn't help but smile at that. "Your point is made, Colonel," he said. His eyes moved to the man to Iapetus's left. "Major Barbarossa—I promote you to Colonel, and offer you the third spot on my council."

Surprise was evident on Berens Barbarossa's dark face. He gathered himself and bowed his head. "Thank you, *Taiko*," he said quickly. "I accept." After a second he glanced carefully at Iapetus; the older man stared straight ahead, exhibiting no emotions whatsoever.

"Sir," Tamerlane said after another few seconds of silence ticked by, "If I may ask—? You have made Barbarossa a colonel—but what of the *leadership* of Second Legion?"

Nakamura appeared to be considering this for a few seconds before meeting Iapetus's eyes again. "Ioan," he said, "your reputation for strength—for *ruthlessness*, as you yourself just described it—is certainly well-known," he said. "And that is why I have saved a particular job for you. One where I believe your very nature will serve as a great asset to the Empire."

Iapetus actually appeared surprised at this. He sat up slightly. "Yes? Sir?"

"I appoint you defender of the Earth," Nakamura said.

"What?" Iapetus was taken aback. "Earth?" He blinked.

"Earth, and all the core planets of the Empire. You and the Second Legion will defend our homeland as First and Third Armies strike out against our many gathered enemies."

Iapetus was trying to process this. "Defend the home worlds? So you're going on the attack—you and your *Lords of Fire*—" He repeated the name the Inquisitor had used, with only a hint of mockery. "—and I'm being left behind?"

"Left behind to protect our billions of souls from any enemy that gets past our forces," Nakamura replied. "You are indeed ruthless, and that is the very quality I want in the person who will direct the defense of our homes."

Iapetus chewed at his lower lip for a few seconds as the others all looked at him, waiting to hear what he would say. With anyone else present, the response would have been extremely predictable: "Thank you, *Taiko*." But with Iapetus, no one could guess what might come next—what arguments he might marshal against his own leader.

When he finally did speak, his answer dumbfounded most of the individuals present. Iapetus nodded to Nakamura and said, "Very well. I accept."

Nakamura recovered from his surprise quickly. "You are promoted to general," he said—as if to sweeten the deal before the man could change his mind.

Iapetus nodded once but didn't speak.

Nakamura hesitated, frowning, his eyes never leaving Iapetus. At last he asked, "Is everything all right, General?"

"Certainly."

"Can you work with us?"

Iapetus was taken aback. "What?"

"Can you *work* with us, General? With me, with Ezekial… With those of us who have gained these powers, these abilities?" He stared intently at the man—almost through him. "Your intensely negative feelings and attitudes with regard to the gods are very well-known, Ioan. *Very* well-known. Now at least two of us have gained powers of a similar nature. So I ask you—can you live alongside us? *Fight* alongside us?"

Iapetus appeared to be considering that thought for the very first time, as if it had never occurred to him before. For a third time in the last five minutes, he shrugged.

"Powers? Abilities? I couldn't care less," he said. "Now—do I like someone who actually claims to speak for a god? Or to *be* one? Do I believe any of those that made that claim in the past ever *were* gods? No. Not hardly." He laughed softly. "I suspect a quad-rifle blast to the skull would've killed them just as easily as it would anybody else. But that's beside the point." He shook his head. "I don't hate people with godlike powers," he said. "Only those who actually *say* they're gods—that say they are somehow *above* me, *better* than me, for no other reason than their birth or some quirk of nature." He looked from Nakamura to Tamerlane and back. "You've just set yourself up as *Taiko*, not god-emperor or even regular emperor. You've made Tamerlane a *Hatamoto*—a trusted advisor—not a demigod. So that all works for me."

Nakamura gazed back at the man for several seconds, as if trying to decide what to make of him.

"That being said, however," Iapetus added just when Nakamura appeared ready to change the subject, "I would like everyone here—and particularly those members of your *Lords of Fire* army—to understand one thing. If I'm being put in charge of protecting the inner worlds, then I plan to do everything in my power to keep them safe. *Everything*. That means safe from outsiders *and* internal threats alike."

"Absolutely, General," Nakamura began, nodding.

"And that means," Iapetus concluded, "that I will be watching *you*, too. *All* of you."

"General!" exclaimed Governor Mehmet. "You tread very close to treason."

Iapetus slowly turned his gaze toward the governor, his expression neutral, but said nothing.

Nakamura meanwhile was still processing Iapetus's words. He considered what the man had said for a moment, weighing it carefully, and reached what he felt was the proper conclusion. "No, no, Governor," he said to Mehmet a second later, as the man started to rise in anger. "The general is within his rights to speak his mind here." He looked from Mehmet to Iapetus and nodded. "Very well, General," he said. "I'm certain we could all benefit from your scrutiny. The scrutiny of an impartial observer with only the best interests of the Empire at heart."

"An observer with his own army," Tamerlane muttered, not any happier than Mehmet.

Nakamura's eyes flicked to Tamerlane for an instant as this registered. Then he chose to let it go.

The meeting ended a short while later. It had resulted in momentous changes for the Empire, and everyone there knew it. It had also resulted in a precarious new balance of power within the upper echelons of government and the military—and everyone knew *that*, too.

4

The soldiers manning the defensive outpost orbiting NR-776 would have loved many more years of life, of course. They would have likely settled for hours more existence, had they known the alternative—known their fate, as it lay before them that very instant, revealing itself to them in the hot, burning terms of a volley of high-intensity energy blasts that ripped their orbital station apart and flung the blazing debris across the sky.

Failing days or hours, they might have contented themselves with minutes—or even seconds. For a few seconds more would have been all they would have required to notice that the fleet of spacecraft dropping out of hyper and opening fire on them were not ships of the Riyahadi Navy, nor of the Chung. Indeed, they were not human ships at all.

They were vessels of sweeping curves and elegant arcs, made all of a gleaming substance that looked like glass but was a thousand times more resilient.

They were vessels of the Dyonari, and they were on the warpath.

The Dyonari, a race ancient when Man was first emerging from the jungles and grasslands of Africa.

The Dyonari, a race of very long lifespans but virtually no reproduction.

The Dyonari, a race that possessed technology far beyond that of humanity, and possessed great psychic gifts as well.

Generally they kept to themselves, remaining within the boundaries established by numerous treaties with the human empires they bordered. They were not liked, and they did not like mankind. But they rarely interfered in human affairs, and that was usually enough.

They were interfering now.

Their ships pulverized the outpost at NR-776 in the blink of an eye, the humans aboard that station obliterated before any word of warning could be sent. Then they zoomed past, seizing the entire star system, sending down landing craft, establishing a beachhead, and evaluating their next move. On their holographic starmaps, arrows pointed inward, toward the heart of the Anatolian Empire. Toward Earth.

The Dyonari generally kept to themselves. They were not keeping to themselves today.

A voice—a very persuasive voice, echoing throughout their minds, throughout their worlds—had told them of the new weakness in the major human empire. Told them that the Emperor was dead and that anarchy loomed. Told them—urged them—*commanded* them—to strike. To unleash their ships and their armies and their massive psychic powers upon humanity. To bring the Empire to its knees—to bring it *down*.

They had listened, and now the Dyonari obeyed.

5

Did you see the new uniforms Iapetus has issued to Second Legion?" Tamerlane asked as he sipped at his coffee on the observation deck of the flagship.

They had dropped out of hyper only a short time earlier and were now streaking into the Sol system at just below lightspeed.

"What? No," Nakamura replied absently, looking from the starfield that filled the broad transparent blister over their heads to the spot where Tamerlane sat, off to his right. They both wore their dress uniforms of red and orange, accented with insignia of gleaming gold here and there. Nakamura had added a sort of sash of purple and white, indicating his new status as *Taiko* of the Empire. He looked down at himself, chuckled, and said, "Gaudier than *this?* I can't imagine."

Tamerlane laughed, too. "Not gaudier, no. But they've ditched their traditional blue for black, to match what his own company's always worn. And—get this—he's added a stylized golden eye to the chest."

"An eye?" Nakamura frowned.

"*Always watching.* Remember?"

Nakamura groaned. He remembered the meeting on Ascanius very clearly—every moment of it—though it had happened weeks earlier.

"He's changed their name, too."

Nakamura was startled by this. "To what?"

"They are now the *Sons of Terra.*"

"Sons of Terror?" Nakamura looked at him in surprise.

"*Terra.* Though I'm sure the double meaning occurred to him, too."

Nakamura weighed this in his mind. "That's fine," he said after a few seconds. "Everyone does call Legion I the *Lords of Fire* now."

"Even though, of everyone who accompanied us on that expedition, only you and I and the Inquisitor have manifested any such abilities," Tamerlane pointed out.

"Even though that, yes. But my point is—I suppose Iapetus is within his rights."

"So you're not going to order him to change the name back?"

Nakamura shrugged. "What harm?"

Tamerlane snorted. "Even so…"

Nakamura crossed his arms over his chest and exhaled heavily. "I know you don't like him, Ezekial. But—"

"Nobody likes him. Sir. And with reason."

Nakamura grimaced. "I know, I know," he admitted at last. "Despite my best efforts… He's going to be a problem, isn't he?"

Tamerlane was hunched forward, his chin in his hands. He rubbed at his face roughly to clear his thoughts—the stars passing slowly outside had nearly lulled him to sleep, even with the coffee—and sat up. "Not necessarily," he replied. "Think of it this way: Iapetus is a gun. A very dangerous gun—a gun with its own army behind it. But still just a gun." He raised his hand and made a pistol-shape with his fingers, pointing at himself. "Guns can go off and shoot their owners." Then he pointed away from himself.

"But, handled properly, they can also eliminate your enemies."

"So I simply have to handle him properly, and keep him pointed at the enemy," Nakamura said. "Fine—but that's much easier said than done."

Tamerlane shrugged. "I would just keep him occupied. Keep him *busy*."

"Now *that* shouldn't be too hard," Nakamura replied. "Our Empire is besieged from nearly every direction, thanks to the actions of our demonically-possessed former Emperor."

"Including from within," Tamerlane stated. "Remember—the old Ecclesiarch, Zoric, was with the Emperor and the Guardsmen in the Below. But after returning—and while you and I were in our little comas— we are to believe he simply *died*." Tamerlane shook his head. "I don't buy that. Not for an instant."

"Then what—?"

"He must have been possessed, as well," Tamerlane explained. "He had to have been, or he would have revealed the truth about the others. But if so, he wouldn't have just *dropped dead* with a demon inside him. It must have *abandoned* him..." He met the *Taiko's* eyes, frowning. "...For another host. A *preferred* host."

Now Nakamura was frowning just as deeply.

"The question, obviously," Tamerlane concluded, "is— *who?*"

Nakamura said nothing for a few seconds, and the question hung there, fouling the air of the room. Finally, "Stanishur is investigating," the *Taiko* replied, somewhat testily. "He will bring all of the considerable might of the Holy Inquisition to bear on this question. We have to believe—we have to *trust*—that he will root out any demonic infiltration. Even at the highest levels of power."

Tamerlane only nodded.

Nakamura looked as if he was going to say something more, but then he simply turned back to the observation blister and the vast starfield beyond.

After a few seconds, Tamerlane stood and stretched. "We'll be arriving at Earth in a couple of hours," he said. "I'll go and make certain all the preparations are moving along."

"We don't need any kind of coronation ceremony, Ezekial."

"Maybe not," Tamerlane said. "But there needs to be *something—some* kind of event—that focuses the public's attention on you and lets them see that you are fully in charge. We *have* to do that. They have to see that the Empire is continuing on as before."

"As before?" Nakamura whispered. "I hope not."

Tamerlane paused at that, licked his lips, and said, "But you see—that's the beauty of it all. Now *you're* in charge—so the Empire will go the way *you* want it to go. Nobody else gets to set the course we follow now. Nobody but you."

Nakamura nodded. "Thank you, Ezekial. I will join you on the bridge shortly."

Tamerlane saluted and turned to exit. As he did, the door opened and three figures entered. Two were soldiers of the Lords of Fire, serving as personal guard to Nakamura. The third, situated between them, was a slender, dark-haired man clad all in black.

Tamerlane hesitated, still standing in front of the trio, inadvertently blocking them. He looked at the man in black and turned back to Nakamura, puzzled. "Sir—"

"It's all right, Ezekial," Nakamura said. "This man and I have business to discuss."

Tamerlane frowned. He'd seen the man before, somewhere—but the memory of it seemed to evaporate from his mind. He looked the guy up and down, hoping something would trigger a recollection, but there was nothing there—it was as if a section of his memories had been cut away.

"Colonel—ah, pardon me, *General*—Tamerlane," the man in black said to him as he stepped forward, extending a hand. "I wanted to thank you for rescuing me from the Above."

"The Above?" Tamerlane said, his frown deepening. "Rescuing you?"

"Yes. I was trapped there along with our late, lamented Emperor. You and your team helped bring me back."

Tamerlane shook his head, now seemingly filled with cobwebs. "Ah—yes, of course," he said. He clasped the man's hand and shook it. "Glad we could help you."

There was something else that came to Tamerlane's mind then, but it danced around the periphery of his consciousness like the gossamer strands of some almost-forgotten dream and he couldn't quite pin it down. Something about a sword—stealing it, and seeing it thrown through a doorway of some kind, or...

No. Gone. All gone.

Tamerlane squeezed his eyes closed, groaning.

"Are you well, General?" the man in black asked, a look of concern crossing his features.

"What?" Tamerlane looked up and the pain receded. Within a couple of seconds it was entirely gone. "Yes—I'm sorry," he said quickly, "just a headache. It's passed."

"Good," said the man in black. A second later, his mouth smiled.

"I will join you on the bridge shortly," Nakamura repeated, and again Tamerlane nodded and saluted. As he moved through the doorway and it began to close behind him, he couldn't help but look back. Something was nagging at him—something very important. Something *critical*. But he had no idea what it could be.

"*Taiko*," the man in black was saying. "Thank you for meeting with me."

"My pleasure, Mr. Goraddon," Nakamura replied, reaching out to clasp his hand.

The last shreds of memory evaporated as the door slid closed in Tamerlane's face.

EPILOGUE

May I say, Governor, that you have never looked better—never appeared healthier—than you do now."

Governor Amon Rameses gazed down at the high priest, his expression dubious. "There is no need to flatter me, Raza. I survived. I'm fortunate to be alive at all. That is more than enough."

The high priest, resplendent in robes of deepest red, bowed respectfully as he backed out of Rameses' way. The planetary governor of Ahknaton swept past him and into the main sanctuary of the Great Cathedral of Anakh. Some two dozen citizens filed in behind him—men, women, and children of all ages, come to participate in a service along with their Imperial governor. They filled in the space at the rear of the sanctuary while Rameses made his way toward the front.

"I am sincere, Governor," Raza said as he followed along behind Rameses and his small retinue of advisors and bodyguards. "Your countenance is one of youth and vigor. Surely the gods favor you in all things—now more than ever!"

Rameses ignored him, used to his underlings saying whatever they felt he wanted to hear. He strode the length of the vast hall and stopped only when he reached the altar, quickly climbing the two steps that led up to it. There he stood, hands on hips, his formal red and gold robes swirling as he turned slowly to take in the beauty of the cathedral's gothic interior, as lit by hundreds or thousands of flickering candles. Leaning on his ever-present staff with its crooked head, he studied the lush tapestries that hung from the walls on either side, filling the space between the stained glass windows. Each tapestry depicted a different figure—one of the many gods of the holy pantheon of the Empire, otherwise known as Those Who Remain. The main window directly ahead, above the altar, had been wrought into a colorful depiction of a tall, slender man in robes of red and gold—precisely the same as what Rameses now wore—with arms outstretched in welcoming. In the luminous glass image, the man was flanked by common people much like those who had entered the hall behind Rameses, and all clad in the customary, Egyptian-themed dress of this world, Ahknaton. The central figure's eyes stared out, comprised of sparkling green gemstones set into the glass.

"Amenophis," the governor intoned reverently. He sank to his knees and repeated the name: "Amenophis. Hear me."

The priests who stood hidden behind opaque paper screens at the rear of the sanctuary began to chant then, the words unintelligible but their meaning—and their reverence—clear. Clouds of scented smoke began to fill the area around the altar, almost obscuring the kneeling governor from the view of the parishioners behind him.

"Hear me, great Amenophis, chosen god of Ahknaton, who favors our world with grace and bounty."

The priests sang louder then, and Rameses repeated the invocation, then recited several lines of standard prayer that matched what was being spoken in churches all across

326

Ahknaton. Finally the governor stood, bowed once more, and turned his back on the windows. He took two steps down from the raised altar steps and froze in place.

The parishioners were all standing and staring, gawking and pointing past him.

Frowning, he turned back and looked at the windows.

The image of Amenophis, patron god of Ahknaton and one of Those Who Remain, was glowing brighter than Rameses had ever seen it. And the *eyes*—those green eyes were practically alight, pale beams spearing down from them to touch the chest of Rameses. He gasped, staggered back a step, and looked down again. The beams had moved as he moved. He stepped to one side, and they followed. They were tracking him.

He turned back to the crowd of people, eyes wide, and then spread his arms in a gesture not unlike the one Amenophis was making in the image. He solemnly nodded to them.

The crowd hesitated a moment and then surged forward, sensing a miracle at work, anxious to touch him.

The beams faded and disappeared. The image of the god returned to its normal brightness.

After all the people had touched him and received his blessings—and those of Amenophis—in turn, they were led back out of the cathedral by the priests. Rameses watched them go, raising a hand in a solemn farewell gesture to those who looked back.

When the last of them had gone, Rameses waited until the doors were closed and locked. Then he gestured for the high priest to approach.

The man bowed deeply to him. "A miracle," he murmured, a blissful smile forming on his dark features. "A sign, and a portent for the future of our world."

"Let us hope so," Rameses said in a loud, clear voice. Then he leaned in and murmured, "Dismantle the lasers immediately. Leave no traces behind. Excellent work, Raza."

He stepped back and the high priest bowed again. Then he turned and motioned for his bodyguards to lead the way out of the cathedral and through the growing throng that was already gathering outside.

One of his top political aides, Haden Moentat, approached. His unfocused eyes indicated that he was currently accessing the Aether network. What he said after he greeted Rameses proved that.

"Word is already spreading of this miracle, Governor," Moentat said, smiling. "The news broadcasts will all lead off with the story tonight. Soon all of Ahknaton will love you even as we who know you so well love you."

"Let us hope so," Rameses repeated. He allowed the guards around him to usher him to a waiting hovercar, a spectacular gilded affair that filled a substantial portion of the square, surrounded by a full company of Sand Kings troops, all resplendent in their Egyptian-motif dress uniforms. As he climbed into the sumptuous passenger cabin, he looked back one last time at the people crowding around the cathedral's doors; most were chanting Amenophis's name, but no small few were chanting, "Rameses." Some of them weren't even in his pay.

"To the Heliopolis," he ordered the driver. "The palace." Then he closed the door and, alone at last, leaned his head forward and breathed deeply, almost hyperventilating.

"Fine work," said the figure in black who was seated across from him. "Well played. Your time has nearly come."

Rameses looked up, saw the man, realized he'd been there all along and understood somehow that it was well and good that this should be so. He nodded his thanks.

"I've left something for you," the man continued, his voice like honey, like silk—but with a very cold edge to it.

"Something you might find useful. At your palace, waiting for you. A gift."

"Oh?" Rameses felt a headache coming on. He squeezed his eyes closed and rubbed at them.

"Or rather, some*one*," the voice went on. "Someone very young, but very valuable, if used properly."

Rameses frowned at this. "What? A *person*?" He opened his eyes and looked up. "What do you mean—?"

But of course there was no one there. *No one.* He had been right the first time— he was all alone. He must have imagined the entire conversation.

"No one. Well," he said aloud. The idea bothered him for a few seconds, but then it faded, forgotten, and his thoughts returned to his successful ruse at the cathedral. He couldn't help grinning at the thought. The people of this world already honored him as their Imperial governor. Soon they would *worship* him.

"That's one small step of the journey complete," he said. "Just one step."

He gazed out the window at the sky and the stars that filled it—stars that stretched on forever and ever.

"One foot on the road to Damascus," he whispered.

To *no one*.

Thanks and appreciation this time around to:
Ami and the girls,
for helping me make the time to work on this series;
Wayne Reinagel,
for talking through some of the original concepts
over nachos;
the gang at the Alabama Phoenix Festival
for their astonishing generosity and hospitality;
the SF Literature Track folks at Dragon*Con
for their continued support and enthusiasm;
Larry Niven, for the "ring" I swiped from him last time,
Gollum-like, and for a lifetime of ideas;
Joe Haldeman, for being such an inspirational force when I
was fortunate enough to share a panel with him at Archon
St. Louis, patiently answering my questions and delighting
us all with his memories;
Alexander Maisey for introducing me
to artist Mark Williams;
and all my readers out there, many of whom communicate
with me regularly on Facebook and/or Twitter.
If you enjoyed what you just read, by all means—
join us there!
@VanAllenPlexico

And an extra-huge THANKS!!! to Mark Williams
for the incredible cover art that graces these new hardcover
and softcover editions.
You can see Mark's work online at
http://marrilliams.deviantart.com
and contact him at Markwilliams3979@gmail.com.

Tamerlane and company will return in
LEGION II: SONS OF TERRA

About the Author

Van Allen Plexico writes and edits New Pulp, science fiction, fantasy, and nonfiction analysis and commentary for a variety of print and online publishers. He's been nominated for numerous writing awards including Author of the Year and Novel of the Year, and won the 2012 PulpArk Award for "Best New Pulp Character." The first volume in this series, *Legion I: Lords of Fire*, was a finalist for Novel of the Year in the 2013 Pulp Factory Awards and the New Pulp Awards. His best-known works include *Lucian*, *Hawk*, the *Assembled!* books, and the groundbreaking and #1 New Pulp Best-Selling *Sentinels* series—the first ongoing, multi-volume cosmic superhero saga in prose form. In his spare time he serves as a professor of political science and history. He has lived in Atlanta, Singapore, Alabama, and Washington, DC, and now resides in the St. Louis area along with his wife, two daughters and assorted river otters.

Van Allen Plexico's Sentinels
Super-hero action illustrated by Chris Kohler
  The Grand Design Trilogy
  Alternate Visions (Anthology)
  The Rivals Trilogy
  The Order Above All Trilogy

Also by Van Allen Plexico
  Lucian: Dark God's Homecoming
  Hawk: Hand of the Machine

Other Great Novels and Anthologies
  Gideon Cain: Demon Hunter
  Blackthorn: Thunder on Mars
  Blackthorn: Dynasty of Mars
   By Ian Watson

Nonfiction:
  Assembled! Five Decades of Earth's Mightiest
  Assembled! 2
  Super-Comics Trivia
  Season of Our Dreams &
  Decades of Dominance (Van Allen Plexico and John
Ringer)

All are available wherever books
are sold, or visit
WWW.WHITEROCKETBOOKS.COM